Hannah Dennison was born in Britain and originally moved to Los Angeles to pursue screenwriting. She has been an obituary reporter, antiques dealer, private-jet flight attendant and Hollywood story analyst. After twenty-five years living on the West Coast, Hannah returned to the UK, where she shares her life with Draco, her high-spirited Vizsla (no relation to Draco Malfoy) in the West Country.

Hannah writes the Honeychurch Hall Mysteries and the Vicky Hill Mysteries, both set in Devon, as well as the Island Sisters Mysteries, set on the fictional island of Tregarrick in the Isles of Scilly.

www.hannahdennison.com
www.facebook.com/hannahdennisonbooks
www.instagram.com/hannahdennisonbooks

Also by Hannah Dennison

Murder at Honeychurch Hall
Deadly Desires at Honeychurch Hall
A Killer Ball at Honeychurch Hall
Murderous Mayhem at Honeychurch Hall
Dangerous Deception at Honeychurch Hall
Tidings of Death at Honeychurch Hall
Death of a Diva at Honeychurch Hall
Murder in Miniature at Honeychurch Hall
A Killer Christmas at Honeychurch Hall
Dagger of Death at Honeychurch Hall

The Island Sisters Mystery series

Death at High Tide
Danger at the Cove

The Vicky Hill Mystery series

Exclusive!
Scoop!
Exposé!
Thieves!
Accused!
Trapped!

A Fatal Feast at Honeychurch Hall

Hannah Dennison

CONSTABLE

First published in Great Britain in 2025 by Constable

Copyright © Hannah Dennison, 2025

Map on p. vi by Liane Payne

1 3 5 7 9 10 8 6 4 2

The moral right of the author has been asserted.

All characters and events in this publication, other than those clearly in the public domain, are fictitious and any resemblance to real persons, living or dead, is purely coincidental.

All rights reserved.
No part of this publication may be reproduced, stored in a retrieval system, or transmitted, in any form, or by any means, without the prior permission in writing of the publisher, nor be otherwise circulated in any form of binding or cover other than that in which it is published and without a similar condition including this condition being imposed on the subsequent purchaser.

A CIP catalogue record for this book is available from the British Library.

ISBN: 978-1-40872-066-0

Typeset in Janson Text LT by SX Composing DTP, Rayleigh, Essex
Printed and bound in Great Britain by Clays Ltd, Elcograf S.p.A.

Papers used by Constable are from well-managed forests
and other responsible sources.

Constable
An imprint of
Little, Brown Book Group
Carmelite House
50 Victoria Embankment
London EC4Y 0DZ

The authorised representative
in the EEA is
Hachette Ireland
8 Castlecourt Centre
Dublin 15, D15 XTP3, Ireland
(email: info@hbgi.ie)

An Hachette UK Company
www.hachette.co.uk

www.littlebrown.co.uk

To Mark Durel,

who keeps me from stepping off that cliff!

The Honeychurch Estate
Jane's cottage
Walled garden
Shepherd's hut
Ice house
Honeychurch cottages
Eric's scrapyard
Caravan
Tradesmen's entrance
Service drive
Grotto
Sunken garden
Stumpery
Stableyard
Servant's entrance
Alfred's flat
Ballroom
Iris' carriage house
Haunted chestnut walk
Formal gardens
Honeychurch Hall
Main drive
To Little Dipperton
Main gate
Gatehouse
Ha ha
Ivy cottage
Equine cemetery
Kat's Collectibles Showroom
Ornamental lake
Summer house
N
W
E
S
Abandoned chapel
River Dart

Cast of Characters

The Honeychurch Hall Estate

Kat Stanford (40), antique dealer and our heroine
Iris Stanford (70), widow and novelist, aka Krystalle Storm
Earl of Grenville, Lord Rupert Honeychurch (early 50s)
Lady Lavinia (mid 30s), Rupert's second wife
The Dowager Countess, Edith Honeychurch (late 80s)
Alfred Bushman (70s), Iris's stepbrother and stable manager

Tenants

Eric Pugsley (40s), handyman, operates a scrapyard on the estate
Delia Evans (60s), Head of House

Little Dipperton

Danny Pritchard (60s), the love-struck vicar
Caroline Pritchard (50s), his prodigal wife

Ruby Pritchard (mid 80s), the vicar's widowed mother
Doreen and Stan Mutters (60s), landlords of the Hare and Hounds
Willow Mutters (early 20s), niece of Doreen and Stan, at home from university
Kizzy and Tom Jones (50s), farmers of Home Farm
Dawn Jones (early 20s), daughter of Kizzy and Tom

The Police

Detective Inspector Greg Mallory (40s), current village police officer
Detective Sergeant Clive Banks (30s), married to Janet
Detective Inspector Shawn Cropper (40s), past village police officer

Honorary Mentions

David Wynne (40s), international art and antiques investigator, and Kat's former fiancé
Piers Pole-Carew (40s), Earl of Denby and Lavinia's brother
Guy Evans (40s), Delia's son

Chapter One

'What have I missed?' I asked my mother as she picked me up from Totnes railway station in her bright red Mini. I'd cut short a three-week trip to the USA and was so happy to be home.

'Nothing much,' Mum said mildly. 'Hop in.'

I tossed my small cabin bag on to the back seat of her car.

'Where's your suitcase?'

'Still on the other side of the Atlantic,' I grumbled. 'It's supposed to arrive tomorrow.'

'At least you got on a flight at the last minute,' said Mum. 'I'm not sure why you're rushing back. I thought you were supposed to be staying on with friends.'

The truth was, I had missed Mallory, my lovely police officer, more than I realised. Although we had tried to speak every day, the eight-hour time difference and both of our busy schedules had made communication very frustrating. Our romantic relationship was still in the early phases and I bounced between being happy and then scared that it would go the same way as my other doomed relationships, which was why we had agreed to keep it secret for the time being. Especially from my mother.

'You look well,' I said neatly avoiding her question. And besides, it was true. My mother was a vibrant seventy and was positively glowing. Her once-permed hair was now styled in a highlighted honey-coloured bob. Large Jackie O-framed sunglasses added a touch of glamour to a simple pale-yellow linen summer dress that showed off her tanned limbs. Open-toed sandals revealed bright blue nail polish.

'I wish I could say the same for you,' Mum teased.

'And I love you too.' I knew I looked a mess, having been travelling for the best part of twenty-four hours. Being naturally clumsy, I had spilt numerous beverages over my khaki trousers, although the coffee stain was due to turbulence.

'How did it all go?' she asked. 'Was it as hot as here?'

'Hotter,' I said. 'But worth it.'

The trip to the United Federation of Doll Clubs annual convention in Los Angeles had been fun but exhausting. The UFDC had been founded by Mary E. Lewis in 1937 and was a big deal. When I'd got the invitation to speak, I jumped at the chance. Much as I enjoyed running Kat's Collectibles and Mobile Valuation Services, I missed the buzz of being around kindred spirits, especially those whose passion for antique dolls and bears matched my own. Living in rural Devon, I was kept busy enough with my private valuations and the space I rented at Dartmouth Antique Emporium, but my work was becoming increasingly generic and run-of-the-mill.

'It was lovely being flown business class and lovely being the keynote speaker, which definitely boosted my ego.' I stifled a yawn. ' I would have thought I would have been forgotten by now.'

'Nonsense,' Mum declared. 'You're still as famous as you've ever been. Who wouldn't flock to hear the former TV host of *Fakes and Treasures* talk about her pet subject?'

I reached over and squeezed her arm. 'You are my biggest fan, thank you.'

'Actually,' Mum said slowly. 'There is something I want to tell you. But I don't want you to be alarmed.'

'Of course I'm alarmed!' I exclaimed. 'What's happened?'

'Nothing yet,' Mum said, 'but her ladyship has been quite poorly. She's been in bed for a week, now.'

'Edith?' I said. The robust octogenarian was never unwell.

'There's a horrible bug sweeping through the village,' Mum went on. 'No one knows what it is. It comes as quickly as it goes but, when it comes, it's really nasty.'

'I'll go and see her tomorrow,' I said.

'Good luck with that,' said Mum. 'You know how Lady Edith hates fuss.'

The dowager countess was stoic to the last. She came from the generation that lived through the Second World War and who kept 'calm and carried on'. The fact that she was in bed was extremely worrying.

Mum's mobile rang. It was in the central console. I glanced down at the caller ID which flashed up, *call-me-Danny*, our vicar.

'I'll answer it since you're driving—'

'No don't!' Mum exclaimed but it was too late. I already had.

'Iris's phone,' I said. 'I'll have to put you on speaker, Danny. She's driving.'

'Iris? Hello. Hot day. How are you? Good. I'm worried,' he boomed without giving Mum a chance to answer any of his questions. 'It's mother. She's not answering her phone and I'm stuck at this church conference in Bath.'

My own mother uttered an exasperated sigh. 'I'm not sure what you want me to do about it, Danny. I'm out and about. Can't you ask someone else? A neighbour perhaps?'

'I've called everyone in the village, but it seems they are too busy.'

'Where is Caroline?' Mum demanded. 'She only lives next door.'

'My wife is not answering her phone either.' Danny's voice sounded tense. 'In fact, I haven't been able to reach Caroline all day.'

'Perhaps she's at a spa.' Mum's voice was laced with scorn. 'From what I've heard, she seems to spend a lot of time and money being pampered.'

There was a brief silence. 'No. That was yesterday.' Danny paused. 'Mother left me a message this morning. She had received a letter and sounded very upset. I won't be home until late this evening. Please, Iris. Would you just pop by and check she is all right? And of course, with this bug going around, I don't want to take any chances.'

Mum gave a heavy sigh. 'Fine.'

'Thank you. Thank you. You are a good woman.' Danny's relief was palpable. 'You know if I wasn't married—'

'But you are. And Kat is with me in the car and you are on speakerphone,' Mum declared. 'Yes, we will check on Ruby. Bye!'

I disconnected the call for her. 'Is he still flirting with you?'

'If he is, I don't care,' said Mum.

'Oh?' I raised a quizzical brow. 'Could there be someone else?'

'Don't be silly,' Mum retorted. 'You'd think *someone* could pop in and check on Ruby. But then who would care? When it comes to the popularity stakes, Ruby is more unpopular than her daughter-in-law.'

'I like Ruby,' I protested. 'And anyway, it's on our way home.' Like the dowager countess, Ruby was also in her eighties and although her mind was sharp, her body, not so much.

'I bought Ruby a complete collection of Wills cigarette cards for her birthday,' I said.

'That's kind of you,' said Mum. 'You're so good at remembering that sort of thing.'

'It's called "A Series of Roses" and they were created in 1912,' I said.

'Ruby doesn't smoke,' Mum said flatly.

'I know,' I said. 'The cigarette cards are not the point. It's the history behind each rose that I think she'd like.'

My mother didn't show the slightest interest when I told her that many of the cultivars no longer existed. 'And each card features a specific rose with a detailed description as to its history, scent, and other anecdotes,' I went on. 'Did you know that many roses date back to the mid 1800s and are still flourishing today?'

'Fascinating.'

'I can give them to her now, oh blast, I can't.' I had packed them in my suitcase. I whipped out my mobile to check for an update alert from British Airways but there was nothing.

We turned off the main road and flew down the first of many narrow Devon country lanes flanked by high hedgebanks, a trademark sight of the South Hams, designated an 'area of outstanding natural beauty' or AONB – although it wasn't particularly beautiful at the moment.

What was usually lush and green was now dry and brown. We were coming to the end of an exceptionally hot summer that had enforced a hosepipe ban across the country. The dead scrubland along the roadside and in the bordering woodland was a fire just waiting to happen.

Dotted at regular intervals were garish posters for Banger Racing. Eric Pugsley, Mum's neighbour and nemesis, ran this noisy event throughout the summer months.

Mum shifted gears and we descended a steep hill much faster than I would have liked. At the bottom was a famously sharp corner that had garnered the nickname

Cropper's Corner because cars and cyclists alike seemed to 'come a cropper' by not making the turn and tearing through the hedge and into the field beyond.

'Mum,' I said quickly. 'Slow down.'

'I am,' she said and frantically pumped the brakes.

Instinctively, I grabbed the handbrake and pulled it up sharply, which did the trick, and we zipped around the corner in one piece, managing to stop just a few yards further on.

My mother was furious. 'There was no need to be so dramatic, Katherine!'

'We nearly went through the hedge!' I said. 'How long have your brakes been like this?'

'Only since yesterday.' Mum set off cautiously. 'The Mini passed her MOT ten days ago. I don't understand it. I've booked the car in on Saturday morning if you must know. I'm not completely useless.'

I knew better than to comment on that remark. When Dad died he had made me promise to keep an eye on my mother. She had always been dependent upon him. After nearly fifty years of marriage, he'd been worried about whether she would be able to look after herself. I had been worried too, which was why I had moved from London to this remote corner of England, retired from *Fakes and Treasures*, and started my own antique business.

An Audi TT Quattro approached, pulled into an open gateway, flashed his lights, and beckoned for us to come forward so we could get by, which made a nice change.

The lanes were notoriously treacherous for motorists. Even though there were passing places and the occasional gateway to pull into, trying to get from A to B in one go was a bit like running the gauntlet. I was getting proficient at reversing and usually did it with good humour. Not so my mother. Many a time she'd stared down the opposition if she felt their passing place was closer than hers. Once, she flatly refused to budge, switched off her car engine and took out a newspaper to read until the exasperated motorist gave in and obliged.

As we drew alongside, the driver indicated for us to stop. Mum opened her window. A face that I could only describe as ferrety, with a pointed chin and bright eyes, smiled back.

He beamed. 'Hello, you.'

'Hello you, back.' I glanced at my mother, who had flushed pink and wore a silly grin on her face.

And now I knew why she was no longer romantically interested in the vicar.

The man was in his late fifties and wore wire-rimmed spectacles and a very neat goatee – in fact everything about him was neat. I noticed a pair of binoculars around his neck.

He caught my eye and said, 'How was your flight?'

Puzzled as to how he knew, I just said, 'Fine, thank you.'

'Your mother has told me all about you,' he went on. 'I thought I wouldn't get to meet you before I left but, here we are.'

'Aren't you going to introduce us?' I asked my mother.

'Yes, of course,' Mum said. 'Crispin, Kat. Kat, Crispin.'

'Crispin Fellowes.' He smiled again. 'How is the eye, Iris? Did you try the raw steak idea?'

A car horn beeped behind us. 'We're holding up the traffic, Mum.'

'Later.' He winked before adding, 'Oh . . . and I would avoid Little Dipperton if you can. The village is teeming with goats.'

Mum laughed. 'You're having us on.'

Crispin laughed too. 'Would I lie to you?'

The car behind beeped his horn again. Mum muttered something derogatory and set off slowly.

'Gosh. I can't leave you alone for five minutes!' I said lightly. 'Is he Danny's successor?'

It was a touchy subject and if this were true, I was glad. A few months earlier, my mother's initial infatuation with our new vicar with his long grey hair and red Harley-Davidson motorbike had been intense but short-lived when his prodigal wife returned and dashed the hopes of all the eligible females in the village. Shortly afterwards, the old vicarage was renovated at huge expense, and Caroline had wasted no time in making her larger-than-life presence clear, elbowing into village affairs and ruling the roost in more ways than one.

'Oh for heaven's sake!' Mum exclaimed. 'If you must know, Crispin has been staying in the shepherd's hut in the walled garden. He's a birdwatcher.'

'Ah. Hence the binoculars,' I nodded. 'Is he married? Perhaps a little young for you but—'

'He's leaving on Saturday,' Mum said firmly. 'We're just friends.'

And that was the end of that.

We continued the rest of our journey in silence and Crispin Fellowes was soon forgotten as the familiar church spire of St Mary's appeared in the distance. Thankfully, Mum navigated the usual series of dangerous hairpin bends more carefully and soon the sign of Little Dipperton loomed into view.

Little Dipperton was a typical chocolate-box Devonshire village consisting of whitewashed, thatched and slate-roofed cottages with a handful of shops and a seventeenth-century pub. There was just one narrow road that snaked around the village green past the Norman church of St Mary's. The cottages, painted in a distinctive blue trim, belonged to the Honeychurch estate and were tenant-occupied. They had no front gardens and there was no pavement. The low front doors opened directly on to the road, with traditional cottage gardens stretching in feudal rows at the rear overlooking woodland and rolling countryside.

The cottages formed a crescent around the graveyard that was encompassed by a low stone wall. Ancient yew trees and hedges flourished among the dozens of gravestones that commemorated the names of the families who had been born, died, and still lived in a village that was mentioned in the Domesday Book.

We joined a long line of stationary traffic just shy of Church Lane where we needed to turn in to check on Ruby.

Little Dipperton seemed more congested than usual. Holidaymakers came in droves to the South Hams to take advantage of the coastal towns of Dartmouth and the nearby beaches of Bigbury-on-Sea and Bantham. With spectacular Dartmoor to the north, and the River Dart, where Greenway, Agatha Christie's former summer home, perched on a bluff, and plenty of stunning National Trust properties to visit, it was easy to see why Devon was such a draw.

A colourful banner on fifteen-foot poles straddled the road announcing next Saturday's Little Dipperton Flower and Produce Festival.

Held in the grounds of Honeychurch Hall the festival was a highly anticipated annual event which seemed to have become more cutthroat of late. Unfortunately, with the county-wide hosepipe ban in force, the impact of the water shortage on their entries was all the villagers could talk about. Backbiting was rife and there was a rumour that neighbours had come to physical blows as to whether a cross between a marrow and a gourd was eligible for the Cucurbit Cup.

And then we saw them.

'Goats!' I exclaimed.

Chapter Two

It was sheer pandemonium, not helped by well-meaning drivers getting out of their cars and windmilling their arms in an effort to drive the goats in a different direction. There were at least twenty. One goat, a billy with horns that must have been over a foot in length, was particularly aggressive and seemed to enjoy charging at anyone who dare approach. Goats dashed down the twittens, the small alleys between terraced and semi-detached cottages alike, only to pop out of others further down the lane.

We were hemmed in and unable to move as a red-faced man, Tom Jones – no relation to the singer – attempted to round the goats up. It was like herding cats. The moment one broke away, the others followed.

The Jones family had bought Home Farm from the Honeychurch Hall estate years ago. They made delicious goats milk, cheese and yogurts that were sold at the community shop.

'I wouldn't want to be in Tom's shoes.' Mum remarked. 'Look at those window boxes. Those goats have eaten all the geraniums!'

A piercing whistle stopped everyone – including the goats – in their tracks. Lord Rupert Honeychurch, the fifteenth Earl of Grenville, materialised along with Mr Chips, the family's feisty Jack Russell. In his early fifties, Rupert was tall and easy to spot with his upright stance and military moustache, and the unmistakable manner that says, 'all this belongs to me!' Despite the hot weather, Rupert wore beige twill trousers, a long-sleeved shirt, tie, and his trademark checked flat cap.

He blew his whistle in a series of short and long peeps which Mr Chips instantly obeyed. Miraculously, the goats were successfully funnelled through the lych-gate and into the enclosed sanctuary of the churchyard.

It can't have taken more than five minutes.

'That dog has missed his vocation,' Mum declared.

Rupert gave a final peep on his whistle and turned away with Mr Chips trotting to heel. The pair melted into the onlookers and vanished.

Traffic finally moved on again, leaving a trail of destruction and a lot of goat droppings in its wake.

We turned into Church Lane, a cul-de-sac which ended in the vicarage and a patch of hard-packed mud that served as a car park, which was where Mum parked. Opposite was another gate that opened into the churchyard. Young Dawn Jones was standing guard just in case any goat clever enough knew how to open a gate.

We got out.

'Dad's gone to get the trailer,' said Dawn. 'We're taking the goats back to the farm and, of course, with Mum poorly we're short-handed.'

'Your mother's got the bug, too?' Mum said. 'I am sorry.'

'The doctor says it's not contagious and since she rarely leaves the farm, I just don't know how she got it.'

'How did the goats escape?' I asked.

'No one knows,' she said. 'The gate to their field must have been left open. The fencing is new and the gate latch is one of those mortice deadlock things. It even swings shut because the gate closes on a downward slope.' Dawn looked upset. 'They've feasted on all the gardens and the allotments on this side of the village.'

It suddenly occurred to me what this really meant. 'Oh. The festival.'

'Yes,' Dawn nodded. 'Dad thinks we'll never live it down.'

'Let's hope that you don't get sued,' Mum said darkly.

Dawn's eyes widened. 'What do you mean?'

Mum shrugged. 'People are funny about this sort of thing these days. Damage to personal property and what-not. I see it on *Judge Judy* all the time.'

Dawn looked blank.

'It's an American TV courtroom show,' I put in.

'Jeremy Kyle meets Doctor Phil,' Mum said. 'Very entertaining.'

Dawn did not seem in the mood to discuss trivia. 'Dad got the phone call from that idiot policeman Clive Banks,' she ran on. 'His wife Janet found them up to their horns in her prize-winning dahlias. She was furious. Poor Capricious is very upset.' Seeing our puzzled looks she explained, 'Capricious Amadeus the billy goat. I'm afraid he's lived up to his name.'

I thought for a moment. 'Where is the goat field?'

She gestured beyond the vicarage. 'Behind there. It runs along the back of the cottage gardens and allotments all the way to the river at the bottom of the hill. At the very least the herd could have been contained in the cart track between because it's fenced on either side. I just don't understand what happened.'

I gave her a sympathetic smile.

My mother's mobile rang again. She glanced at the screen and groaned. 'Hello Danny. No, we just got here. Don't call me. I'll call you.' And she jabbed the end call button. 'I suppose we had better go and find Ruby or he'll just keep ringing.'

We left Dawn perched on the gate and crossed the narrow lane to End Cottage, Ruby's home.

The moment Caroline had returned to Danny's arms and moved into the vicarage Ruby moved out. Fortunately, the dowager countess stepped in. Ruby and Edith shared an unusual history which dated back to the Second World War, when Ruby was one of the thousands of children who were evacuated to the countryside from London to escape the bombing. Ruby ended up being billeted on the Honeychurch Hall estate.

When she found herself – unwillingly – back in the area again, the pair had reconnected and become friends. Edith had given Ruby one of the estate cottages to live in, rent free. To be honest, it wasn't one of the best in the village. In fact, it was called End Cottage because it was literally at the end of the lane, with the front door opening directly into the church car park. Only a screen of mature conifers separated the shabby wooden-clad building from the adjacent vicarage.

'What a depressing place to live,' Mum remarked as we knocked on the front door. 'It looks like a garden shed.'

A net curtain covered the only front window, making it impossible to see inside. After a few more knocks and a shout through the letter box, we decided to go around the back.

A side alley led us to a cobbled path that ran behind the cottages parallel to Church Lane all the way to the main road – if you could call the single-lane that ran through the village a 'main' anything.

Each cottage had a rear entrance with a brick-paved area which, in the old days, would have housed a washing line, a concrete coal bunker and an outside loo. Although it had been years since a coal fire had burned in any of the grates in Little Dipperton, there was still that feel of dust and grime. There was also the usual muddle of recycling bins – the South Hams Council had strict rules which involved a lot of faffing around – dividing bottles, containers, cardboard, and tins into their appropriate containers – which hopefully went towards saving the planet but certainly took up a lot of space. Beyond that, a spindly hedge comprising a mixture of hawthorn, hazel and holly swept along a dilapidated picket fence that was interspersed with lop-sided latch-gates. These opened into fenced strips of garden with a bottom latch-gate that backed on to the cart track flanked by sheep wire.

Mum touched Ruby's back door and it swung open. 'You go in first.'

Tentatively I stepped into the kitchen. With its low ceiling, small window, and quarry-tiled floor, it was dark but cool.

'Good grief!' My mother exclaimed. 'This place could do with a coat of paint.' She wrinkled her nose. 'And what's that smell? Drains?'

I'd been in Ruby's kitchen many times and remembered my dismay at the condition of the place the first time I saw it, too. It was scheduled for a face-lift at some point, but Ruby had been happy to live there just to get away from her daughter-in-law. It was one-up, one-down with a cat-slide roof that housed the narrow kitchen we stood in now. An ancient gas stove, fridge, and an old stone sink with a wooden draining board crowded one corner. A square table was pushed in the other, with two wooden chairs tucked beneath. Other than BBC Radio Devon playing on low, the cottage was silent.

On the draining board were bird feeders in various stages of being filled with seeds and suet balls. The kitchen table was strewn with magazines and what looked like the remains of breakfast – a half-eaten piece of toast, the lid still off the marmalade jar and a full cup of tea that had to be cold.

'It's almost three thirty,' said Mum. 'Where can she be? Why don't you take a look upstairs?'

In my experience, when someone was missing and it was left to me to 'take a look upstairs' the answer was laid out on a cold stone floor. Happily, it wasn't the case today.

Ruby wasn't in her bedroom that overlooked the car park, nor was she in the bathroom, which was a ghastly shade of avocado green. Even with the tiny window open, there was a strange sweet and spicy smell. In the empty bath sat a large washing-up bowl filled with brownish sludge. A five-litre white plastic bottle with spray nozzle stood on the floor. On top of the windowsill was half a bottle of Fairy Liquid washing-up detergent and a book with *Aunt Muriel's Home Remedies* printed on the spine.

I headed back down the narrow staircase to the kitchen. 'She must be in the garden— Oh Mum! What on earth have you done to your eye!'

My mother had removed her sunglasses to reveal a livid purple, yellow and orange bruise on her cheekbone which had been neatly hidden by her large-framed sunglasses. This must have been what Crispin had been referring to earlier.

'Oh, that,' she said. 'I fell off a ladder.'

'What!' I exclaimed. 'When? Where?'

'A few days ago,' she said. 'I had to get a box down from the hayloft.'

'But . . . but . . . Why didn't you ask Alfred to help you?' I exclaimed. 'Or Crispin, since he seemed to be so concerned.'

'It was Crispin who broke my fall,' Mum said, 'We tumbled to the floor together, which was quite exciting.'

'Ugh,' I said but then had a thought. 'If Crispin was there, why didn't he get the box for you?'

Mum gave a mischievous grin. 'Because he said he wanted to admire my legs.'

'You really need to grow up,' I muttered.

'I found this on the kitchen table.' She handed me an official- looking letter from the water company.

With growing astonishment I read that it had come to their attention that Mrs Ruby Pritchard had been using her hosepipe despite the ban being in place, not once but three times in one week, and warning her that she could be fined up to a maximum of £1,000.

I was stunned. 'No wonder Ruby was upset. I would be, too. How on earth did the water company find out?'

'Rumour has it that someone is reporting people who use their hosepipes. Apparently, there is an' – she used air quotes – '"incentive" for sharing information.'

I gasped. 'I don't believe it! Are you sure?'

'Guess what the incentive is?'

'I have no idea,' I said.

'A free watering can.'

'That seems most unfair,' I said. 'Ruby can hardly be expected to lug a watering can from her kitchen to her garden. She can't walk without her stick!'

I replaced the letter on the table and saw what looked like a very fancy mobile phone with a distinctive cover emblazoned in pink roses. It was peeping out from underneath a newsletter called *The Nightjar Network*.

I picked up the phone. 'Oh, it's password protected.' I put it back on top of the newsletter.

'That's an expensive phone,' Mum said. 'It's much better than mine! I bet she doesn't know how to use it. That's probably why she didn't answer it.'

'I wish I could share your confidence, and it doesn't explain the half-eaten breakfast,' I pointed out. 'Ruby must be in the garden.'

We exited the kitchen and stepped into bright sunshine. Mum replaced her sunglasses. The offending hosepipe was attached to an outside tap and snaked across the brick path and through a gap in the fence.

As we opened the latch-gate it was obvious that the goats had been in and done their worst.

Ruby's once neatly laid out vegetable plots and cut flower beds were destroyed. The low, wire-hooped borders that divided each area lay broken. Even the fruit cage had not escaped the goats' greed – the netting was torn and the flimsy bamboo stick frames lay in pieces.

Ruby's garden was an unusual L-shape. It was long and narrow and peppered with bird tables and stone bird baths.

Dangling from the solitary apple tree were so many suet ball feeders that it resembled a Christmas tree.

'Let's try the greenhouse, Mum.'

Gingerly, I pushed open the door. It was stifling inside. There was an abundance of healthy tomato plants and a spectacular array of peaches but no sign of Ruby.

'I'll check the rest of the garden,' I said. 'You stay here.'

It was just before I turned into an arched, rose-covered trellis that opened into her rose garden that my fears for Ruby's safety were confirmed. Her walking stick lay on the grass along with suet balls, random pots, and plastic plant trays as well as a white five-litre plastic bottle with its spray nozzle detached – the same kind of bottle I had seen on her bathroom floor.

And then I saw her.

Ruby was lying on her side with her knees tucked up. She was still wearing a white broderie anglaise nightdress, blotched with brown stains.

Her eyes stared at nothing.

I didn't need to touch her. I already knew she was dead.

Chapter Three

It was another hour before Mum and I were able to leave Mallory to do his job. Other than a brief hug to make sure that I was okay, he whispered that he would still see me later as planned.

When Mum and I left End Cottage, there was still no sign of Caroline or Danny.

I was very shaken up about Ruby's death and a little puzzled. She'd managed to keep the goats from entering her rose garden by hurling suet balls and garden-tool missiles and shooing them away. I couldn't see any visible wounds. Had she been charged by Capricious and suffered internal injuries? Or perhaps the shock had brought on a heart attack. I suppose anything was possible.

And why were the top and bottom gates still closed? How had the goats got in and, for that matter, out!

'Well, I'm sorry to say that she's not going to be missed,' Mum suddenly declared.

I knew it was true. Even though I had a soft spot for Ruby, she had been a strange creature. She was fiercely loyal to Danny and very outspoken about just how much she despised her daughter-in-law, and most of the village if the truth be known. Ruby had never wanted to move to Little Dipperton and she had made that clear to all and sundry. On the few occasions I had talked to Ruby, she'd made no secret that her goal was to win every trophy at the upcoming festival just to put noses out of joint.

'Edith is going to be devastated,' I said. 'Mallory will have to break the news to her.'

'Ah. Your *lovely* Mallory, you mean.' Mum gave a knowing look. 'Even in such tragic surroundings you could see just how much he wanted to take you in his arms and—'

'Stop,' I said quickly. 'We're just friends.'

Mum raised an eyebrow. 'Friendship? Is that what you call it?'

I just smiled, determined not to rise to the bait.

I was still cautious and so was Mallory, who had extricated himself from a very awkward situation with his former superior officer. We were just enjoying each other's company. We hadn't even taken that 'physical' step yet, either, although I knew he wanted to just as much as I did. Both of us had agreed to go slow and be friends first just to make sure we weren't on a mutual rebound.

When the whole village follows your love life and things don't work out, it's embarrassing. I can't remember how many people came up to me after Shawn and I parted ways with condolences and opinions. It was horrible. I'd suffered the same thing when my fiancé of ten years and I had broken up, although that was a million times worse. That story appeared on the front page of *Star Stalkers!* and the usual tabloids. It had made me all the more determined to keep my private life private.

Mallory had his own past and I had mine. We had decided to be discreet and give our relationship the best chance we could.

Mum and I spoke very little on our drive home. She seemed as lost in her thoughts as I was in mine. I suspected she was noodling with a story idea for her next Krystalle Storm blockbuster romance. Soon, the familiar sight of the elegant eighteenth-century gatehouses where I operated my business loomed ahead.

The main entrance to Honeychurch Hall was very grand with two towering granite pillars topped with statues of hawks with their wings outstretched. Etched into one were the words Honeychurch Hall. It didn't seem to matter how many times I saw them I always felt a twinge of pride that I was now part of such a beautiful piece of history.

Mum drove past and on to the next set of pillars – smaller but no less impressive – and a sign that said: 'Tradesmen'. We turned in and followed the service drive that eventually ended at Jane's Cottage, perched at the top of a hill.

Jane's Cottage had been built as a summerhouse in the 1800s on the original site of Warren Lodge where – back in the day – the warrener lived to keep an eye on the

Honeychurch rabbits. Poaching was a serious crime, as evidenced by the warning signs that still peppered the estate.

The cottage was built from red brick under a pyramidal slate roof with two bay windows that flanked the Venetian entrance and ionic pilasters. A fanlight over a pediment door made the finishing touch. Jane's was my home and I absolutely loved it.

I'd transformed the front area to an outside flagstone terrace with a panel of woven hazel to enclose the east end where I'd hung fairy lights. The terrace was my favourite place to sit of a summer's evening to take in the peace of the spectacular surroundings.

To the north was wild, beautiful Dartmoor with its magnificent tors that were outlined on the horizon; to the south-east lay Honeychurch Hall, the grounds, and woodland surrounding my mother's Carriage House; to the south stood the gatehouses and, in the distance, the village of Little Dipperton. There was very little to see to the east since the walled garden, stable block and Honeychurch Cottages were hidden by dense woodland along with – thankfully – Eric's scrapyard and the field where he held his summer banger racing.

How different my life was now! I thought of bustling London where the view from my bedroom window was the platform at Putney Bridge tube station.

'What's she doing here?' Mum groaned as her on-again, off-again best friend Delia Evans, head of house at the Hall, came rushing towards us. Dressed in her usual black garb that closely resembled the clothes worn by Mrs Hughes the housekeeper in *Downton Abbey*, Delia was sweating profusely. Seeing her bicycle propped against a tree, I assume she had cycled here in a hurry.

Delia wrenched open the driver's door unable to stem her excitement, and all but dragged my mother out of the car. 'You were so long! I've been waiting for ages!' and 'Have you heard? Have you heard?'

'What's wrong?' Mum said in a panic. 'Is it her ladyship? Has she got worse?'

'No, thank heavens. Lady Edith is still hanging on.'

'I've been so worried,' Mum said before adding, 'So why are you here?'

Delia beamed. 'It's to do with someone else, and you'll never guess who.'

'Ha!' Mum crowed. 'We will because we found her!'

Delia faltered. 'Found who?'

'She doesn't know.' Mum shot me a look of triumph. The race to get the juiciest gossip first was becoming the stuff of legends. 'So you haven't heard.'

'That depends on what you're going to tell me,' Delia said warily. 'What have you heard?'

'You tell me what you heard first,' Mum shot back.

'Oh for heaven's sake you two!' I exclaimed. 'It's awful, Delia. Poor Ruby Pritchard is dead.'

Delia's jaw dropped.

'And we found her!' Mum said again, barely able to hide her glee. 'In the rose garden. Lying in a pool of blood. Covered in flies.'

I rolled my eyes. My mother just loved to exaggerate. Of course it was untrue but Delia wasn't to know that.

'Oh well.' Delia thought for a moment. 'Do you think anyone would mind if I helped myself to those peaches? I have a new recipe I want to try out for peach jam.'

'That sounds pretty callous,' I said, although I wasn't surprised. Delia was the consummate opportunist.

She shrugged. 'Not callous, Kat. Just practical. And I can guarantee that Ruby's death won't be mourned,' Delia raced on. 'Apparently, Stan has won first prize for his plums every year in the stone fruit category. Ruby introducing peaches set the cat among the pigeons because it was seen as cheating.'

'Cheating? How?' I demanded.

'Because she built a greenhouse with all the modern gadgets to get the edge. And, according to my sources, Ruby didn't apply for planning permission either.' Delia shook her head. 'And don't get me started on the roses.'

'Oh go on *do*, Delia,' Mum said. 'I'm bursting with curiosity. Start away.'

'Ruby took it upon herself to grab some of the garden next door. Verger's Cottage. You know, the bit at the end with the roses,' said Delia. 'It really belongs to the church.'

'But surely that's up to the vicar to decide,' I said. 'If it belongs to the church, why shouldn't his mother enjoy it?'

'Try telling Caroline that,' Delia continued. 'That's why Caroline's not competing. She's backed out of the festival, although frankly, with everyone dropping like flies with this bug, the festival might end up being cancelled.'

'That's not what I heard,' Mum declared. 'Caroline backed out because she wanted to hand out the trophies with her ladyship and her ladyship said no.'

'Yes. I know about that, Iris.' Delia pursed her lips. 'But what you don't know is that there are some very old roses in that bit, going back a hundred years or more. Caroline would have won the Veteran Rose Cup hands down. Instead, Ruby would have got the glory.'

'If she was still alive,' I reminded them. Honestly, the pair of them were dreadful!

'You seem to be well informed, Delia,' Mum said clearly annoyed that she wasn't.

'It's my job to be informed, Iris,' Delia said with no effort to disguise her pride. 'As head of house, I have to keep my ear to the ground to see what the mood is in the village and report straight back to her ladyship.'

'So you're the mole!' Mum exclaimed. 'You're the person sneaking to the water company.'

Delia's face turned red. 'That is not true and well you know it. But I must agree that it seems unfair that those who use a hosepipe have an advantage over those who struggle to use a watering can.'

'Perhaps you should suggest a handicap,' Mum said.

'That's a very good idea,' Delia nodded. 'It might soften the blow for those who got a letter from the water company threatening a massive fine! I think Doreen from the pub got one.'

'Ruby got one as well,' Mum put in.

'Someone in the village is telling tales.' Delia's head was nodding so furiously that I feared it might fall off. 'It's like living in Berlin before the wall came down! No one knows who the mole is.'

'I didn't know you lived in Berlin,' I said, but all too late I remembered Delia's now ex-husband – still serving a sentence for murder – had been in the Army and they'd lived overseas for most of her married life.

Delia gave me a mutinous glare.

'Ah, but did you hear about the goats?' Mum said hopefully. 'Eaten every flower in the window boxes in the village and decimated the allotments. Decimated! Like a plague of locusts!'

'Goats?' Delia's jaw dropped. 'No!'

'Sabotage,' Mum declared and then shrugged. 'Anyway, do you want to tell us what you've heard? I doubt if it's going to be as exciting as our news.'

Delia smirked. 'Hah! It is very exciting. Certainly more exciting than goats.'

Mum thrust out her jaw. 'More exciting than finding Ruby dead?'

'Oh yes, definitely.' Delia gave a dramatic pause. 'Eric Pugsley is getting married on Saturday!'

Chapter Four

Mum's eyes widened in astonishment and I was just as shocked.

'But . . . who to?' Mum demanded.

'*This* Saturday?' I said. 'Gosh. I've only been away for three weeks!'

'Who do you think?' Delia's grin became so wide I could see her back teeth.

'I don't know, Delia,' Mum snapped. 'After Vera, he swore he'd never marry again.'

'Well, he changed his mind.' Delia paused again to enjoy her triumph. 'All right, I'll tell you. You know those friends he has staying with him?'

'I didn't pay much attention, why?' Mum thought for a moment. 'Wait? The woman in the black muumuu? But she's far too old for him.'

Delia's smile remained. 'Not her. Not Banu. No, it's the daughter.'

'Right. In the kitchen. Now!' Mum exclaimed. 'Gin and tonic?'

'I shouldn't really,' Delia said. 'I'm supposed to be working. But go on, twist my arm.'

'Excuse me,' I protested. 'I've just flown halfway around the world and I'm really tired.'

'You don't have to join us,' Mum said. 'Go and have your shower. I did a little bit of shopping for you, knowing your cupboards would be bare and I know where everything is kept. Oh, and I left your post on the kitchen counter.'

As I hesitated, the irony wasn't lost on me. I despised gossip, but perhaps in special circumstances like this one, I'd have to make an exception. I relented. 'Okay. Perhaps a small gin.'

The significance of this news could not be underestimated. Forty-something Eric Pugsley with his beetle brows and inability to say a complete sentence without peppering it with grunts, had not only fallen in love but it would seem that he'd brought his bride-to-be to the Hall and kept it a secret. After a volatile marriage to Vera – Mum said it was Little Dipperton's version of an Elizabeth Taylor–Richard Burton love affair – that ended in her untimely death shortly after I moved here, Eric was adamant that he would remain single for the rest of his life.

Mum bombarded Delia with questions but she refused to tell us any details until we were sitting on the terrace with our drinks.

'But isn't the daughter about twelve years old?' Mum said.

I was surprised. 'I thought you hadn't seen her.'

'Only from a distance,' said Mum. 'A tiny little thing.'

'She's young, I'll give you that,' Delia nodded. 'But guess what else?' She waited until Mum and I were leaning in. 'They're Turkish. Or maybe it's Romanian. Hungarian. Anyway, it doesn't matter. Neither speaks a word of English!'

Mum gasped. 'No! You're making it up.'

'So hang on a moment, does Eric speak whatever language she does?'

'No,' said Delia. 'I have no idea how they communicate.'

'I do,' Mum flexed her fingers and leered. 'Braille.'

Delia laughed. 'Oh, you are naughty, Iris.'

'If you ask me, she's a mail order bride,' Mum said suddenly. 'That's what she is. I can't imagine anyone normal would have him. I bet he bought her online.'

This was juicy gossip indeed. Poor Ruby's awful accident was soon forgotten.

'No.' Delia's grin grew broad again. 'Remember that raffle ticket Eric won last Christmas?'

'I don't remember,' I said.

'Eric met her on holiday,' said Delia.

'No!' Mum burst into laughter. 'You're having me on.'

'It's true!' Delia protested.

'But that was only a few months ago,' Mum pointed out.

'And he kept it quiet,' Delia ran on. 'I thought there was something fishy going on when Eric asked if they could stay in number two.'

'I thought they were staying with Eric in number three,' Mum said.

'They are,' Delia declared. 'I told him no. I've got to keep number two ready for the new housekeeper. I've been advertising for weeks. You know how picky I am.'

'So are her family and friends flying in for this wedding?' I asked.

'No,' Delia shook her head. 'They're getting married here on Saturday, going on their honeymoon and then having a big party in . . . wherever it is they come from.' She lowered her voice as if about to reveal a secret. 'They come from money. A lot of money.'

'Marry in haste, repent at leisure,' Mum said. 'And what's the attraction? I don't get it. It's not like Eric's got any money and, let's face it, he's not exactly pin-up material, is he?'

It was unkind, but Mum's description was spot on. Eric had more excess hair than a gorilla – not that he could help that – and his life was his scrapyard and racing his old cars.

'You'd be surprised,' Delia declared. 'He's bought himself a BMW and well . . . I heard that he won the Premium Bonds back in the nineties and has been very clever with his investments.'

'How do you know?' Mum demanded.

Delia reddened. 'I . . . I just know.'

Mum cocked her head. 'Snooping you mean.'

Delia pulled herself to her feet. 'If you are going to insult me, I'm leaving.'

'Oh sit down!' Mum caught my eye and winked. 'Can't you take a joke?'

Delia sat down. 'And you'll never guess what else!' She gave another dramatic pause.

'You're killing me,' Mum said. 'What?'

'She's . . . she's . . .' Delia's face turned pink.

'Spit it out!' Mum prompted.

'I have it on very good authority that she won't sleep with him until they're wed.' Delia's nodding had gone into overdrive. 'She's holding out.'

'Who does she think she is?' Mum sneered. 'Anne Boleyn? Does she want to be Queen of the Scrapyard?'

'Her mother watches her like a hawk,' Delia said. 'Maybe it's a tradition. A culture thing.'

'Back in the dark ages, maybe,' Mum declared. 'But in the twenty-first century? You're making it up!'

'I'm just telling you what I know,' Delia said with a sniff. 'Banu's all right. One of my dailies is on holiday so she offered to help with dusting and whatnot for free.'

'There's no such thing as a free lunch,' Mum pointed out.

'Can we stop referring to this poor young girl as she,' I said.

'Yasmine – that's her name, with an emphasis on the e – as in Yasmeene. I must go.' Delia downed her gin and tonic. 'You'll meet her at the Safari Supper tomorrow evening, which reminds me, I've been trying to reach Caroline to confirm the timing, but I suppose she's too caught up in the death of her mother-in-law to answer her phone now.'

'You'd like to think so,' Mum said and told Delia we had been to End Cottage in the first place because Danny had been worried about his mother and couldn't reach Caroline. 'What do you mean, confirm the timing?'

Delia shrugged. 'You know what Caroline is like. Always changing her mind. Let's see . . . it starts at six at the Carriage House.'

'Six!' Mum shrieked. 'I thought it was six-thirty!'

'Ah. You see! Always best to check.' Delia raised her hand and, ticking off each finger said, 'Appetisers at your place, Iris. Main Course at the vicarage. Pudding in the beer garden at the Hare and Hounds and petits fours and digestifs down in the summer house by the lake.'

'That seems inefficient,' I said. 'Going back and forth to the village.'

'She's got transportation laid on by Bob-the-Bus,' said Delia. 'Caroline has gone all out to make a big splash and now Eric's getting wed, she's decided it's going to be in their honour. Hired tables and chairs, glasses, and plates from Festive Fun Planners. Why else do you think the tickets were so expensive? Supposedly all the proceeds are going to her Hats Off charity, but once she's paid for all that, I doubt if there will be much left. And of course, those who are too ill to attend will expect a refund on their ticket, which is only fair.'

'Well. I hope the time is all Caroline is going to change.' Mum grumbled. 'I've boiled twenty-seven eggs for my Oeuf à la Russe starter.'

'Make it thirty,' Delia said. 'We've got three extras. Banu and Yasmine and I invited the birdwatcher, that lovely man who has been staying in the shepherd's hut. Crispin. He goes home on Saturday so I thought it would be a nice gesture.'

Mum's face fell. 'Why? Whatever for? He's . . . he's a holidaymaker.'

It was obvious that Delia was unaware of my mother's friendship with Crispin.

'If that's the case, you may as well invite everyone who is on holiday in Devon,' Mum went on.

Delia frowned. 'Crispin said he'd like to come.'

'You mean, you'd like him to come,' Mum snapped.

Delia seemed taken aback. 'It was a casual invitation. Why?' Her eyes narrowed. 'Are you after him romantically?'

'No, of course I'm not! He can't be more than fifty-odd,' Mum retorted but I could tell from her face that she was miffed.

'He's fifty-eight,' said Delia. 'He told me. We're going together.'

'Knock yourself out,' Mum said. 'I just think it's strange inviting . . . inviting a holidaymaker to something in the village, that's all.'

'Well, he's coming and that's final.' Delia's voice was firm. 'And since you're not interested, I'll take a crack at him. I'm quite partial to a younger man and he was definitely giving me the eye.'

The friends fell into an awkward silence.

Delia took in the terrace with my planters and twinkling fairy lights. 'You've made it nice here, Kat,' she said. 'Done a fair bit of decorating, too.'

I smiled. 'Thank you.'

Delia looked around again and gave a grunt. 'Well, don't get too comfortable. You never know what's around the corner.'

'Hadn't you better be going?' Mum stood up. 'You told us you couldn't stay long.'

'I *am* going!' Delia stood up, too. 'Don't forget to boil three more eggs. Unless . . .' She turned to me with her mean little eyes. 'Are you bringing anyone, Kat? A plus one?'

I gritted my teeth. Here we go again. Delia just couldn't help digging at my single status every time we met. 'Not this time.'

'Oh, poor you.' Delia shot me a look of pity before returning to her ever-efficient self.

'Iris, do me a favour. Would you stop at Eric's and tell him it starts at six, not six-thirty? Her ladyship is expecting me at the Hall in fifteen minutes to go through the digestifs. His lordship is talking about opening a bottle of Graham's vintage port but I think it will be wasted on the villagers.'

'I suppose I can,' Mum said, feigning reluctance. But I knew she would be anxious to meet the bride-to-be officially and to be honest, so was I.

'Oh – and we're all supposed to wear hats,' Delia added.

'Hats?' Mum ventured. 'What do you mean, hats?'

'Safari hats.' Delia rolled her eyes. 'Caroline wants everyone in fancy dress but she said she'd provide the hats. For a donation.'

'So not only have we bought tickets for the Safari Supper and have had to buy the food, we now have to pay for the hats,' Mum moaned. 'I'm not wearing a pith helmet.'

'They're Panama hats, and try at least to get into the spirit of things,' Delia scolded. 'It's for charity, after all.'

'All right,' Mum said. 'But I'm not wearing fancy dress.'

'I won't, if you won't,' said Delia.

They agreed neither would with a handshake.

'And by the way, that bruise on your eye looks worse,' Delia went on. 'You should try Muriel's Miracle Spray from her book of home remedies. Excellent for skin conditions. Arthritis. Cleaning an oven. Fixing a squeaky door. Repelling mosquitoes – although I prefer Avon's Skin So Soft. It's supposed to be nature's answer to WD40.'

'WD40? No thanks!' Mum scoffed. 'A packet of frozen peas is good enough for me.'

And with that, Delia mounted her bicycle and pedalled away.

'Do you want to come with me and meet the blushing bride-to-be?' Mum suggested.

I grinned. 'What do you think?'

Chapter Five

Moments later we pulled up outside the three terraced cottages that were adjacent to the Victorian walled garden. Honeychurch Cottages had been built for the gardeners towards the end of the nineteenth century when the Hall was in its heyday.

One of the things I loved about living on the old Honeychurch Hall estate was the sense of history. The Earl of Grenville title had been bestowed on the Honeychurch family by King Henry V in 1414. A Honeychurch had lived at the Hall ever since.

I'd noticed a sense of pride and loyalty among the villagers, many of whom still lived in the cottages owned by the estate and whose ancestors were one of the five main families – Stark, Pugsley, Cropper, Banks, and Jones – who had worked below stairs, in the extensive grounds or had farmed the land – most of which had been sold off to keep the old Hall habitable. Even a basic repair like replacing the guttering cost hundreds of thousands of pounds, not to mention the sash windows – most of which didn't open.

Mum and I were newcomers or 'blow-ins', which was the derogatory term used by the locals, but we'd slowly been accepted into the close-knit community, as had Delia, too.

Delia lived in number one, the larger of the three cottages – and marked her status with an abundance of flowering geraniums in window boxes and planters. She had surprised everyone with her managerial skills and turned the Hall and gardens around. The Hall had even been accepted into the Historic Houses Association and had hosted two open garden days this summer that had been very successful.

There were two cars parked outside the cottages. One was a battered blue Skoda with the passenger door painted in pink primer, and the other was a shiny silver BMW convertible that had the roof down – presumably, this was Eric's new car.

Mum knocked on Eric's front door and waited. She pointed to a handwritten sign in the front window with a crude sketch of a skull and crossbones with the words 'Smoking Strictly Prohibited Anywhere on the Honeychurch Hall Estate!'

The door flew open and a hard-looking woman in her mid-fifties with a heavy unibrow and iron-grey short hair stood in front of us with a cigarette dangling defiantly from her lips. She was dressed in a shapeless black dress.

I assumed this must be the mother of the bride.

'Ah, you must be Banu,' Mum said warmly. 'I'm Iris and this is my daughter Kat. Welcome.'

'Yes.' Banu smiled with a surprisingly dazzling set of white teeth which seemed at odds with her dowdy appearance.

'Is Eric there?' Mum said brightly. 'There's been a time change for the Safari Supper tomorrow night.'

Banu dragged on her cigarette. 'Repeat please.'

'Ay-up!' came a cry and we turned to see Eric and a very young woman emerge from Honeywell Woods opposite, hand in hand.

The first thing I noticed was how sleek Eric's eyebrows were. They were perfectly groomed. He had shaved off his stubble and his face looked remarkably smooth underneath. He wore a clean blue-checked shirt, beige chinos and gleaming white trainers. The woman next to him was – there were only two words for it – utterly stunning. Petite, lightly tanned with long dark-brown hair and a set of teeth that matched her mother's, which I now assumed was a nod to Turkish dentistry. Yasmine wore impossibly tight jeans and a tiny white T-shirt that showed off perfect breasts and a toned midriff. Her peach-coloured nails were long and possibly fake.

I was trying to reconcile this miserable, grumpy specimen who I'd known for the past several years to the beaming love-struck middle-aged man that stood before me. I was speechless. I'd never seen Eric happy before and it completely transformed his features. In fact, he was quite attractive.

'This is Yasmine,' he said holding his girlfriend's arm up as if he'd just won a trophy – which I suppose, he had. 'Yasmine this is Kat and Iris.' He introduced us by speaking in a very slow voice.

Yasmine showed us her perfectly white teeth. 'Yes.'

'Congratulations and welcome,' I said.

Yasmine nodded with enthusiasm and warmth. 'Yes.'

'Yes. Congratulations.' Mum pointed to the ring on Yasmine's finger. It was distinctive in that it wasn't a traditional engagement ring. It was Etruscan and highly decorative. 'What a lovely ring.'

'It's been in Yasmine's family for generations,' Eric beamed again. In fact, he reminded me of the Cheshire cat from *Alice's Adventures in Wonderland*. He had quite a nice smile, too. And what's more, I hadn't detected a single grunt. Yet.

'And you're getting married this Saturday,' I said.

'Everyone is invited.' Eric looked at his new bride with adoration. 'Yasmine loves England so we wanted to get married here so she can meet everyone.'

'And then you're going on your honeymoon,' Mum said.

'We're flying to Istanbul on Tuesday,' said Eric. 'We're staying at the Kale Konak Cave hotel. It's like sleeping in a cave. That's why it's called the Kale Konak *Cave* hotel. We're going to do hot air ballooning, mountain hiking. Anything my girl wants.' He gave Yasmine a happy smile which she returned with a coy giggle.

My mother gestured to Banu, who was framed in the doorway lighting up another cigarette. She tossed the match on to the ground where it smouldered for a few seconds before going out.

Mum lowered her voice. 'You know there's no smoking on the estate, Eric. Delia will have a fit.'

'It okay, Eric,' Yasmine said in halting English, giving us that beautiful smile again. 'I tell her no smoke. She start the patch tomorrow. She promise me. "Yasmine. If you want no smoke. I no smoke."'

'Ah, the nicotine patch,' Mum nodded. 'Good idea. And your English is excellent, Yasmine. Delia told us you didn't understand our language.'

'Delia!' Yasmine laughed a tinkly girlish laugh. 'She so funny. My English not so good but I try.' She pointed to my hair. 'Very pretty.'

'And so are you,' Eric blurted out and Yasmine giggled again.

Mum stifled a groan.

'Thank you,' I said to Yasmine. My mane had earned me the nickname Rapunzel. It was rather sweet to see them grin and nod and giggle. I felt a pang of something I couldn't quite put my finger on. Not longing – there was no question of me wanting to be with Eric – but perhaps the innocence of young love that radiated from Yasmine's face. We were all young once, weren't we?

'The Safari Supper starts at six tomorrow, not six-thirty, Eric,' Mum went on. 'I'm sure everyone is excited about meeting you, Yasmine. I hear the party is to celebrate your nuptials.'

Yasmine frowned. 'What is the nuptial?'

'She means our marriage,' said Eric. Yasmine draped her arms around his neck and nibbled his ear. Eric turned pink with pleasure.

I refused to look at my mother, who I was quite sure felt as nauseous as I did at the blatant display of public affection.

'We'll leave you lovebirds to it,' Mum said. 'Oh. Apparently we're all to wear fancy dress and Panama hats for this event. Presumably Caroline will hand them out at the door.'

Eric attempted to extricate himself from Yasmine's embrace but she clung on tightly.

'You in tomorrow, Kat?' he managed to croak.

'In where?' I asked.

'Working, like,' he said. 'There are a few things I want to talk to you about.'

'I can be,' I said. 'What time?'

'How about eleven and, oh—' Whatever Eric had been about to say was lost as Yasmine dragged him towards the front door where Banu was waiting. Her action reminded me of a little girl dragging a parent to the ice cream van.

He shot us another happy smile, nearly missed his footing and all but fell on top of Banu.

'I'll run you back up the hill, Kat,' said Mum and we piled into the Mini once more and set off.

'Well,' I said. 'What do you think of that?'

'He's certainly changed,' Mum mused. 'It looks like his eyebrows have been, what do they call it, threaded?'

'I wonder what he wants to see me about,' I mused.

Mum laughed. 'Maybe he's going to ask you to be a bridesmaid.'

'Very funny,' I said.

I was dropped off at Jane's Cottage and, with a cheerful peep on the horn, I was alone at last.

I wandered inside and gave the pile of post on the kitchen counter a passing glance. An elaborate business card from Bespoke Interiors: Manifester of Dream Homes, was on the top with a note written in calligraphy that said, 'Sorry we missed you. Please call Natalie,' along with a London phone number. Puzzled, I set the card aside. I'd ring whoever Natalie was tomorrow and tell her she had called at the wrong house. In fact, I'd do everything tomorrow. The only thing that was keeping me awake was the prospect of seeing Mallory.

I took a long shower and wondered what to wear. I chose an olive-green linen shift. Mallory had said he would come by but, given Ruby's death, I wasn't sure what to expect. Mum had been as good as her word and stocked up my fridge. There was even a bottle of chilled white wine in the door and six bottles of Peroni. I also had some mineral water on hand just in case he was still on duty.

I felt the usual butterflies and reminded myself of something that my mother liked to say. '*Enjoy this part of the relationship. It's the most exciting of all. It's the promise of the unknown that can be far more thrilling than washing his socks.*'

Mum always believed in keeping the mystery in marriage alive and, since my parents had been happily married for almost fifty years, whatever she had done must have worked.

It wasn't yet six. I watered my geraniums with my watering can and did a bit of dead heading so it looked as orderly as the heatwave would allow. I checked my mobile for the umpteenth time to see where my luggage was, and according to the text I had received, it was 'last tracked at LAX', which was the airport code for Los Angeles. It was infuriating.

I had about an hour to wait so I grabbed a catalogue for an upcoming estate sale at Luxton's auction house. The owner had a small collection of antique dolls that I had my eye on. I kicked off my flip-flops and settled into one of the wicker chairs outside on the terrace.

It must only have been a few minutes later when I saw, rather than heard, a car appear. It was Caroline's 'I'm saving-the-planet' silver Mercedes Smart EQ forfour cabriolet.

I watched her check her reflection in the rear-view mirror, then only just manage to extricate her voluptuous curves from the driver's seat. Dressed in white trousers belted tightly around her waist with a pink, long-sleeved floral shirt-waister, her feminine assets only just stayed within the realm of decency. A wide Alice band kept her shoulder-length chestnut hair off her face. It was hard to judge Caroline's age because, as Mum unkindly pointed out, she put her make-up on with a garden trowel. Caroline favoured bright red lipstick and was never seen without it. It was her trademark and the first thing you noticed about her. She was handsome rather than beautiful but there was none of the warmth that one would expect a vicar's wife to possess.

Plastering a fake smile on my face, I stood up and went to meet her.

Chapter Six

'One for you and one for Iris.' Caroline handed me two Panama hats. 'She wasn't home when I stopped by. That will be ten pounds per hat. I can wait while you get the money. Cash only.'

'Oh. Right.' I was taken aback. She hadn't even mentioned Ruby! I left her and returned moments later with a twenty-pound note and passed it over. 'That's a lot of hats you've had to buy.'

'I've borrowed them from the Gipping Bards amateur dramatics,' Caroline went on. 'The wardrobe mistress is a personal friend.'

I was about to point out that if they were on loan, why should we have to pay for them?

'The proceeds are split between the Bards and my charity,' said Caroline who must have guessed what was going through my mind.

'Oh, right,' I said. 'I'm . . . so sorry to hear about Ruby. So sad.'

Caroline looked away and a small cry escaped her lips. 'Yes. Poor Ruby. Such a darling. Danny is devastated. He drove like the wind to get home. And you found her! How frightful. How distressing.'

'It was,' I said as I tried to push the image of Ruby lying in her stained nightdress out of my mind.

'I feel terrible,' Caroline ran on. 'I should have been there. As it happened, I was at Crafty Pleasures, frantically finishing up the table decorations for our Safari Supper. Crafty Pleasures is in Bovey Tracy by the House of Marbles? Do you know it? Quite fun. I was there all day.'

'Oh,' I said.

'Yes,' Caroline nodded. 'Painting stripes on zebras and sticking eyeballs on giraffes. They're going on the tables and I thought if people wanted to take one home, ten pounds would be fair. Otherwise, I'll sell them at the community shop. Would you like to see them?'

'What? Now?' The segue from Ruby's death to her craft project threw me completely. Caroline didn't seem to notice. She popped the boot of her car and gestured for me to join her to admire her handiwork.

Giraffes painted in uneven splodges of brown with bright-red beaded eyes, zebras with wobbly stripes and elephants, who could have done with another coat of grey paint, were arranged in two open cardboard boxes. The wooden animals were crudely made and badly painted but I suppose they did the trick.

'How lovely,' I said politely. 'Although I've never seen a giraffe with red eyes.'

'I bought the beads on Amazon,' said Caroline. 'With the little black spots, they do look like eyes, don't they? It was so fiddly to glue them on. No wonder it took me all day. And I had my mobile off otherwise I'd have got Danny's call. I only found out about Ruby when I got back home. Ambulance. The police.' She paused for a moment. 'Would you know why the police would get involved? I know you and . . . Shawn Cropper – is that his name? – are an item.'

'That was the former detective inspector,' I said. 'He transferred to Exeter a few months ago.'

'Oh what a shame,' said Caroline. 'You do seem to have bad luck.'

'The police were there,' I continued, 'because there is always an autopsy when a death has occurred in unusual circumstances.'

'An autopsy!' Caroline sounded horrified. 'I heard that the goats had got into her garden and that she died from shock.'

'I really don't know, Caroline.'

We stared at each other.

'What about Iris? She was there, too. What does Iris think?' Caroline didn't wait for an answer. She plunged on again. 'I didn't get any sense out of that buffoon. You know. The one who looks like Captain Pugwash.'

'Clive Banks,' I stifled a smile because she was right. Detective Sergeant Banks did resemble the children's cartoon character with his barrel-shaped body and thick black beard.

'Perhaps, out of respect for Ruby, we should cancel the Safari Supper.'

'I wish we could,' Caroline sounded pained. 'But that wouldn't be fair on Eric and Yasmine, would it? Or for those who have already gone to the trouble of hiring fancy dress outfits.'

I was struck by a sudden thought. Since Delia had seemed genuinely surprised at Eric's upcoming nuptials, had Caroline just found out, too? 'When did you know they were getting married?'

'We were sworn to secrecy,' Caroline said.

'It must have been the best kept secret in the village.'

'Naturally, Danny knew because he's going to marry them,' said Caroline. 'Eric wanted to elope to Turkey but Yasmine wouldn't have any of it. She insisted on an English church wedding with all Eric's friends followed by a reception at the Hare and Hounds. Of course, Eric had hoped that his lordship would host that in the ballroom at the Hall, but apparently he refused.'

'What about her own family,' I asked.

'I think,' Caroline lowered her voice and gestured for me to stand closer even though there wasn't a soul for miles around. 'I think it's because there's some opposition to the marriage.'

'From Lord Rupert? Is that why he wouldn't host the reception?' Although surely it had nothing to do with him!

'No, no,' Caroline shook her head. '*Her* family. Once they're wed, Yasmine's kin will have to get over themselves.'

I hated gossip but I just couldn't help myself. 'Why the opposition? Banu seems okay with the nuptials.'

Caroline rubbed her thumb and the top of her index finger together. 'Money.' She lowered her voice again. 'Yasmine's father passed and left her a lot of money. She's quite the catch. I think the phrase "punching above his weight" might apply in this instance.'

I thought of Eric and had to agree but would never say so aloud.

'And what about you?' Caroline said. 'We really need to find you a nice man and perhaps not one in uniform – although it was the dog collar that attracted me to Danny in the first place.' Caroline smiled. It was the first time I noticed the snaggle-tooth which gave her a curious vulnerability, especially as there was a tiny smudge of red lipstick on it.

She gestured to my planters with my poor dried-up flowers. 'I'm glad to see someone is following the Devon county guidelines. I am appalled at the lack of consideration shown in the village for our planet. And all this fuss over a flower show! It's so . . . parochial. I suppose I'll have to step in and judge if the dowager countess doesn't get better.'

And that's when I noticed the damage to her car. There was a nasty scrape that ran the entire length of the body.

Caroline noticed and scowled. 'I know,' she said. 'Wretched holidaymaker! I should have listened to my instincts but he just insisted I could get by. It's going to cost thousands of pounds. He didn't even stop! I got his number plate. Trust me. He won't get away with it.'

'You're now officially a local with a country car,' I said lightly and gestured to my Golf, which bore plenty of scratches and dents from similar escapades.

I was getting agitated and wanted Caroline to leave. Mallory might be here at any minute, which could be awkward.

'Well, thank you for bringing up the hats,' I said. 'Delia had mentioned the Safari Supper is starting at six tomorrow, not six-thirty.'

'Yes,' Caroline nodded. 'At the vicarage.'

'At the vicarage,' I repeated. 'Aren't the appetisers at the Carriage House?'

'Oh it didn't make sense to do it that way,' Caroline said dismissively. 'No, I'm doing the starter now – canapés, little mini quiches, spinach tartlets and other yummy nibbles. Iris can do the main course – perhaps a summer salad – nothing too fancy. She could poach a salmon or something. Then we'll have the puddings in the summer house by the lake and finish up in the drawing room at the Hall for digestifs and petits fours.'

I thought of my mother and her soon-to-be-thirty Oeufs à la Russe. Good luck telling her of that change. Delia wasn't going to be too pleased either.

Caroline returned to her car and attempted to turn around. With each turn on the steering wheel, her face contorted with pain.

As luck would have it, Mallory's black Peugeot came into view. As he pulled over to allow Caroline to pass, she stopped and opened her window. Whatever she said seemed to take a long time to say.

Finally, the Mercedes disappeared from view and Mallory parked and got out. My stomach turned over as it always did when I saw him now. Tall, at over six foot three, he was incredibly handsome with cropped dark hair and grey-green eyes. My mother had used his likeness for one of her Krystalle Storm promotional Thermos flasks once, which now we could laugh about, but at the time, given that Mallory knew it was him, was mortifying.

I strolled over to meet him and he caught me up in his arms, kissing me long and hard. My head spun and I felt ridiculously happy.

'I'm hot and sticky,' he said, nuzzling into my ear.

I stepped back, conscious of my heart hammering in my chest.

His eyes met mine. 'I missed you, Kat. And I want to hear all about your trip but,' he took a deep breath, 'I can't stay long this evening. I expect you're tired anyway.'

'I am,' I admitted. 'But never too tired for you. What's happened? Is it to do with Ruby?'

He nodded. 'Things have changed. I need to move quickly.'

'It's okay,' I said. 'I know you can't tell me.'

'Not everything, perhaps,' he said grimly. 'But I'm afraid it looks like the cause of death is not as straightforward as I thought. Shall we go and sit down?'

Chapter Seven

'How well do you know the vicar's wife?' Mallory asked once we had settled down with cold drinks – me with a glass of white wine and him with Perrier water and ice.

'As well as anyone in the village,' I said carefully. I was still at the stage in a new relationship where I wanted Mallory to think I was perfect. What I had wanted to say was that I couldn't stand Caroline and that she was a pushy cow who had broken our eccentric vicar's heart.

'What was Caroline doing here?'

I pointed to the Panama hats that I'd left on a wicker chair. 'Dropping those off. They're for the Safari Supper tomorrow night.' I pulled a face. 'And we're all expected to dress up.'

He raised an eyebrow and the corners of his mouth twitched. 'You don't like her?'

'I do!' I blushed then added ruefully. 'How can you tell?'

'I'm trained to tell.' Mallory gestured to where he had stopped to allow Caroline's car to pass. 'She seemed unusually chatty about her movements today. Crafty Pleasures, eh?' He grinned. 'Not exactly the name I would choose for a craft workshop!'

Mallory took out his notebook and hunted for a pen in his top shirt pocket. It was short-sleeved and I couldn't help noticing his tanned forearms and had to look away. What on earth was wrong with me? I was acting like one of Krystalle Storm's breathless heroines.

I said the first thing that came into my head. 'I suppose Caroline told you about her altercation with a holidaymaker who scraped her car and drove off.'

'Yes, although she couldn't tell me exactly when it happened,' said Mallory, 'And yet she was very specific about painting zebras, sticking eyeballs on giraffes and struggling to find the right shade of grey paint for the elephants.'

'She showed them to me,' I said. 'They're table decorations and if you love them enough, you can buy one for ten pounds!'

Mallory's expression grew serious. 'So let's run through the afternoon's events. The vicar called Iris to say he couldn't reach Ruby or Caroline and asked if Iris would check to make sure Ruby was all right.'

'Yes,' I said. 'He was away at a conference in Bath.'

'Was your mother close to Ruby?'

'Not at all,' I said. 'Unfortunately, Ruby wasn't very popular in the village. I think my mother was Danny's last resort. He told us that he was concerned because Ruby had received a letter and was very upset.'

'What kind of letter?' said Mallory.

'I know that you already know,' I teased.

'You're right, I do,' he said. 'But I like to be thorough.'

'Mum and I found a letter from the water company on her kitchen table. She'd been threatened with a fine for using a hosepipe – not once, but three times! I'm sure you know about the county-wide ban.'

He nodded. 'We've had a few complaints but it will only become a police matter if people start hurling watering cans about and someone gets hurt.'

'And you know about the upcoming Flower and Produce Festival at the Hall?'

'It's very hard not to,' said Mallory. 'But please, carry on.'

'The festival has been in the grounds at Honeychurch Hall since Victorian times and always on the first weekend in September. Originally the contest was just for the estate workers, which was basically everyone in Little Dipperton but, of course, that's no longer the case.'

'Ah yes,' said Mallory. 'The infamous five families. Let me see, Pugsley, Banks, Cropper, Stark and Jones.'

I was impressed. 'You're learning.'

'How do they regard the er . . . blow-ins taking part? Like you and Iris, perhaps?'

'I'm not taking part,' I said. 'But my mother is entering her heirloom tomatoes.'

'And Ruby? She would have been classed as a blow-in, surely.'

'Definitely,' I agreed and proceeded to fill him in on the feud over who owned the rose garden at the bottom of End Cottage. 'Caroline says it should be hers, but Danny gave it to his mother.'

'The church?' Mallory asked. 'But I thought all the cottages in Little Dipperton belonged to the Honeychurch Hall estate.'

'Only the ones with the blue doors and windows,' I said. 'That's about eighty per cent of the village.' I thought for a moment. 'And then we have the hosepipe ban. It's caused a lot of upset since many of the original contestants are elderly now and find it hard to ferry watering cans back and forth to their allotment or garden. You have to admit it's not exactly a level playing field, is it?'

I watched him writing notes on his pad and realised that he was lefthanded, holding his pen in the cramped, awkward way that many lefthanded people do. I felt a surge of affection and wondered if he had been teased at school like I had.

'It wasn't just Ruby's garden that was destroyed,' I went on. 'The goats had escaped for hours. They were still out when Mum and I got to Little Dipperton just before three. It was only when Lord Rupert arrived shortly afterwards with Mr Chips that they were corralled in the churchyard.'

Mallory turned to a fresh page in his notebook. 'The general consensus in the village is that the festival should be cancelled given that so many of the entries have been destroyed,' he said. 'So we have Ruby, the blow-in, who is using her hosepipe which is not only illegal but could be viewed by her fellow competitors as having an unfair advantage. And not only that, she's got the monopoly on those award-winning roses. I would say that provides a good motive for mischief which, unfortunately, went horribly wrong.'

'Are you saying that if the goats were deliberately let out and inadvertently caused Ruby's death, the culprit could be charged with manslaughter?'

'I can't see Capricious in the dock,' said Mallory. 'But let's remember the ABCs of policing.'

I rolled my eyes in mock surrender. 'Assume nothing, believe nobody and challenge everything.'

'Now *you're* learning,' said Mallory.

'What bothers me is that both gates to Ruby's garden – top and bottom, were still latched when Mum and I got there. Whoever let them in, must have let them out.'

'Or not,' said Mallory with a smile. 'This is why it's important not to jump to conclusions. The greenhouse backs up against a line of conifers where we found a sizable hole big enough for the animals to get through into the alleyway.'

'Oh.'

'You sound disappointed,' Mallory said. 'But how they escaped from their field is still under investigation.'

'You think Ruby heard them in her garden?' I said. 'And that's why she ran outside dressed only in her nightdress?'

'It's possible,' he said. 'Most of the time the simpler explanation is usually the answer.'

'Occam's razor,' I said. 'Isn't that what you call it?'

'I *am* impressed,' Mallory grinned.

I'd learned the theory verbatim and quoted, 'A principle of theory construction or evaluation according to which, other things equal, explanations that posit fewer entities, or fewer kinds of entities, are to be preferred to explanations that posit more.'

He laughed, drained his glass, and stood up. 'I've got to go.'

I walked with him back to his car. He stopped to gaze out at the view and, turning back to me, suddenly said, 'I think it's time we went public. Isn't that the celebrity term for showing we are a couple?'

My stomach flipped over. I wasn't sure and I could see by Mallory's expression he knew that. It wasn't that I didn't want him. I did. But I was scared of another mistake and besides, how did I know that he would stay in the area. Shawn hadn't.

Mallory was living in temporary accommodation. He had been used to dealing with hardened criminals and OCGs – Organised Crime Groups. How would goats and petty rivalries stack up to that?

Apart from my ten-year relationship with David – what a different life that seemed now – I'd briefly gone out with Lady Lavinia's brother Piers, unaware he had an insane ex-girlfriend who wouldn't let go; Delia's son, Guy, the navy helicopter pilot, and then of course, there was the agonising on-again-off again relationship with Mallory's predecessor Shawn Cropper. There had been no physical relationship with Piers and Guy but no one in the village knew that other than my mother. And, judging by the gossip in the community shop, it sounded like I was getting some kind of fallen woman reputation!

Each time I'd been hopeful when a relationship began and, each time when it failed, everyone in the village knew about it. It was so strange. When I was host of 'Fakes and Treasures' my personal life appeared on the front page of the trashy tabloids regularly – particularly my wardrobe malfunctions, of which there were many. Yes, it had bothered me but there had been a distance between my real life and my public façade. Here in the village, it felt personal.

Mallory gently lifted my chin. 'It's time, Kat. I don't want gossip when I'm spotted leaving your house the following morning or you're seen leaving mine.'

'Oh,' I whispered, knowing full well what Mallory was implying. Of course we'd talked about our relationship going to the 'next level', which for me, would be a one hundred per cent commitment. 'I think I'm just nervous.'

'Don't be.' He looked into my eyes again. 'I'll never hurt you, I promise.'

'You can't promise something like that,' I said quietly.

'I just have.'

Warmth flooded my heart but so did fear. 'Does that mean you're coming to the Safari Supper tomorrow night?'

'It does,' he grinned.

'I'd better ask my mother to boil an extra egg.'

He laughed. 'And I suppose I'll need one of those hats. Oh, and while you were away, I signed a two-year lease on a lovely barn conversion just a couple of miles from here.'

I couldn't believe it. 'So you *are* staying in the area?'

'Yes, I'm staying.'

Mallory pulled me into his arms. 'And I also want that moment to be a special time, far away from here. Have you ever been to the Isles of Scilly?'

My butterflies went into overdrive. 'No,' I croaked. 'I've heard it's beautiful there.'

'There is a hotel on an islet only accessible at low tide called Tregarrick Rock.' He pulled away and looked deeply into my eyes. 'We should go. You tell me when it works for your schedule – estate sales, auctions, valuations or whatever – and I'll take some days off.'

He leaned down and kissed me again and, even though it was quick, it made me dizzy.

I waved his car out of sight and had to pinch myself. Was this really happening? Poor Ruby and the goats, Caroline and her Safari Supper and my mother and her gazillion boiled eggs, seemed a distant memory.

Back indoors I stared at the pile of post. I was far too excited to think about going to sleep. Most of it was junk mail but then at the bottom was a cream vellum envelope with the Grenville coat-of-arms embossed in the upper right-hand corner. *Delivered by Hand* was written alongside my name.

Curious, I tore it open and stared at the handwritten letter with growing astonishment and utter dismay.

It was signed by Lord Rupert Honeychurch. I had to read it twice and even then I felt there had to be a mistake.

The Earl of Grenville had given me three weeks to vacate Jane's Cottage and both the east and west gatehouses.

I was being evicted.

Chapter Eight

'What do you mean, evicted?' My mother said on the other end of the line. 'That's ridiculous!'

'I tried to call the Hall to speak to Rupert but there was no answer.' I was still in shock. 'I just don't understand. My arrangement is with Edith. There's no explanation. Nothing. Three weeks' notice! Not so much as "I'm sorry".'

'I'm afraid my magic wand stopped working when you turned twenty-one,' said Mum. 'Do you want to me to come up and give you a cuddle?'

Tears stung my eyes, which was silly. It was just a house, wasn't it? But it wasn't! Not really. This was my home.

'Are you still there?' Mum said.

I swallowed hard and tried to keep my voice steady. 'I'll go to the Hall first thing tomorrow and see if I can talk to Edith.'

'Perhaps it's happened,' Mum said.

'What?'

'Lady Edith has finally decided to pass the torch to his lordship,' said Mum. 'Why don't you offer to buy Jane's and the gatehouses?'

'I didn't think they wanted to sell any more of the estate off.'

'I was lucky with the Carriage House,' said Mum. 'And I dealt with Lady Edith directly at a time when the estate had some financial problems. You could afford it. How much do you think you'd get for your place in London? I bet it would more than cover it.'

Now that I was no longer earning a good salary on the TV show, I had been renting my flat out for the past several years to cover the mortgage. 'Except that I have a tenant with a lease,' I reminded her. 'And it could take months to sell.'

I'd also wanted to hang on to my flat just in case things didn't work out in Devon. Just as it tends to happen in life, you never appreciate what you've got until you realise you might lose it.

'Why is Rupert in such a hurry to get me out?' I wailed. 'Three weeks!'

'Take a breath,' Mum said gently. 'Let's get all the information first. Talk to him tomorrow, and if you can't get to him during the day, we'll corner him at the Safari Supper.'

'Oh, that.' I told Mum about the change of venue for the main course.

'Typical,' Mum muttered. 'I'll just add a piece of lettuce. Oeufs à la Russe it is and Oeufs à la Russe it will stay.'

'You know . . .' I began slowly. 'Just a few moments ago I was so happy because Mallory wants to make our relationship official.'

'I knew it!' Mum exclaimed. 'That's wonderful! So not all bad. Perhaps you can move in with him.'

'No,' I said firmly. 'Call me old-fashioned but if that happens, I'll have a ring on my finger.'

Mum laughed. 'Goodness. I never expected that to come from you.'

We ended the call with me promising to stop by the Carriage House in the morning after I'd spoken to Edith or Rupert.

There was no way I would be able to sleep tonight. Jetlag, mixed with the excitement of Mallory and me being a couple, was dampened by worry over losing my home.

I thought of the money I had put into making the cottage habitable – not just painting it but installing a new bathroom and kitchen. The same went for the gatehouse. I'd put in wall cabinets, display cabinets, bespoke shelves, and upgraded the little kitchen. Edith had assured me I could stay for as long as I liked. It wasn't as if I was living there rent-free, either.

My contract to lease Jane's Cottage and the two gatehouses for my business had been a one-page document that I'd written down myself. Edith and I had agreed verbally but I'd had the foresight to record our conversation and get her to sign it. It had never occurred to me to get our agreement notarised. If something happened to Edith, would this stand up as a legally binding contract?

Again I picked up the business card for the interior designer, which now seemed ominous. Perhaps this Natalie person might know something that I didn't. And then there was that cryptic comment that Delia had made earlier when we were sitting out on the terrace. She'd warned me not to get too comfortable. I wouldn't be surprised if she knew something too.

Needless to say, sleep didn't come for hours. To distract myself I researched the Isles of Scilly, the cluster of islands twenty-eight miles off the Cornish coast and found the hotel Mallory mentioned which sounded wonderfully romantic. On a whim, I googled Eric's honeymoon destination. I read, 'No matter how many images of the awesome landscape of Cappadocia they see, nothing can prepare the visitor for the reality. The fairy chimneys and other bizarre rock formations dominate the landscape and give the impression of a barren, dry lunarscape . . .' Although offering hot-air ballooning and mountain hikes, it seemed a bit remote to me and rather an odd choice for a honeymoon.

Friday morning dawned misty with a slow burn shedding a reddish glow over distant Dartmoor. By eight thirty, it already registered 18 °C on my outdoor barometer. An alert on my mobile said that my luggage was going to arrive sometime today between ten and two. Jane's Cottage was notoriously difficult for couriers to find, so I always used the West Gatehouse for my official address.

My anxiety about moving had only increased during the night. I knew exactly where I had put the agreement

– in a box in the gatehouse I used for storage – but it was tricky to get to.

Rather than telephone with the possibility of being fobbed off by Delia – who always answered the phone in an affected voice announcing I had reached, 'The Earl of Grenville's residence' – I drove to the rear of the Hall and pulled up next to Rupert's Range Rover.

It was just before nine.

The courtyard looked spotless in the morning sun with none of the assortment of farmyard appliances, random pieces of wood, and sheets of corrugated iron that used to litter the area. I was always fascinated by the different architectural periods that were visible here. A series of exposed wooden beams hinted at a Tudor beginning. It was as if the Hall kept being swallowed up by bigger and more fashionable additions as time went by.

I pushed open the glass-panelled door that led to the low-ceilinged, flagstone passage where, high on the wall, was a long row of service bells with indicators. This was the original entrance to the servants' quarters. Half a dozen or so doors lined the gloomy corridor. Each bore a wooden plaque that indicated the purpose of those rooms, long abandoned now.

There was an assortment of larders including dry, fish, meat and dairy along with a lamp room, gun room, stillroom and, of course, a wine cellar. I'd heard plans that these were to be revived for educational purposes when the Hall would eventually be open to the public on a regular basis. Perhaps, I thought bitterly, Rupert had earmarked Jane's Cottage as a tea room.

I paused at the open door to the kitchen, struck by the memory of my first impression: the cobwebs and grime that draped from the high-gabled roof and clerestory windows, the wooden shelves lined with dusty crockery and various dull copper saucepans and fish kettles stacked higgledy-piggledy on the counter tops.

Back then, the old-fashioned grate with its elaborate arrangement of roasting-spits was encrusted with the grimy remnants of cooked food. The warming cabinets and counter tops had looked as if they hadn't seen a damp cloth since the turn of the century – the last century, at that! But now, all sparkled and shone.

Much as I wasn't a fan of Delia's, there was no denying she had excellent managerial skills. Not only did she produce a variety of daily meals for the household from scratch, she managed the various dailies and gardeners with military precision which, I suppose, wasn't really surprising considering she used to be an Army wife.

Arranged on the enormous farmhouse table were various mixing bowls and basins bearing the Grenville coat-of-arms, a set of scales, a rolling pin and wooden spoons. A handful of recipe books had been marked with Post-its, presumably for today's fare and tonight's Safari Supper.

Delia was perched on a stool at a small table in a corner which served as a computer station with her laptop out, a pen and pad to hand.

I knocked on the door.

Delia looked up and closed her laptop with a snap. 'Goodness. What are you doing here so early? Why didn't you call?'

I kicked myself for not bringing something for Edith, grapes perhaps, or flowers.

'I was hoping I could see Lady Edith.'

Delia regarded me with curiosity. 'Why? Is something wrong?'

'Not at all.' I smiled. 'I've just been worried about her.'

'We all are,' said Delia. 'Ah, let's ask Banu.'

I hoped my surprise didn't show when Banu appeared carrying a bed-tray table laid up with a white cloth and a rose in a crystal posy vase. The breakfast – scrambled eggs, mushrooms on toast – looked as if it hadn't been touched. Also on the tray was a small spray bottle labelled Muriel's Miracle Spray.

'She no eats,' said Banu shaking her head. 'I try.'

Delia frowned. 'Oh dear. Her ladyship must stay hydrated. She's got to keep her fluids up.'

'She sick when she drink.' Banu looked worried. 'She like leg massage with miracle.'

Just like Yasmine's, it appeared that Banu's English was better than Delia had led us to believe.

'What's wrong with Lady Edith's legs?' I asked.

'Rheumatoid arthritis. Very nasty.' Delia turned to me. 'So no, her ladyship won't be seeing any visitors.'

I hesitated. 'I'd like to talk to his lordship in that case. Would he be in the library?'

Delia cocked her head. 'This sounds important.'

There was an expectant pause which I did not fill.

'Very well.' Delia got to her feet. 'Please wait here. I'll see if his lordship is home.'

'He is,' I cut in. 'His Range Rover is parked outside.' But Delia had already gone, leaving Banu and I together.

Banu headed to the vast stone sink to sort out the breakfast tray, scraping the untouched eggs into a compost bin on the draining board. I attempted to make polite conversation, asking if she liked being in England, but my questions were drowned out by the taps being turned on full blast.

Delia returned. 'His lordship is busy, I'm afraid. Perhaps tomorrow?'

'I need to see him today, Delia,' I said. 'I only want five minutes.'

Delia cocked her head again. 'It's happened, hasn't it?'

'What do you mean?'

Delia made an annoying tut-tutting sound. 'I told you so. I warned you! How long have you got to get out?'

Every fibre in my being told me not to confide in Delia, but I was too worried to care. 'Three weeks,' I said. 'How do you know?'

'As I told Iris, it's my business to know what's going on in the village, luv.' To my surprise, Delia's expression softened. 'There's a pot of hot coffee on the range. Let me pour you a cup. Sit down for a moment.'

So I did.

'Banu, why don't you take a break?' Delia said.

Banu pointed to a wooden tray piled with silver cutlery, a tin of Silvo, rags, and a duster. 'I clean. Yes? For tonight?'

Delia saw from my face that I didn't want her there. 'You can do that later.'

'I clean now.' Banu insisted. 'Lots. Lots.'

'Later.' Delia's voice was firm.

'Later.' Banu rewarded us with her bright white smile. And left.

Delia gave a sigh. 'It's all very well Banu volunteering to help with tonight's event, but she appeared first thing in my kitchen offering to help at the Hall, like we were old friends.'

'That does seem odd,' I murmured as I waited for Delia to pour my coffee, and wished I hadn't agreed to it now. I'd already decided I was going to see Rupert regardless, and if it meant leaving by the back door and sneaking around to the front, I'd do it.

'It's very awkward.' Delia stirred a spoonful of sugar into her cup. 'I still don't know how I was kept in the dark about the nuptials.' She shot me a rueful smile. 'I suppose I don't know everything after all.'

'Do you know why I've been asked to leave?'

'Now, I might be wrong but . . .' Delia continued stirring her coffee. 'I think it's Eric.'

'What's Eric got to do with it?' I said sharply.

Delia raised her hands in mock defence. 'They can hardly live in number three.'

'Eric? You mean Eric and Yasmine want to live in my house?' I was stunned. 'In Jane's Cottage?'

'But that's the thing, isn't it?' Delia's face oozed mock sympathy. 'It's not your house, is it?'

And she was right. It wasn't.

'Did I ever tell you about the gamekeeper and his wife over Modbury way—'

'Yes Delia. You have.' I had heard the story many times before and it had struck fear into the tenant-occupied cottages in the village.

'The gamekeeper and his wife lived in an estate cottage for twenty-five years,' Delia went on regardless. 'One day, the old earl decided to convert half the estate into holiday lets and turned them out. No compensation. Nothing. Maybe you can take over Ruby's cottage now she's gone? I'm assuming that Banu will move into number three after Eric vacates.'

End Cottage? That dump! I drained my cup and stood up and made a monumental effort to be polite. 'Thank you for the coffee and chat.'

I was due to see Eric in an hour. I would ask him outright, but first I was going to find his lordship.

Chapter Nine

I didn't have to look very far.

As I left the servant's quarters and stepped into the courtyard, Banu was chatting to Rupert by his Range Rover. Not only that, she was smoking!

The moment he saw me, I saw a flicker of panic cross his features. I took a deep breath and strode up to join them.

'Ah, here they are,' said Rupert quickly, and I turned to see Lavinia and Yasmine walking together.

Both were dressed for riding – Lavinia in her usual jodhpurs with her blond hair clamped under a hair net but Yasmine . . . She looked as if she had stepped out of *Tatler* magazine. Dressed impeccably in skin-tight jodhpurs with a tiny shirt that hugged her minute frame, she wore her dark hair in a long plait. I noticed she'd repainted her nails in pink.

I felt like I'd stepped into the twilight zone. I also felt something I couldn't quite put my finger on. Was it jealousy?

Lavinia, brandishing a bottle of Muriel's Miracle Spray, made the introductions. Yasmine said we'd already met.

'Yasmine is riding out,' said Lavinia. 'Super rider.'

Lavinia spoke in the strangled vowels of the upper-classes and also in the curious stilted way she had that was never in complete sentences. With Yasmine's halting English I suspected they would get along. But I felt weird about it. I was Lavinia's riding companion, not Yasmine.

Lavinia proceeded to spray her bare arms. She offered it to Yasmine, who shook her head.

Banu tossed her cigarette to the ground and crushed it under her heel. I waited for Rupert to say something, but he didn't. He seemed too mesmerised by Yasmine's beauty.

Yasmine touched Lavinia's shoulder and said, 'We go before too hot. Yes?' She offered Lavinia her arm and Lavinia took it. I couldn't believe it. Banu looked on with a strange indulgent smile before strolling back to the Hall.

I felt like an outsider. I was an outsider.

I heard the car door slam and spun around to see that Rupert had started the engine. Swiftly, I stepped up to the driver's door and knocked smartly on the window.

He reluctantly opened it. 'I'm in a bit of a hurry.'

'I was hoping to speak to you about your letter.'

'Can we talk about this tomorrow, Kat?' he said. 'I've got a meeting at my solicitor's and need to be in Exeter within the hour.'

'I just need five minutes.' Without waiting for an answer, I darted around to the passenger side of the Range Rover, opened the door and scrambled in.

He kept the engine running. 'Now is not a good time.'

'Lady Edith said I could stay here for as long as I wanted. I have a contract to prove it.'

Rupert turned off the engine. 'I'm afraid Mother isn't well, and whatever she said to you then, no longer applies. Now, if you don't mind . . .'

I didn't move. 'I'd like to buy Jane's and the gatehouses,' I blurted out. 'I love it here.'

Rupert kept his eyes firmly ahead. 'They're not for sale.'

'Okay,' I said knowing I sounded desperate. 'Perhaps you could raise my rent a little? Would that help?'

Rupert's hands gripped the steering wheel. He still wouldn't look at me. 'I'm sorry. I can't.'

'This is to do with Eric, isn't it?' I said bluntly.

'Please Kat,' Rupert said quietly. 'We can find you somewhere else. Perhaps in the village? I believe that—'

'No! Not End Cottage,' I said rudely. 'I've spent a lot of money on Jane's and both gatehouses. Lady Edith had given me her blessing and a promise that I could live there for as long as I wanted.' I struggled to keep my voice steady.

'It's not up to my mother anymore,' said Rupert, still refusing to look at me. 'She's an elderly lady. She's extremely ill, so I am asking you not to involve her in all of this.'

'At least give me time to look elsewhere,' I said. 'Three weeks is nothing – oh! Of course, silly me. That's when Eric and Yasmine will be back from their honeymoon.'

Rupert finally looked at me. 'If you were offering to buy the properties without even knowing how much they are worth, it sounds to me that you can probably find something elsewhere. Perhaps even better.'

He was right. I could. So why did this matter so much?

'I'm sorry,' he said again. 'The decision has been made.' He turned the engine back on.

I got out and slammed the car door harder than I intended. I suppose I'd felt that in some way I was part of the family but, obviously, I wasn't. I was just a blow-in.

Delia's words about the divide between those upstairs and those downstairs hit home. She was right. But I wasn't going to take the wretched Earl of Grenville's dismissive eviction lying down.

And as for Eric! Of course he would take precedence over me. I thought of Yasmine and her new friendship with Lavinia; of Banu helping Delia in the kitchen. The pair hadn't taken long to muscle in and it really bothered me. But what bothered me all the more was how Rupert seemed to have already taken over the Honeychurch reins! Was Edith so very ill?

I had to talk to Mum.

I found her in the courtyard liberally watering her planters with her hosepipe. No nosy neighbours here to spy on her. The planters were overfilled with lush geraniums, begonias, and petunias. Roses climbed over the roof of the wishing well and scrambled up the walls of the stone outbuildings that formed two sides of the quadrangle. The condition of the ruined barn that stretched along the third was hidden by clematis and honeysuckle that was probably the only thing that was holding it together.

The Carriage House looked stunning and seemed a lifetime away from the neglected semi-derelict building that my mother had recklessly bought several years ago. The two-storey red-brick building had a spectacular arch-braced roof. There were adorable lunettes in the clerestory and small hatches led to a hayloft. An arched double carriageway door spanned both storeys. Above that was a small window trimmed in pale-blue paint and, above that, a timber cupola topped with an ogee dome and a horse weathervane.

My mother had spent a lot of money renovating the property, taking great care to retain all the original fixtures and features inside the building, too. In its heyday, there had been room for four horse-drawn carriages in the carriageway. A row of stalls stood on either side, accessed through red-brick arches bearing the Grenville crest of arms and motto, *ad perseverate est ad triumphum* – To Endure is To Triumph.

Mum had bought the Carriage House from the estate so why wouldn't Rupert sell Jane's Cottage to me? Surely it was going to be far too small for Eric and Yasmine especially if – not that I wanted to think too much about that aspect – they were going to start a family. And surely, with Eric's money and Yasmine's wealth, they could afford something so much better – maybe somewhere for Banu, a guest house or an annexe or a granny flat.

I turned off the tap, and with a cry of frustrated surprise, Mum swung around. I winced at the sight of the bruises on her face. Her expression changed to one of concern. 'Bad news. I can tell.'

'Rupert is in charge,' I declared. 'He refuses to sell to me and even rejected my offer of paying more rent.'

'Oh dear,' Mum said.

'Eric and Yasmine will be moving into Jane's Cottage.' I hadn't even pursued the topic of the gatehouses with Rupert. 'And guess what, Lavinia and Yasmine seem to be bosom pals. They were just going out riding together!'

'What?' Mum seemed shocked. 'Well, it certainly hasn't taken her long to get her feet under the table.'

'And let's not forget about Banu,' I wailed and went on to tell my mother that Banu was 'helping' Delia in the kitchen and more besides.

'And massaged her ladyship's legs?' Mum was shocked. 'But . . . that's outrageous! Into the piggery right this minute. Coffee?'

I shook my head. 'No thanks. I had a cup with Delia. Who knows everything, by the way.'

'Except for Eric and Yasmine's nuptials,' Mum reminded me. 'She didn't know anything about that.'

'True,' I said miserably.

'We can't allow this to happen,' Mum declared. 'I have an idea. Come with me.'

I followed her into the converted piggery aka her writing house, which didn't seem so cosy in the summer but was nice and cool.

I scanned the room, impressed with everything my mother had accomplished all by herself and with no encouragement from anyone, simply because we just hadn't known about her writing skills.

Floor-to-ceiling custom-made bookshelves covered one wall, displaying all her writing awards. Her first-edition books ran for entire shelves, and I knew that she had boxes of copies up in the attic in the Carriage House too.

A grey metal filing cabinet five drawers high stood in one corner. In another was a standard lamp and Dad's battered leather wingback chair that she used for reading. Next to that was a hexagonal table piled with editions of *The Lady* magazine and the *Dipperton Deal*, our weekly local newspaper.

Another wall held a corkboard showing the official Honeychurch family trees, both above stairs and below. Mum had been appointed the unofficial family historian – something she relished and something that provided her with a bona fide reason for being closeted in her lair for hours on end.

'Go and sit down.' She pointed to the two-seater and headed to a neat corner unit where she'd set up a coffee machine on top and a small fridge underneath.

'What's your idea?' I said.

'Don't you have a contract?' said Mum.

'It's a one-page agreement between me and Edith,' I said. 'But it's written in my handwriting. It wasn't recorded or anything like that.'

'It's still an agreement,' Mum said as she joined me on the sofa with her coffee. 'We're going to ask Crispin. He's amazing.'

'Crispin?' I said. 'The birdwatcher?'

Mum took a sip of coffee. 'I wasn't completely honest with you. He's my financial adviser.'

My jaw dropped. 'So he's not a birdwatcher at all?' I was exasperated. Why couldn't she have said so in the first place?

'Actually, that's his hobby,' Mum said. 'He's obsessed with birds, especially the nocturnal nightjar. Apparently there's one in the forest behind the walled garden. They're quite large you know. Crispin says some can be up to twelve inches in length! And their wingspan is huge! Quite unusual creatures with cryptic plumage—'

'Cryptic what?'

'It's camouflage,' Mum said. 'Like tree bark. So they can't be seen.'

'Mum, I'm really not interested in birds at the moment,' I said. 'Since you conveniently forgot to tell me he is your financial adviser, I'm assuming it's because he's a friend of Alfred's.'

Currently going straight, the stable manager had a history of forgery, fraud and embezzlement and had been a guest of our former Queen more times than I cared to remember.

'Alfred? Of course not!' Mum sounded hurt. 'And frankly, young lady, I would watch your tone if I were you. You're very lucky that you came home early, otherwise you wouldn't have met Crispin at all.'

'Sorry. I'm just upset, that's all.'

'Do you want help or not?'

'Of course I do,' I said meekly.

'I met Crispin at Goldfinch.'

'Goldfinch Publishing? Your publisher?' I wasn't expecting that. 'You mean he worked there?'

'Yes Katherine,' Mum said. 'Do you think I'm an idiot? Crispin was in the accounting department and was handling my contract. I've known him for decades.'

'Go on,' I said.

'It was my first contract in the Star-Crossed Lovers series and the advance was so much money that I wasn't sure how to handle it. I asked them if I should get an accountant and Crispin volunteered.'

'But he must have just been an assistant back then,' I pointed out.

'Back then, yes,' Mum agreed. 'It was at the beginning of his career. Crispin continued working for Goldfinch while he built up his client list and went independent. Of course, I didn't want your father to find out about the money because . . . Well, you know why.'

I certainly did. Dad was prudish to a fault. He wouldn't have just been horrified at what my mother had written; he would have been disgusted. Writing what could only be described as soft porn would definitely have been too much for him. If there was even a chaste kiss on the television, he would change channels. I often thought about my parents relationship, and couldn't reconcile my mother's gaiety to my father's seriousness, but perhaps they balanced each other out. Mum said he grounded her and she livened him up.

'I also wanted my own money,' my mother went on. 'Your father kept me on a strict budget as if we grew up in the Depression! I didn't start drawing the money out until he died and by then it was too much to count and too late to declare it. I wasn't to know that Krystalle Storm was going to be . . . well . . .'

'A global bestseller!' I couldn't keep the pride out of my voice, but then was struck by the obvious. 'Mum,' I said slowly, 'if you met in the contracts department at your publishers, your income would have been reported to HMRC from the get-go.'

'I know that *now*,' she said. 'He told me. I don't know why I thought I hadn't been paying any taxes. Oh, I wish I'd paid more attention to all that sort of thing, but you know, in my day, we always let the men do that.'

Perhaps it was a mixture of jetlag, the possibility of losing my home mixed with keeping a secret from everyone on the planet, to say nothing of her tax issues, that just made me snap.

'Why didn't you tell me who he was when I asked you?' I demanded. 'Why the secrecy? Is he staying in the shepherd's hut? Are you having a relationship with him?'

Mum looked startled and then annoyed. 'It's none of your business.'

'I'm sorry,' I relented. 'I'm just so confused. One moment Crispin is wonderful and the next minute you're sulking because Delia invited him to the Safari Supper.'

'I wasn't sulking,' Mum said. 'I just don't want Delia to know he's my financial adviser, that's all, but I spoke to Crispin about that and he promised to keep it quiet. Next question?'

I didn't have one.

'Look, darling,' Mum began. 'Just talk to him. Show him the agreement. He can look at your legal rights.'

'But what's the point?' I wailed.

'Pouting won't solve anything,' said Mum. 'Let's just see what Crispin says.' She gave my hand a pat. 'Come on. Give me a smile.'

'Maybe I will have that coffee after all.' But it was when I returned with my cup that I saw a dozen or so bulging black plastic dustbin liners stashed behind the sofa.

'Mum?' I said. 'What are all these bags doing here?'

'Oh those?' Mum said airily. 'Just having a clear out.'

'A clear out?' I set down my coffee and picked a bag up. It was light. 'What's inside?'

'Nothing much,' Mum said.

I spied a large shredder tucked next to the filing cabinet that I hadn't noticed before. When I squeezed one of the bags it felt scrunchy. 'It's paper. Shredded paper.'

'I know,' said Mum.

'Is this anything to do with the box of documents you were getting out of the hayloft?' I asked. 'When you fell off the ladder?'

'A little bit,' Mum admitted. 'And honestly, what is it to you?'

'A lot,' I said and gave a heavy sigh. 'You'd better start at the beginning.'

Chapter Ten

'There was an incident in Poole,' said Mum.

'Pool? A swimming pool?'

'Not a pool. Poole! The town called Poole in Hampshire.'

Now I was thoroughly confused.

'It's Alfred's fault really,' Mum went on.

'Alfred?' I echoed.

'Fergal was arrested.'

'Fergal was arrested,' I echoed again having no clue as to what she was talking about.

'Oh for goodness sakes! Is there a parrot in the room?' Mum exclaimed. 'Everything is fine now. I told you. Crispin has sorted it all out.'

'You're not making sense!' I protested. 'What's in Poole? Who is Fergal? And what's Alfred got to do with the bin bags?'

Mum rolled her eyes in exasperation. 'This is why I don't tell you things. When Fergal got off the ferry in Poole he was arrested by Border Control.'

I was still confused. 'The ferry in Poole? Not the ferry in Plymouth?'

'Poole,' Mum said. 'One ferry goes to the Channel Islands from Poole. The other ferry goes to Brittany from Plymouth.'

'I wanted you to start at the beginning,' I said crossly.

'This is the beginning.'

It would appear that for the first time ever, Alfred had been unable to make the 'channel dash,' as my mother liked to call it, to withdraw the usual cash from her bank account in Jersey because Alfred had been kicked by Tinkerbell, Edith's highly strung mare.

Mum told me that it was legal to bring ten thousand pounds into the country, but not a pound more. Unfortunately, Fergal – whose connection to Alfred was still unclear – had gone on Alfred's behalf and, not being very bright, had tacked on his commission. Upon arriving at the Poole Ferry Terminal, Fergal was stopped and searched by Border Control. The money was confiscated and he was arrested. Fergal was allowed one phone call. He called Alfred. Alfred told my mother and Mum called Crispin.

'Being the lovely man he is,' said Mum, 'Crispin got in his car and came straight down to Devon. I asked Lady Lavinia if anyone was using the shepherd's hut and they had a cancellation, otherwise he would have stayed at the Hare and Hounds in the village.'

I frowned. 'But why would he need to stay anywhere at all? Couldn't he just have talked to you about it on the phone?'

'Crispin had already been planning a trip to the West Country and when he found out about this elusive nightjar being spotted in the area, well,' she smiled, 'it was a no-brainer.'

'Okay,' I said slowly. 'But that doesn't explain what you are shredding.'

'Just old papers,' Mum said.

'Did he tell you to do that?'

'It's just a precaution,' said Mum. 'We've been doing some creative accounting. Crispin suggested getting rid of a few documents and what not. If your father was alive, he would admit that everyone does that.'

'I don't,' I said.

'We're not all perfect like you,' Mum retorted. 'Why do you always have to be so suspicious!'

I needed to think. I knew that the publisher sent my mother hard copies of her royalty statements every quarter because they were addressed to me and were sent to my post box at the post office. Her bank statements were a different matter.

'Mum,' I said patiently. 'Just destroying the paper copies doesn't make your creative accounting go away. Everything will still be available online – bank statements, royalty statements, contracts – the lot.'

'Oh,' Mum's face fell. 'He didn't mention that.'

'Apart from the early ones of course,' I said. 'Those wouldn't have been digitised. Those, you should keep.'

Mum gave me a pained expression. 'I have no idea which bag *those* would be in and besides, it's too late now.'

I thought for a moment. 'Is Crispin expecting an audit? Maybe when Fergal was stopped it might have triggered something like that. A look into your finances perhaps.'

Mum shook her head. 'Alfred told me that Fergal was let off with a caution. The money was confiscated. My name didn't come into it and, since it was cash, Alfred said it can't be traced.'

'That can't be the end of it, surely?' I said. 'What did Crispin say about it?'

'He told me not to worry.'

'This Crispin,' I said slowly, 'do you trust him?'

'Of course. With my life,' said Mum. 'I told you. He came through my publisher. I've used him for over two decades and we've never had any problems at all.'

'Do you have his business card?'

'Why? Are you going to do a background check?' Her voice was laced with scorn. 'Go ahead. Be my guest. And frankly, if you're going to be like that, it's better that he doesn't get involved in your mess.'

'Mess!' I shot back. 'Thanks a lot! I'm just asking for his business card.'

'Fine.' Mum got up and went over to her desk. She returned with a card which said Fellowes Financial Consultants est. 1995 with an office address, website, and an email address. The logo was embossed in silver and the card stock was good quality. I resolved to check it out the moment I got to the showroom.

We both heard the rattly grumble of a Land Rover enter the courtyard.

'That'll be Alfred,' said Mum. 'He's come to pick up the bags.'

This was unusual. Alfred rarely left the stable yard unless he was running an errand for the dowager countess.

'And take them where?' I demanded.

'To the recycling centre,' Mum said. 'It's all been shredded. Crispin wanted us to light a bonfire but I didn't want to risk a wildfire, which would be just my luck.'

'Let me talk to Alfred,' I said. 'I think this is a bad idea. At the very least you should wait, just in case you are audited.'

'What's the point?' Mum grumbled, 'you can hardly glue the paper back together.'

'You'd be surprised,' I said. 'There are shredder reconstruction machines and all kinds of advanced software these days. The German government used them to reassemble the shredded files of the Stasi after the Berlin Wall came down.'

Mum rolled her eyes. 'Now you sound like Delia.'

We stepped outside into the sunshine.

Alfred Bushman kept himself to himself. Mum had got him the job as the stable manager several years ago following his stint – one of many – at Wormwood Scrubs prison. Instead of telling the dowager countess the truth, she'd invented an elaborate tale, namely that Alfred had been training circus horses out in Spain and supposedly could communicate with them through his psychic gifts. Alfred did have an uncanny gift with animals, however, so at least that part was true.

Upon first meeting Alfred, it would be easy to mistake him for a harmless little old man with his thatch of white hair and wire-rimmed spectacles, but looks sure were deceiving. Wiry and compact, Alfred had a jaw like a French bulldog and a nose that had been broken many times. His forearms were heavily tattooed with birds of prey and his knuckles bore the scars from a lifetime in the boxing ring – or doing things I'd rather not think about.

Alfred extricated himself from the front seat of the Land Rover. I say 'extricated' because it was obvious that he was in a lot of pain and could hardly bear the weight of his left foot on the cobbled courtyard. I had no idea how he had managed to drive. I thought of Ruby lying in her rose garden, Caroline's discomfort getting in and out of her car, and then there was my mother's bruised face. Was Mercury retrograde? I didn't usually believe in blaming a planet for things that went wrong, but having lost my luggage – to say nothing of losing my home – perhaps there was something to it after all.

Alfred limped over.

'I really think this is a bad idea,' I said and told Alfred why. To my relief, he agreed.

'Perhaps Alfred can store these bags somewhere until things settle down,' I suggested 'How about one of those old potting sheds in the walled garden?'

Mum hesitated. 'Well, since Crispin is staying in the shepherd's hut we can hardly put them in there without him noticing. I don't know. Crispin was very clear on what he advised us to do.'

'I'll store 'em somewhere,' Alfred agreed. 'Just in case.'

'All right,' said Mum reluctantly.

'I'll help you put them into the Land Rover,' I said.

It was easy lifting and didn't take long but just as we loaded the last bag, Crispin's Audi drove into the courtyard.

'Oh no,' Mum whispered. 'He's going to be awfully cross. Let's get away from the Land Rover. Stand over by the wishing well.'

I regarded her with concern. She seemed almost nervous of him.

'Don't worry,' I said firmly. 'I'll deal with Crispin.'

Chapter Eleven

Crispin slid out of the driver's seat, all smiles. I took in his appearance. Binoculars at the ready, summer shorts, a short-sleeved pale-blue polo shirt, Paisley ankle socks and open-toed sandals – never a good look in my opinion. In his top pocket was a pencil and a small notebook.

Crispin greeted my mother with a warm hug.

'Kat's got a problem,' Mum blurted out. 'I was hoping you could help her.'

And, before I could say a word, my mother had told him everything about my possible eviction.

'Don't worry,' he said. 'I'm sure we can sort something out. Do you have the agreement?'

Mum jumped in again and said it was handwritten, and more of a verbal summary of what the dowager countess and I had agreed upon.

'I don't think I have a leg to stand on,' I said.

'We'll see about that.' Crispin smirked. 'And you think this . . . What was his name, Eric—?'

'Pugsley. He lives in number 3,' Mum said helpfully. 'Runs the scrapyard that I've always complained about to say nothing of the noisy banger racing meetings all summer. He's getting married to a *very* young girl called Yasmine. Turkish.'

'So they'll move in?' Crispin asked.

'It's not confirmed but yes, I think so,' I said. 'Eric wants to meet with me this morning. I'm going to ask him outright.'

'Good, good.' Crispin nodded. 'I'll want her full name as well. And bring the agreement to the shepherd's hut this afternoon and we'll take a look.'

'Okay,' I said.

'I hope you haven't spoken to the landlord yet,' said Crispin.

My heart sank. 'I did. I offered to buy the properties, or at the very least, pay more rent.'

'Oh dear,' Crispin shook his head. 'That could put you at a disadvantage.'

'I'm already at a disadvantage,' I said. 'I'm just the tenant.'

'Can he offer you somewhere else to live on the estate?' said Crispin.

I pulled a face. 'He already did. End Cottage, by the church car park.'

'Ruby Pritchard. Poor love.' Crispin's face fell. 'Very upsetting. Ruby was a fine lady.'

I was surprised. 'You knew her?'

Crispin nodded. 'The birding network is very small and the nightjar network even smaller.' He cocked his head, eyes alert – he even looked like a bird. 'Yes, Ruby and I shared a passion for our little feathered friends. She'll be a great loss to the birding community. Her knowledge of the elusive nightjar's habitat was second to none. There's supposed to be one in that forest behind the walled garden but I've yet to see it. Poor Ruby,' he said again, and seemed overcome with sadness.

It didn't last. Mere seconds later he brightened up. 'I wonder if the vicar would be interested in selling me her wildlife camera. She's got a Ceyomur Solar with Night Vision and vision motion activation.'

'Wait,' I said sharply. 'Did you say *wildlife* camera?'

Crispin nodded. 'He bought it for her birthday.'

'That's why she had the latest smart phone,' I said half to myself. 'It would have synced with an app.'

I barely heard the list of birds that Ruby had captured in her garden. I was too excited about telling Mallory that it just might give us a clue as to what had happened to Ruby that fateful morning. For a moment, my own problems were forgotten.

'It was Ruby's suggestion that, since I was already this far down country,' Crispin continued, 'my sister – who will be joining me – and I should go on to the Isles of Scilly.'

My ears perked up at the mention of the Isles of Scilly and Mallory's proposed romantic getaway.

'The islands are supposed to be a cross between the Mediterranean and the Scottish Highlands,' I said having researched them the night before. 'I've never been there—'

'You don't want to take the ferry,' Mum broke in. 'The *Scillonian*. They call it the great white stomach pump. I've heard that even dogs get sick on the crossing.'

'No danger of that,' said Crispin. 'We're going by helicopter. You won't get me in a boat ever again.'

'Oh? Why?' Mum said.

'I'd rather not talk about it.' A shadow passed over Crispin's face but was quickly gone as he continued to enthuse on his pet subject. 'I'm hoping to see the Icterine Warbler or perhaps a Rosefinch. If I'm lucky, it could be a Lesser Grey Shrike. If that happens, I'd die a happy man.'

'I thought you said you would die a happy man if you saw a nightjar,' Mum teased.

'Ah, sadly I think that's unlikely, after all,' said Crispin. 'Unless I get lucky tonight.' He wriggled his eyebrows. The innuendo was clear.

Mum scowled. 'Knock yourself out.'

'Have you tried saying no to Delia?' Crispin chuckled. 'She's a pushy one – hello? Are those what I think they are?' He pointed to the Land Rover. 'I thought you were going to burn the bags here.'

'I don't think you should burn them at all,' I said. 'What if Mum gets audited?'

'Audited?' Crispin seemed to find that concept amusing. 'Why would Iris get audited?'

'Some of those statements are the originals, before digitalisation,' I said. 'They should never have been shredded.'

'I was under the impression Iris wanted them shredded,' said Crispin. 'It was you who suggested it, Iris.'

'I said no such thing! It was your idea.' Mum looked uncomfortable. 'Kat has a point. I didn't think about the earlier statements.'

'You sound worried, Iris.' Crispin turned to me. 'She doesn't need to be. I always said I'd look after her and I have.'

There was something that had really been bothering me. 'You know, for years Mum has been worried that she hadn't been paying her taxes,' I said, 'And suddenly, she finds out you've been paying them all along.'

Crispin roared with laughter. 'You're kidding! That's what she pays me for. I take care of everything so she doesn't have to worry about it. Oh Iris! What do you think you were signing every January?'

Mum opened her mouth and shut it again.

'You do remember signing your tax returns, don't you?' he persisted.

Mum shook her head. 'I . . . well . . . how? Did you post them?'

'My mother doesn't do email,' I said. 'She's old-school and prefers hard copies.' I turned back to Mum. '*Do* you remember signing them?'

'I . . .' My mother seemed to wither beneath Crispin's confident gaze and I found that alarming.

'Come on, Iris,' Crispin scolded. 'Don't you remember? You didn't want your husband to find out about the extra income so you snuck up to meet me in London. Then, when digital signatures came into play, you told me to sign on your behalf.'

Mum grew even smaller. 'I don't remember meeting you to sign anything.'

Crispin laughed again. 'Oh Iris, Iris! Of course we did.' He looked at me as if to say that my mother's memory was failing, but I knew it wasn't.

'And let's face it, you went against my advice about these cash withdrawals.' He turned his attention to Alfred. 'Ten thousand pounds is the limit and frankly, we wouldn't be in this mess if your man hadn't been picked up at the border. Fortunately I've got some connections and Grimes has been let off with a caution.' Crispin checked his watch. 'Look. Let's talk more about this in the car.'

'Car?' said Mum. 'Where are we going?'

'You promised to accompany me to Hope Cove this morning,' said Crispin. 'Don't you remember?'

'Did I?' Mum's frown deepened. 'I am quite sure I wouldn't have agreed to go with you because tonight is the Safari Supper and I'd be too busy.'

'I told you I wanted to show you the view of Thurlestone Rock from Bolt Tail,' Crispin persisted.

'No, I would definitely never have agreed to that,' Mum said firmly 'I haven't got a head for heights. Perhaps you said that to Delia.'

'In your dreams.' Crispin laughed. 'Surely you remember? I said we'd be back by lunchtime and besides, I've got a date with your daughter to sort out her little problem.'

'No,' Mum declared. 'I've got far too much to do.'

'A word, Iris,' Alfred broke in.

I'd forgotten that Alfred had been standing there all this time listening to our conversation. He gestured for my mother to step aside and out of earshot.

I don't know what was said but when Mum re-joined us she was smiling broadly. 'It's a lovely idea, Crispin – I'm quite sure that Kat doesn't mind picking up some lettuce for the main course.'

'Excellent, excellent.' Crispin gestured for Mum to accompany him to his car.

'Give me a moment,' Mum said. 'I need to lock up the piggery and get sunscreen and a towel to sit on.'

'I've got all that,' Crispin said. 'Kat will lock up, won't you, Kat? The sooner we go, the sooner we'll be back.'

I grabbed Mum's arm and said, 'Why the sudden change of heart? What did Alfred say to you?'

'It's better that you don't know,' she whispered.

And with that cryptic comment, Mum slipped into the front seat of the Audi, Crispin gallantly closed her door, and they roared out of the courtyard.

Alfred didn't move and nor did I.

He was a man of very few words but I could tell that something was bothering him and I could guarantee it was the same thing that was bothering me.

'You don't like him, do you?' I said.

'Best you stay out of this, Kat,' he grunted. 'Let me handle it.'

'Handle what?' I said. 'What are you going to do?'

But Alfred didn't answer. He clambered into the Land Rover and rumbled out of the courtyard.

I felt very unsettled. I turned my attention to the next appointment of the day.

Eric Pugsley.

Chapter Twelve

By the time I heard Eric's car pull up outside the gatehouse, I had found my agreement with Edith. 'Agreement' was perhaps the wrong word. It was basically a bullet-point list of our conversation, stating that I paid the princely sum of five hundred pounds a month for Jane's Cottage and a further five hundred pounds a month for the pair of gatehouses, the date I'd moved in and that all repairs and renovations were approved unseen, providing I left the property as I found it. There was no clause that gave me any notice to vacate and I suppose I hadn't thought to ask for one.

Like so many situations that started as temporary and morphed into permanent, this one had snuck up on me and I had never thought twice about it up until now.

Eric appeared in the open doorway holding a leather man bag, looking smart in beige chinos – although I did notice a smudge of grease on the knee.

I gestured for him to take the chair on the opposite side of my desk but he didn't. He stood there, taking in the showroom as if he'd not seen it before.

The gatehouse consisted of one large living area, one-and-a-half storeys high with a vaulted ceiling. Two tiny dormer windows were set into the pitched roof. The place was light and airy with three bay windows that looked on to the driveway.

At one point there had been a mezzanine level with a ladder that led up to a sleeping area, but the floorboards had been rotten and, as per my contract, I felt free to take them out. I suppose I'd have to put them back now, although those boards had ended up on a bonfire.

'Do you want to sit down?' I said but Eric just made a dismissive gesture and began to roam around the room, inspecting the shelving, opening a cupboard here and there, before disappearing through the archway to the galley kitchen.

I darted after him. 'Excuse me, Eric. What are you doing?'

Eric turned around and smiled. 'Just taking a look like. I suppose it will do for now.' He gestured to the new units that I had installed a year ago. 'Where's the toilet?'

I pointed to a door leading off. He opened it. The bathroom was small, with just a washbasin. A small window backed on to woodland.

Eric pushed past, back into the showroom and started tapping walls. I trailed after him, feeling that my worst fears were coming true.

'Is the other place the same?' Eric asked. 'You know, old Jones used to live in that gatehouse when I was a nipper.'

'It's the same size,' I said, 'But obviously I use it as a storeroom. Why?'

'I reckon I could get planning permission,' he said. 'Tack on an extension. What do you think?'

'I'm sorry, Eric, but I rent both gatehouses from the dowager countess,' I said firmly. 'I'm not moving anywhere. I've got a lease here and on Jane's Cottage. If you have a problem with that, you'll have to take it up with her.'

Eric smirked.

I could feel my temper start to rise. 'Wouldn't you rather buy something somewhere else, especially if you are thinking about starting a family?'

Eric shook his head. 'Yasmine loves it here.'

'Here?' I said. 'As in the gatehouse?'

'For a studio. She paints and whatnot.' He took in the space again.

'I see,' I said. 'So not to live in.'

'She likes Jane's,' said Eric. 'We took a look when you were away.'

I was furious. I'd left in a hurry to catch the train to the airport. My underwear had been on a drying rack in the bathroom and I knew I hadn't made my bed.

Stupidly, I never locked my doors. None of us did on the estate. Only the showroom and the gatehouse which I used for storage were alarmed. 'You went inside my house without my permission!'

'You can't deny access to your landlord,' he said.

'Excuse me?' I said sharply. 'What do you mean by that?'

Eric smirked again. 'Yasmine liked the spiral staircase. We'll keep that.'

'*That*, as you say, was put in by me,' I said. 'When, *if*, I leave, I'll take it with me!' Which was a stupid thing to say and Eric smirked yet again.

'Is that why I found a business card from an interior designer? Natalie someone or other.'

'Oh, she came, did she?' said Eric mildly. 'She was supposed to call first.'

I thought my head was going to explode, especially since Eric seemed to be thoroughly enjoying my discomfort.

'Of course, Yasmine prefers the Carriage House.'

I regarded Eric with astonishment. 'What are you talking about? You know my mother bought it from the estate.'

Eric shrugged. 'Maybe we'll convert Honeychurch Cottages to one house.'

I just didn't know what to say so I didn't say anything.

'Yasmine comes from a good family,' Eric went on. 'They own a big villa in Bodrum.'

One of my colleagues at the Dartmouth Antique Emporium had just come back from Bodrum. It was on the Aegean coast and well-known for attracting the rich and famous.

'I want to keep her in the style to which she's accustomed.' Eric brought out his mobile and started scrolling through his photographs. 'Take a look.'

Standing so close to Eric for the first time in my life, I was painfully aware of a musky odour and a coarseness that could never be erased. I thought of Yasmine's sophistication and just couldn't figure out the attraction.

I reluctantly made admiring noises as he skimmed through a gazillion selfies – he and Yasmine on the beach, on a yacht, frolicking in the waves, at a restaurant eating lobster – before he paused on a magnificent white villa adorned with fuchsia-coloured bougainvillea overlooking the azure sea.

'That's her parents' place – well, her ma's now,' he said. 'Her dad died last year. Left them quite a bit of money.'

Crispin wanted information, so I was going to get it. 'Ah yes. I read about it in the newspaper,' I lied. 'He was quite a big deal in Istanbul.'

Eric seemed surprised. 'You did?'

'What was his name again?' I pretended to think. 'Uz? Az?'

'Aydin,' said Eric. 'That's her surname. Yeah.'

'He made his fortune in . . .' I frowned. 'Was it carpets?'

Eric looked blank. 'I don't know.'

'How did you meet Yasmine anyway?' I gestured yet again for him to sit at my desk. Finally, he did.

'I met her in the hotel bar where I was staying,' said Eric. 'It was her ma who introduced us. She was waiting for her daughter and we just started talking.'

'Banu introduced you?' I repeated, just to be sure that I'd heard correctly.

'She knew I was from England,' said Eric. 'Yasmine arrived and well . . . she was bloody gorgeous.' His face grew wistful. 'I went the next night but they weren't there. But the next night, Yasmine was just leaving with another man and—' He shook his head as if he could hardly believe his luck. 'She changed her mind and came and sat with me.'

'So you've known Yasmine for how long?' I said.

'We talked on the phone for weeks,' he said.

'Weeks.' I couldn't keep the sarcasm out of my voice. *Weeks*! There was no way this marriage was going to last.

'She wanted to know all about England,' Eric went on. 'I showed her pictures of Honeychurch Hall and all the cottages and the church in the village, like.'

It suddenly occurred to me that Yasmine might have thought Eric owned Honeychurch Hall! That would explain everything. She thought he was loaded.

I recalled Caroline's comment about the family disapproval. 'What does her family think?'

Eric's face fell. 'Oh that. Yeah. Well, it'll be too late after we're wed. Banu is throwing us a big party after the honeymoon so I'll meet everyone then.'

'Oh? You mean, you've only met Banu?' I said. 'Are you implying that everyone disapproves of the match?'

Eric grinned. 'That's because Yasmine was supposed to marry a family friend but she turned him down.' He puffed out his chest. 'We've gone against the family. We're like Romeo and Juliet.'

'I certainly hope not,' I said drily. 'Their relationship didn't end well.'

Eric looked blank. 'Didn't it?'

'They both die,' I said bluntly.

'Oh.'

There was an awkward silence. Eric was being a complete idiot if he thought this relationship would last. If I hadn't been directly affected, I would have just let him get on with it, but there was no question of me being pushed out for a relationship that was only going to last five minutes.

'You wanted to see me about something,' I said coldly.

'Oh yeah,' Eric seemed to come to his senses. 'Do you have one of those tray things for displaying jewellery?'

I pulled out one of the drawers from my desk and retrieved a large velvet tray. I plonked it down in front of him.

Eric unzipped his leather man bag – another sign of his mid-life crisis if you ask me – and brought out a ring box and a small cloth pouch. He opened the first, which held an exquisite engagement ring made of 18-carat white gold with a white-yellow diamond that looked well over a carat. It was expensive.

'We chose her engagement ring in Turkey,' said Eric.

'What's in the cloth pouch?'

He removed the Etruscan ring I'd seen Yasmine wear when we first met. 'It's an heirloom that has been in the family for generations. I thought, as you're valuing this one, you can value the other.'

I took my loupe out of my top drawer and switched on the angle light. 'Do you know much about Etruscan jewellery? It's a specific style.' Eric didn't answer so I enlightened him. 'This ring is probably late nineteenth century. It's actually Victorian. It's not Turkish.' I let that piece of information hang in the air, given that Eric had told me it had been in Banu's family for generations.

'Yeah. But Yasmine told me it was given to her ancestor by a British soldier who was stationed there during the Ottoman Empire.'

I was annoyed, but more with myself for letting my personal feelings get in the way of being professional. 'Ah, that explains it.'

It was a very pretty ring but not particularly valuable. Perhaps a few thousand pounds at the most. Made of 18 carat yellow gold, the ring featured detailed beading and granulation. It was centred by a gleaming half carat old European diamond that doubled as a door to a hidden compartment.

I knew the original purpose of such a ring and, call it revenge, felt a surge of malicious pleasure at what I was about to tell him.

I flipped the door gently upwards. 'This type of ring was used to slip poison into an enemy's food or drink, or to facilitate the suicide of the wearer who might be captured or tortured.'

'Poison?' Eric whispered. 'No. It's for locks of hair or perfume or something isn't it? That's what Yasmine said.'

'She's right,' I reluctantly agreed. 'And by the seventeenth century, jewellers were creating locket rings in the shape of caskets which doubled as mementos for mourners or funeral rings.'

'Funerals?' Eric whispered again.

'Yep. Funerals. But *traditionally*, it was used for poison,' I insisted and decided to educate him. 'The historian Pliny the Elder recounts how a Roman government official escaped torture by taking a bite out of his ring. The thin shell was the container for the poison.'

'Oh,' said Eric.

'So you'd better watch out if she's after your money. That scrapyard must be worth a small fortune.' I laughed, but it came out how I felt. Mean-spirited. Then I felt guilty. 'Just kidding, Eric.'

I picked up the engagement ring and popped in my loupe. 'Now this . . . is stunning. Are you familiar with the four Cs?'

Eric shook his head.

'When selecting a diamond you want to look at the colour, cut, clarity and carat.' In a rush of remorse I handed him my loupe. 'Take a look.'

Eric barely glanced at the stone and I realised that I was wasting my time.

'I'll write up the valuation certificates,' I said. 'If you want to come back a little later, I can have them ready by the end of the day.'

'I'll wait.' Eric sat there. I would much rather he wouldn't, but he did and I felt his eyes watching my every move.

I finished up the detailed description of both pieces putting a value of £3,500 for the Etruscan ring and £15,000 for the diamond, endorsing them both with a stamp of authenticity and my name.

I tucked the certificates into an envelope and handed them over. 'I'll invoice you for the valuation.'

'Oh.' Eric was taken aback.

'Should I make the invoice out to you, or perhaps someone else?'

Eric hesitated for just a split second. 'Make it out to Pugsley's Scrap and leave the description blank.'

My heart gave a tiny leap. The only reason he would have said that was to create his own description on my headed paper! Eric had slipped up, and if he did this with me, what was the betting he did it with others? I filed that juicy piece of information to tell Crispin later. I grabbed a blank invoice with my company logo and paused. 'Do you want me to write in the amount?'

'Friends and family rate, yeah?'

'Three hundred pounds.' I wrote in the amount, thinking he could easily add on a few more zeros. In the 'To' box in the left-hand corner I paused again before addressing it to Pugsley's Scrap, Honeychurch Hall Estate, Little Dipperton.

'I'll just take a photo of this invoice—' I began, but Eric was too fast. He snatched it up and tucked it into his top shirt pocket. Then, he withdrew some cash from his man bag and peeled off the notes.

Before I had a chance to ask if he wanted a receipt, his mobile rang.

He stared at the screen with a frown and answered it with a tentative. 'Hello?'

Although I could hear Caroline's voice booming from the other side of the desk, I couldn't hear what she was saying. But whatever it was, seemed to upset him.

Eric's face turned red and when he hit the end button without saying goodbye and flung the phone on to my desk with a clatter, I knew something was wrong.

'Bad news?' I ventured.

All the wind seemed to have gone out of his sails. 'The vicar's cancelled the wedding.'

Chapter Thirteen

'It's cancelled because the vicar's mother has just died,' I said. 'Didn't you hear about Ruby's accident.'

Eric scowled. 'A two-week delay! We can't wait two weeks.'

'What about tonight's Safari Supper?' I said hopefully. 'Did Caroline say anything about that?'

'No. She said, "See you later, Eric."'

Eric picked up the ring box and the pouch and stuffed them back into his man bag.

'Maybe you can marry when you get back from your honeymoon?' I suggested.

He swallowed hard, drawing my attention to an enormous Adam's apple which I had never noticed before.

'Some honeymoon *that's* going to be,' he muttered.

My mother's comment about Anne Boleyn saving herself for her wedding night to get the crown hit me afresh – although, like Romeo and Juliet, that didn't end too well either.

'Are you sure you can't get married in Bodrum?' From what I knew about Turkish customs, weddings were huge celebrations with three days of feasting starting with flag planting at dawn and with the bride being taken from the family home in a cart to the venue. 'Don't you think Yasmine might feel a little cheated by having a small affair here?'

'No,' Eric said firmly. 'She wants it among my kin. Her new people.'

As far as I was concerned, things had happened so quickly between them, the sooner they got married, the sooner they would get divorced and, with any luck, I just might come through it with my home and business intact. I knew I had three weeks' grace and, with both of them overseas, at best Edith would have recovered; at worst, I could work on Rupert. I hadn't handled it very well that morning. Crispin had been right. I'd shown Rupert I was desperate.

'How about getting married in a registry office?' I suggested. 'Maybe they can squeeze you in before you go away. Follaton House in Totnes is lovely.'

'Registry office, eh?' He nodded. 'Yeah. That could work – oh, here she is!'

Yasmine stepped into the showroom. She skipped over to her fiancé and kissed him on the cheek. She had changed from her jodhpurs into a flimsy T-shirt and tiny white shorts that showed off her tanned legs and barely covered her rear.

'You're back early,' said Eric.

Yasmine made a sad face. 'Poor Lady Lavinia. She *hashta*. She *ishal*.'

'Excuse me,' I said concerned. 'What happened? Is her ladyship okay?'

Yasmine shook her head. 'She sick. Loose bowels. We come back quickly.'

'Cripes!' Eric blanched. 'Is it contagious?'

Yasmine shrugged. 'Who knows?'

'So much for a romantic honeymoon,' I said but my comment was lost as Eric pulled Yasmine into his arms, swearing he'd look after her 'till death us do part.'

Yasmine pushed him away and regarded him with affection. 'You funny man.' She stroked his chin. 'You my little *kucak köpeği*.'

Eric turned pink at what I assumed was an endearment.

Eric unzipped his man bag and removed both rings. He slipped the diamond on to the fourth finger on Yasmine's left hand and put the Etruscan ring on to the middle finger of her right hand.

Yasmine kissed him again and Eric returned the favour but this time on the lips. I've heard giraffe's have long tongues but Eric's was something else. It certainly put me off my lunch.

And then they were gone and I was glad, but I was also concerned about Lavinia and called the Hall.

'The Earl of Grenville's residence,' boomed Delia on the phone. 'Yes,' she said in answer to my question. 'I popped her ladyship into the bath, poor luv, and now she's resting.'

'Do you know what happened?' I said.

'They got as far as Larcombe,' said Delia. 'Her ladyship said she felt dizzy and nauseous. It came on very quickly. It's just as well Yasmine was with her.'

'Do you think this bug is contagious?' I asked.

'I don't get ill,' Delia replied stoutly. 'I haven't had a cold for years.'

Nor had the dowager countess who had boasted of having a constitution like a Sherman tank.

'Did you talk to his lordship about your situation?' Delia said suddenly. 'I was thinking that End Cottage would suit you very well now that Ruby is dead. I can put in a good word if you like.'

I bit back what I really wanted to say and instead said, 'Please don't worry, Delia. I'll be fine. I'd also rather keep this quiet for the time being. Will you promise not to say anything?'

'Mum's the word,' said Delia but somehow I didn't believe her.

We disconnected the line.

I finally got an alert to say my luggage would be with me within fifteen minutes. Time was moving on. I still had to go into the village to pick up some ingredients for the main course before meeting Crispin later.

I opened my laptop and checked Crispin's credentials. I don't know what I expected to find, but it seemed he ran a bona-fide financial advisory business in Newcastle with a slew of testimonials. I checked Company's House and saw Fellowes Financial Advisory Service had been registered in 1995 and his sister Nancy was listed as a shareholder. Everything looked above board. But he wasn't on LinkedIn which, for a businessman, was unusual.

I googled his name with various keywords like fraud, scam, court case which drew a blank. What did surprise me, however, was a newspaper article from a decade earlier naming Crispin Fellowes who, along with a Nancy Fellowes and three others, were swept overboard when a motorboat ran into difficulties crossing the Channel. Crispin was effusive in his thanks to the RNLI who had saved his life because he couldn't swim. I assumed there couldn't be two Crispins with a sister called Nancy, and besides, I distinctly remembered his comment about never going on a boat again.

My luggage arrived. I popped it into the Golf to unpack later in the afternoon and then set off for the village.

The former post office was managed by twenty-something Bethany and her partner Simon Payne. They lived in the flat above and had taken over from Bethany's Aunt Muriel and, rather than face closure, which was the fate of too many village stores, moved it into the twenty-first century by turning it into a community shop. It now resembled the Agrabah Bazaar from Disney's *Aladdin*. There was nothing this place did not sell.

The industrious couple had kept the soul of the old village shop alive. The original brass bell sat on the counter and they still used the old-fashioned cash register and still accepted cash! The back wall behind the counter housed shelves of large glass jars containing traditional sweets like Sherbet Pips, Fruit Chews, Black Jacks, and the kind of treacle toffee that cracked teeth.

Volunteers from the village gave up an hour or two of their time to help out. Bethany was proud to support local vendors and sold wine and the most amazing cheeses from the Sharpham estate nearby, along with a vast array of homemade wares from honey, jewellery, and knitted scarves. Even my mother's Krystalle Storm novels were displayed on a carousel along with picturesque postcards of the South Hams. Of course, no one knew that this world-famous author lived in their midst.

Even I couldn't escape community expectations. Kat's Collectibles and Valuation Services was promoted and, in return, I gave a discount on valuations for locals and, whenever there was an event in the village, be it a flower show, the harvest festival, or a book drive, I always helped out.

Bethany had also started a White Elephant corner where unwanted items were left and could be swapped out for other unwanted items for free. Some of the objects on the table were bizarre and always provided a source of amusement. Someone once left an inflatable sheep there, which definitely generated a few bawdy comments from the farming community. And of course the annual Naked Farmer Calendars were hugely popular at Christmas. My mother had one hanging in her office and claimed it helped her describe her male heroes in her novels.

But this afternoon, as I stepped down into the welcome coolness of the low-beamed shop, I couldn't help noticing

Caroline's hat charity – Hats Off! – was slowly creeping out of her assigned corner space by the 'staff only' door to the loo. The modest hat stand that carried an assortment of colourful hats with various adornments (feathers, fruit, ribbons) 'suitable for a happy bridal party' or 'to cheer up your funeral' was now accompanied by a small table stacked high with Panama hats with a £10 rental tag.

Caroline had also displayed three of her wooden safari animal models – a giraffe was already missing one red eye – with a note saying these 'exquisite carvings' would be on sale after the event, too. There was an honesty box, heavily Sellotaped with 'notes only, no coins' written in black Sharpie. I took a Panama hat for Mallory and tucked ten pounds into the box.

Grabbing a wicker shopping basket, I headed for the back of the shop to pick up the salad ingredients from the chilled food cabinets and returned to the counter to pay. No one seemed to be around. I hit the bell and waited.

Below the counter stood a low bench spread with a selection of local newspapers – the *Dipperton Deal*, *Dartmouth Packet*, and *Totnes Times* – as well as trashy magazines and national newspapers. I noticed *Star Stalkers!*, which used to be the bane of my life. When I was a TV anchor for *Fakes and Treasures* whatever I did appeared in that wretched newspaper. I hated it.

A notice board bore the usual-coloured flyers, but front and centre was the upcoming Little Dipperton Flower and Produce Festival at Honeychurch Hall. Another was an announcement from the water company reminding villagers of the hosepipe ban along with a phone number promising anonymity and a free watering can for 'concerned citizens'. But what really caught my eye was a sign in neon orange. Written in large letters were the words: REWARD FOR INFORMATION LEADING TO FATAL GOAT INCIDENT. It had been signed by the vicar. In smaller print underneath was the announcement that Danny would be taking a two-week compassionate leave of absence.

Doreen Mutters, the landlady of the Hare and Hounds and possibly the worst gossip in the village, emerged from the door behind the plexiglass window that led to the post office sorting room.

'No Bethany today?' I asked.

'She's got that bug,' said Doreen. 'Simon too, but it seems to come and go. And of course we've had to cancel Eric's wedding reception tomorrow night now he's not getting wed.'

'Don't you think the Safari Supper should be cancelled too?' I said for the umpteenth time.

'It's not contagious,' Doreen declared. 'Caroline's determined to go on with it. And those wooden animals she's made? The eyes fall out. It's a rip-off.' She lowered her voice. 'If you want my opinion, she can't cancel because she's already spent the ticket money.'

Doreen was probably right but I knew better than to agree with her, otherwise it would be another 'Kat thinks' rumour circling the village.

Doreen pulled out a hidden stool and settled down for a chat.

'Three more warnings last week,' Doreen declared.

'Excuse me?'

'With the water company,' she went on. 'And now this goat business. The vicar is beside himself with grief. Poor Ruby. Not that I knew her that well, you understand.' She nodded at the neon orange sign. 'I've heard that it was deliberate. Manslaughter. That'll be the charge. Danny's not going to let it go. He's demanding a full investigation.'

'Ah,' I said carefully. 'That sounds like a good idea.'

'Why?' Doreen said sharply. 'So you *do* know what happened! I said to my husband, Stan, I said, if anyone knows what happened it's Kat Stanford.' She leaned in. 'So, what happened?'

I supressed a heavy sigh.

'Go on. Tell.' Doreen leaned in even further. 'After all, you were the one to find the body. I heard it was a bloodbath.'

'I don't know who told you that,' I said, knowing full well who had. Delia Evans had heard it from my own mother's lips 'And besides, I don't think anyone will know the cause of death until after the autopsy.'

'An autopsy!' Doreen exclaimed. 'So it's true! She was murdered!'

I suppressed another heavy sigh. 'There's usually an autopsy in cases where death is unexpected or there is an accident of some kind.'

'Oh.' Doreen sounded disappointed, before adding hopefully, 'But that's not to say it isn't murder.'

'I really don't know.' I transferred the items from the wicker basket into my hessian shopping bag. Doreen picked up a book from a pile next to the cash register. It was *Aunt Muriel's Home Remedies* – the same one that I'd noticed in Ruby's bathroom. The cover was embellished with insects and flowers.

'You should take one of these,' said Doreen. 'They're selling like hotcakes. It's in aid of the RNLI. Ten pounds.'

I wondered if everything was ten pounds these days.

Doreen didn't wait for me to say yes or no. She just put it in my basket. 'You were here when Muriel was alive, weren't you?'

'The former postmistress, yes,' I said.

'A lot of these remedies were passed down from her grandmother who worked at the Hall for Lady Edith's mother,' Doreen declared. 'But her miracle spray . . . now that's something else! Unfortunately, we've run out. Bethany was making up batches and couldn't keep them on the shelves! But the recipe is in there.' She tapped the cover to make a point. 'And it's all natural!'

I thought of the brown trays of sludge and wondered if Ruby had been doing just that.

Doreen spied the hat in my basket and scowled. 'We're not going. We were supposed to do the puddings but Caroline changed her mind and Stan just told her to get stuffed.'

I couldn't wait to get away. Thanking Doreen, I picked up my supplies and stepped out into the sunshine.

I'd parked my car at the entrance to Church Lane. Returning, I glanced up the road to End Cottage and wondered if Mallory had had a chance to watch the wildlife footage on Ruby's mobile.

On a whim, I decided to go and see. After all, it had been my tip!

A police car was parked outside with Malcolm, who usually manned the desk at our local satellite police station, at the wheel. He was reading a newspaper and, as usual, eating a sandwich.

His window was open. We made small talk until I nodded towards the cottage which now bore Police-do-not-cross yellow tape stretched across the entrance to the side alley.

It looked like Doreen was right. Danny was not going to let this goat incident go.

'Is Mallory back there in the garden?' I asked Malcolm.

'No,' said Malcolm. 'He's got the rest of the afternoon off.'

I thought I had misheard. 'Off? You mean, he's been called elsewhere?' Mallory would never have disappeared in the middle of an investigation. 'Are you quite sure?'

Malcolm nodded. 'He took a phone call about an hour ago and said he wouldn't be coming back this afternoon. I've got special instructions to make sure that no one goes into the house or the garden.'

'Do you know if Mallory picked up Ruby's mobile? He would definitely want to look at it,' I said. 'I left it on the kitchen table.'

Malcolm shrugged. 'I didn't see a mobile so perhaps he did.'

I headed back to my car and wondered if I should call Mallory myself to see what was going on. Or perhaps I should just wait until he picked me up this evening at six-fifteen.

My mobile rang and for a moment I thought it was him, but it was my mother and she sounded upset.

'Please come and get me,' she said.

'Where are you?'

'I'll wait by the church in Kingsbridge.'

'Kingsbridge?' I repeated, knowing that Kingsbridge was half an hour inland from the coast. 'But I thought you went to Hope Cove? What's happened? Is everything all right?'

'Just get here quickly,' she said and rang off.

Chapter Fourteen

It took at least an hour to navigate the steady stream of holiday traffic en route to the many beaches that dotted the south Devon coast. All I could think about was that my mother and Crispin must have had an argument. By the time I got to the assigned meeting place at the church there was no sign of Mum at all. I was worried. But then she broke away from the shadows of an overhanging bank of trees.

I leaned over and opened the passenger door. 'Oh Mum! Didn't you wear any sunscreen?'

My mother was as red as a lobster and she had one or two nasty looking mosquito bites. 'Where's Crispin?'

As she slid into the passenger seat, she didn't meet my eye. 'He wanted to stay longer. I told him you could come and pick me up.'

'We'll need to put some ointment on those bites,' I said.

'Oh, it could have been a hundred times worse,' Mum muttered. 'I used that miracle spray and must have missed those bits.'

She leaned back on the headrest and closed her eyes.

'Are you feeling okay?'

'I just feel a bit nauseous that's all,' she said. 'I'll be all right in a minute.'

I thought for a moment. 'How did you get as far as Kingsbridge? I don't understand. It's miles from Hope Cove.'

'I caught a bus. I don't want to talk about it.'

'Something happened, didn't it?' I persisted. 'What? Did you fall out?'

Mum hesitated. 'You were there when I told him I didn't have a head for heights.'

'Yes,' I said. 'He wanted to show you the view of Thurlestone Rock from Bolt Tail and you said no.'

'Well, Crispin doesn't take no for an answer,' she declared. 'He tricked me into a stroll along the southwest coast path and before I knew what was happening we were right on the edge of the cliff. I felt dizzy and . . . well . . . there's no barrier or fence there and . . .'

'Go on,' I said.

'I thought . . .' She hesitated again. 'I thought he was going to push me over the edge.'

'Don't be silly!' I said, exasperated. 'Why would he do that? It's obvious you had too much sun and you hate heights.'

'I hope you're right.' She gave a nervous laugh. 'If it hadn't been for the young couple and their dog – on a lead thankfully – appearing out of nowhere . . .' Mum closed her eyes again as if to blot out the memory. 'Tell me about your day. What did Eric have to say for himself.'

'A lot,' I said and told her everything. 'And when I gave him the invoice for valuing the rings, he told me to leave the description blank.'

Mum yawned. 'You should definitely tell Crispin. It sounds like a bit of creative accounting to me.'

'And guess what,' I said. 'When I was away, Eric and Yasmine actually went into my house and had a good snoop around.'

'Ah, I wondered how that business card from the interior designer had got there.' Mum opened one eye. 'You should definitely tell Crispin that, too. What a cheek!'

The traffic was still crawling along but for once, my mother didn't seem to notice. 'Is the air conditioning on? I'm very hot.'

I glanced over and saw she was sweating. 'It's the lowest it can go. Are you sure you're all right?'

'Just feel a bit sick, that's all. I'll be fine.'

The traffic was excruciatingly slow. We began to crawl behind a large tractor along the A381. It was just before the turn-off to Dartmouth that I saw it.

It was Mallory's black Peugeot and it was parked on the apron of the petrol station.

The car in front of me slowed to a stop to make a right turn against the traffic so I had to stop too.

A young woman in her early twenties emerged from the service station shop with a plastic carrier bag bulging with groceries. She strolled over to Mallory's car and got into the front passenger seat.

I must be dreaming. The driver had to be someone who looked just like my boyfriend.

A car horn abruptly brought me to my senses.

'Are you going to sit there all day?' Mum mumbled.

I slammed the accelerator but stalled, exasperating the man behind who hit the horn again. My hands were shaking a little as I pulled away.

The woman was young – not much older than Yasmine. It was hard to tell at such a distance, but she was pretty, with long hair pulled up into a messy topknot. She wore leggings, heavy Doc Marten boots and a large flannel check shirt which looked suspiciously like one I had seen Mallory wear. I felt sick to my stomach and confused.

Once, I had misunderstood a situation when I was dating Shawn and had felt foolish when he had explained that far from being a secret girlfriend, the woman in question was a work colleague.

There had to be a logical explanation. I was just overreacting. I'd be seeing him this evening and I would take the bull by the horns and ask him outright.

Finally, we turned into the courtyard and came upon an astonishing scene. In the hour or two since I'd been away, Festive Fun Planners had delivered and set up the trestle tables and benches and strung fairy lights and balloons around the buildings. It looked amazing!

Along with the existing flowering geraniums and begonias, the courtyard could easily have been somewhere in the South of France– not exactly on safari in Africa – but definitely good enough for an outdoor summer party.

As I continued on and drove into the arch-braced roof carriageway, I spied a bicycle leaning against the stone mounting block. 'Delia's here, Mum.'

Delia emerged from Mum's kitchen. She looked hot and annoyed. 'Where on earth have you been?'

I got out. 'Mum's not feeling well.'

Delia's face fell. 'Why? Has she caught that bug?'

'I don't know, but she doesn't look too good.'

Delia opened the passenger door and her face fell. 'I see what you mean. Come along, luv, let's get you indoors.' She turned to me. 'Look at her face! She's all hot and clammy.'

'What are you doing here, Delia?' Mum said in a weak voice. 'Sorry. I just feel awful.'

'Don't you worry about anything now,' Delia said briskly. 'Kat and I will take care of everything.'

'Thank you,' Mum whispered.

'No Safari Supper for you tonight,' Delia went on. 'We'll manage, won't we, Kat?'

'But I still want to know why you are here,' said Mum.

'With all the changes that Caroline insists on making, everyone is confused. I wanted to make sure you knew what was going on.' Delia took my mother's arm and led her inside. 'Kat, put the groceries in the kitchen. We'll take care of those in a moment. I'm going to pop Iris into bed.'

I did as I was told and set them down next to a mound of plastic utensils, paper plates and cups with a lion motif.

A box of glass tumblers and another of wine glasses were on the counter.

When I joined them upstairs, they were in the middle of an argument.

'I don't need your help taking off my clothes,' Mum batted Delia's hand away. 'I just need to lie down.'

Delia stood staring, arms akimbo. 'We'll make your apologies. Fortunately, everyone is going to be outside in the courtyard but I can't guarantee we will be able to keep the noise down.'

Mum climbed under the duvet fully dressed but she allowed me to remove her shoes.

'Perhaps we should get her a bucket. If she's got that bug she'll be throwing up everywhere.' Delia clicked her fingers at me. 'Go and find one, Kat. And a glass of water.'

I left the bedroom and returned a few minutes later with a plastic bucket that I put on the floor. I set the glass of water on the nightstand.

Delia drew the curtains and ushered me out of the room and on to the landing, closing the bedroom door gently behind us.

'I couldn't help noticing some sand on her shoes,' Delia said. 'Was she at the beach?'

I hesitated to get into a conversation with Delia about why my mother had gone to the beach, who she had been with and how I had ended up bringing her home.

Why was life so complicated?

'It's a long story,' I said. 'What do you need me to do?'

We trooped downstairs to the kitchen where Delia had already started preparations and didn't press me for details. She seemed preoccupied with the evening ahead and, thankfully, didn't even mention my upcoming eviction.

I chopped up the salad ingredients whilst she put everything together right down to whipping up a delicious-looking potato salad without consulting a recipe book. I would have agonised over every detail.

Finally, we were finished. The dishes that needed to be refrigerated were put in the fridge, and those that didn't, were set on the oak dresser covered in clingfilm.

Delia surveyed the immaculate kitchen that was far cleaner than my mother had ever left it. 'Well, I think we're as organised as we're going to be.'

'Thank you again,' I said for the umpteenth time. 'I know Mum really appreciates it.'

Delia's expression softened. 'She overdoes it sometimes. Let's hope she doesn't miss all the fun.'

I followed Delia back to the courtyard, where she retrieved her bicycle and slid on to the saddle. 'Oh, isn't it a funny coincidence,' she began, 'about that lovely new detective, Greg Mallory?'

At the mention of his name, my stomach lurched as I thought of Mallory and the young woman at the service station again. With all the fuss surrounding my mother and getting ready for the evening, I'd managed to push him to the back of my mind. 'What do you mean? Coincidence?'

'Iris texted me earlier today to give me the news that you're going steady,' she said. 'Of course, he's not a patch on my dear Guy, but Guy is so happy with Amélie. She's French, you know.'

'And I'm happy that he's happy,' I said and meant it. 'But what do you mean by a coincidence?'

'With Guy back in Germany he decided to rent his home out for a year or two, so guess who his new tenant is?'

I had a sinking feeling that I could.

'You can't guess?' Delia smirked again. 'Such a smart investment for my clever son.' She took a pause, as if readying herself to reveal a big secret. 'It's Mallory! Mallory is Guy's new tenant!'

I was right. Of course I knew that Mallory had signed a two-year lease because he had told me, but not in a million years did it cross my mind that the property would belong to Guy!

'You didn't know?' Delia's eyes gleamed with triumph.

And this was why I didn't like Delia Evans. At times she could be kind – compassionate even – and then she'd suddenly stick in the knife.

'Moving in with Mallory would certainly solve your living situation, wouldn't it?' she said. 'Although in my experience, you don't want to push things when you've only just started dating. You don't want to frighten him off like you . . . well . . . least said about that the better.'

I knew exactly what she was implying, even if it wasn't true, but all I did was smile and say, 'You're right. I don't.'

I watched Delia cycle off and braced myself for the next ordeal.

It was time to meet with Crispin.

Chapter Fifteen

As Crispin read my handwritten agreement I scanned the shepherd's hut. We were seated at a small fold-out table on the only two chairs. In front of him were his laptop, a Mont Blanc fountain pen and a yellow legal pad covered in neat print.

The interior of the shepherd's hut was lovely.

Wooden steps led up to a stable half-door that opened into the living space, with a wood burner, a queenie stove, and a stone sink with a small draining board. A cool bag, Muriel's Miracle Spray and his binoculars sat on the countertop. A two-seater sofa in a cheerful yellow print hugged the opposite wall. On the sofa were a pile of books, an ordnance survey map, and a leather computer bag with a combination padlock on the zipper.

A half-packed suitcase lay on top of the raised bed that spanned the width of the hut. It was framed with carved wood and painted with primroses and violets.

Crispin sat back in his chair, his expression grave. 'This is not a contract but rather a licence to occupy.'

'What does that mean?'

'You have no rights,' said Crispin. 'It can be terminated at short notice but the good news is that it's vague enough for us to work with. Does the dowager countess have a copy?'

'No,' I said.

'And has the earl seen this piece of paper?'

'No,' I said again.

'Good,' he said. 'So since this is in your handwriting, there's nothing to stop you from adding another page – perhaps one more specific about the terms of the agreement. I can notarize it retrospectively, which will make it legally binding.'

I was shocked. What Crispin was suggesting was clearly illegal and I told him so.

He shrugged. 'It's your call. But that's what I would do.'

'Sorry to waste your time.' I got to my feet, feeling very uncomfortable. 'Surely there is another way that doesn't involve . . .' I paused for a moment before adding pointedly, '*Fraud*.'

'There is always a way, Katherine,' he said. 'It depends on how far you want to go and how much you want to stay here.'

'I don't want to do anything illegal,' I said somewhat primly.

Crispin acknowledged my comment. 'I'm just giving you all your options, dear.'

'I know,' I said. 'And thank you.' I headed for the door.

'What if Eric Pugsley was doing something illegal?' said Crispin, stopping me in my tracks. 'Would that salve your conscience? Or perhaps the earl?'

Before Crispin had suggested blatant fraud, I had been going to tell him about Eric's invoice, but I had changed my mind. If Crispin found something out, I didn't want it coming from me.

'There is nothing illegal about doing background checks,' Crispin went on. 'Imagine you're selling a property or buying something, or even hiring someone for a job. Wouldn't you want to make sure whoever you were dealing with didn't have a criminal record?'

'I suppose so.'

'What we're looking for is *leverage*.' Crispin's eyes gleamed. 'All I need to do is make a few phone calls. He runs Pugsley's Scrap, isn't that right? And what about his banger-racing enterprise?'

'I don't want to get Eric into trouble—'

Crispin waved my concerns away. He wrote down Pugsley's Scrap on the pad. 'And what's the full name of his wife to be? Iris told me she came from a wealthy family in Turkey.'

I was changing my mind by the minute. 'I'm not sure.'

'No problem,' he said. 'That's easy enough to find out. Since they are getting married, she would have had to provide identification to your vicar in order for him to marry them. A passport, a driver's licence. Leave it with me.'

I didn't want to leave it with Crispin. 'Look, I made a mistake with the agreement' I said. 'That's on me—'

'Now, off you go and get ready for tonight,' he said. 'And leave me to do my job.' He stood up and gallantly ushered me out of the door. 'How is Iris feeling now? I tried to call her but she wasn't answering her phone.'

'Mum's not feeling well,' I said. 'Either she had too much sun or she's coming down with the bug that is making the rounds.'

Far from seeming concerned, Crispin rolled his eyes in exasperation. 'Was that the problem? Why on earth didn't she say so instead of walking off in a huff and abandoning me?'

'Abandoned *you*?' I exclaimed. 'That's not what my mother said.'

Crispin's eyes widened in amusement. 'Yes. She abandoned me! I only wanted another half an hour but she wanted to go straight home. I've known Iris for a very long time and when she wants something, she wants it straight away.'

I had to admit that part was true. If impatience was measured on a scale of one to ten, my mother would be a twelve. 'I don't think she'll be well enough to join in tonight.'

I left the shepherd's hut feeling more unsettled than ever. I couldn't believe that Crispin had suggested that I forge my agreement with Edith! The dustbin liners full of shredded documents that he had wanted Mum to burn now took on a more sinister air. I needed to talk to someone about this and my first thought was Mallory. But what if my mother was up to something illegal? I needed to speak to her first. So far, I wasn't at all impressed with Crispin.

Back at Jane's Cottage I remembered that I had my suitcase in the back of my car and took it indoors to unpack later. I was assuming that Mallory would come back this evening and didn't want him to see a pile of unwashed laundry on my kitchen floor. I thought of the young woman at the service station again and how I planned on asking him who she was without sounding like a possessive girlfriend. Of course, finding Ruby's body had been horrifying but, selfishly, last night I felt as if things were finally falling into place. But now I had never felt so unsure about my future.

After showering and donning a pair of sand-coloured capri pants with a white shirt, it was almost six-fifteen. But six-thirty came and went with no sign of my boyfriend and when my mobile rang and the caller ID flashed up his name, I just knew what he was going to say.

The word 'disappointment' didn't even cut it. He explained that something unexpected had come up and he wouldn't be able to be with me tonight after all.

Intuitively, I already knew the real answer, but I had to ask. 'Is this connected to Ruby's death?'

There was a pause and then, 'No. It's not work-related.'

My heart sank. I didn't speak.

'I can't tell you at the moment, but you've got to trust me, Kat.' Mallory lowered his voice as if someone was there. *She* was there. 'I'll make it up to you. I will.'

I was desperate to say, 'I saw you! Who is she?' But the words just wouldn't come out and I realised it was because I didn't want to hear the answer. I just didn't want to get hurt again.

'By the way, Malcolm told me you saw Ruby's mobile phone on the kitchen table.' Mallory broke into my thoughts.

'Yes,' I said. 'It needed a password.' I went on to tell him about the wildlife camera app.

'Are you sure that's where you saw it because it's not—'

'I told you I did.' I knew that my voice sounded clipped, but I couldn't help it. He had let me down. *He* had been the one to say we were going public, not me. I should never have believed him.

'Kat, I've got to go,' he said. 'Have fun to—'

I had already hung up.

Chapter Sixteen

I left for the village straight away but first made a quick stop to check in on my mother. The house was silent. I headed upstairs. Her bedroom door was still closed.

I opened it a crack. The room was in darkness. Mum was still in bed and it looked like she was sleeping. I left her to it.

I turned into Church Lane and managed to park behind Banu's blue Skoda outside End Cottage. The police caution tape was still there but I couldn't see a police officer.

Crispin's Audi pulled up, with Delia riding shotgun. The pair piled out wearing their Panama hats, both in good spirits. Crispin hadn't changed clothes but Delia had squeezed into white trousers and matched them with a zebra print blouse.

He beckoned me over. 'We're in luck.'

'Who's in luck?' Delia demanded as she joined us.

Crispin nudged her. 'I'm in luck having such a lovely lady on my arm tonight.'

'You're such a flirt!' Delia beamed with pleasure, but then her face fell. 'Still no Iris?'

'No. I checked on her and she was sleeping,' I said.

Delia placed a hand on Crispin's arm in a possessive manner. 'Maybe we'll pop up and see her when we get to the main course and take her a sausage roll.'

'How is Lady Lavinia feeling? I heard she had to cut her ride short with Yasmine.'

'Oh, you know what those horsey people are like,' said Delia. 'Cast-iron stomachs. She's fine now.'

'Why don't you go on ahead, Delia,' said Crispin. 'I'll meet you inside. I just want a quick word with Kat.'

Delia stood her ground.

'In private,' he said and winked. 'Off you go.'

Delia winked back and left us.

Crispin steered me away from a group of arriving partygoers. He wore an expression that I could only describe as the cat who had got the cream.

Despite my misgivings, I had to ask. 'Well?'

Glancing over to make sure we were out of earshot he said, 'Not to put too fine a point on it, your Earl of Grenville is sinking fast. He's taken out several hefty loans to stay afloat.'

I didn't want to hear this. It felt as if I was rifling through someone's underwear drawer.

'Now Pugsley's Scrap?' He grinned again. 'Ha! Dodgy ticket sales? Creative accounting like you'd not believe. I can't move on this until Monday but I thought I'd have a little chat with him tonight.'

My heart sank. 'I've been thinking about this,' I began, 'and I'm truly grateful but—'

'Wait!' he exclaimed and held up his hand. 'I haven't told you the best part yet. Do you know how Banu entered the country?'

'*Banu*? Don't you mean Yasmine?' I was puzzled. 'I have no idea. What do you mean *how*?'

'She wasn't travelling with her daughter, that's for sure,' he said. 'A bit of a mystery and— Holy moly!' his jaw dropped in amazement. 'Will you look at that! It's Betty Rubble!'

I turned to see what had halted him in his tracks and felt my jaw drop too.

Eric and Yasmine were strolling towards us hand in hand, but Yasmine was not dressed as Betty Rubble. She was dressed as Jungle Jane, in the tiniest leopard faux-fur bikini adorned with a plastic necklace and bangles strung with bones. Suede ankle boots completed her outfit.

With her hair tousled as if she had just fought off a sabre-tooth tiger, Yasmine looked radiant. Fortunately, Eric had decided to keep all his clothes on. It must be pure torment for a red-blooded man like Eric to be around a beautiful woman who oozed sex appeal. Mum's comment about Yasmine doing an 'Anne Boleyn' hit me afresh.

Crispin was mesmerised and, to be honest, so was I.

'We'll talk later,' said Crispin and zoomed in on the happy couple who were being mobbed by admirers.

I headed for the entrance where Caroline, perspiring freely and dressed in full-on safari gear, was greeting her guests. Along with the Panama hat, she wore matching khaki trousers, with a gazillion zipper pockets, a long-sleeved insect repellent shirt – which was probably a good idea since the mosquitoes were out in force – a bandana, and heavy hiking boots.

'No Iris?' Caroline asked.

'She's not feeling well,' I said, 'But the main course is under control.' But Caroline's attention was already on Crispin, who had caught me up.

She stepped forward to welcome him. 'Ah, and you're the birdwatcher.'

'That's right,' said Crispin. 'And I'm sorry for your loss. I knew your mother-in-law.'

Caroline looked startled. 'You knew Ruby? How?'

'We shared a love for our little feathered friends,' said Crispin. 'Such a terrible accident. Of course the police will soon find out what really happened.'

Caroline's expression changed from surprise to annoyance. Her eyes narrowed. 'Wait, I know who you are! You're the idiot who hit my car!'

Crispin looked taken aback. 'Excuse me?'

'Do you drive an Audi TT Quattro in slate grey? Number plate FFS 123?'

'Well, yes. Goodness!' He snapped his fingers. 'Are you the lady in the Mercedes?'

'Yes I am!' Caroline exclaimed. 'And you're going to have to pay for the damage. I've already filed a police report.'

'Whoa, steady on,' Crispin sounded amused. 'With all due respect, I did not hit your car and I think you'll find that since there is no damage to mine, it's going to be a he-said-she-said, situation.'

Caroline reddened. 'But that's not fair!' She caught my eye. 'Is that not fair, Kat? He should pay!'

I just stood there wondering how I got caught in the middle of situations that had nothing to do with me.

'You forced me into the hedge!' Caroline protested.

'Whoa!' Crispin said again. 'No need to get upset. I'm a fair man. Tell you what. Why don't we talk about this tomorrow afternoon and not spoil your lovely party. I'm staying in the shepherd's hut.'

'Yes I know,' said Caroline.

'Why don't you come by say, around four?'

I opened my mouth to point out that Crispin was checking out in the morning, but was stopped by his mobile ringing. He raised one finger, looked at the caller ID and his face lit up. 'I've got to take this. It's for us, Kat.'

Us?

Crispin turned away giving me a chance to dart past Caroline and into the vicarage.

Inside the entrance hall was a large, framed photograph of Ruby on a side table flanked by lighted candles, a crystal vase filled with the most exquisite roses and a placard edged in black that said, *RIP Ruby: You will be missed.* At least she was being acknowledged, although I suspected that it was arranged by the vicar – who I couldn't yet see.

'Go through to the terrace, please!' Caroline cried from the front door. 'Mind the rugs! They're new! No one can go upstairs! Go on through! Go on through!'

Although I had not been here before, I could tell that no expense had been spared with the refurbishment. Most doors were closed, with one bearing a placard saying 'Toilette'. Upstairs was roped off using another French word: 'Interdit', for some bizarre reason.

'Kat!' hissed a familiar voice. A door opened. 'I thought it was you.' It was Danny and he gestured for me to follow him into a room full of hats.

Danny looked a wreck. His long hair, usually swept back in a man-bun, fell about his face; his clerical collar was unbuttoned and dangled over the neck of a tatty long-sleeved sweatshirt. 'Did anyone see you come in?'

'Er. I don't think so,' I said.

Danny headed for an armchair as if settling in for a chat. I hovered by the door.

'How are you holding up?' I said.

'I can't . . . I can't be frivolous when Mother . . .' He trailed off.

'I'm so sorry,' I said.

'I am not alone,' Danny went on. 'The Lord walks by my side. I just . . .' He put his head in his hands. Conveniently, there was a box of Kleenex on a computer work station. I offered him a tissue.

'I'm so sorry for your loss.'

'I've offered a reward you know,' Danny said suddenly. 'Someone knows something. My mother was as strong as an ox and she wasn't afraid of anything. She lived through the Blitz for heaven's sake!

'We're hoping there is a clue on Ruby's mobile's phone,' I said. 'But no one seems to have found it.'

'The police have already asked me but I don't know what she did with it.'

'It was on the kitchen table,' I said.

'Are you positive?' Danny said.

'Yes,' I nodded. 'It was next to *The Nightjar Network* newsletter. I distinctly remember it because the mobile was the latest model and Mum and I were impressed.'

'Iris!' He brightened up. 'She's the only person I can face seeing tonight.'

'My mother isn't here,' I said. 'She's not feeling well.'

'Oh no!' Danny was worried. 'You don't think she's caught that bug?'

'Let's hope not,' I said. 'I think it's sunstroke.'

'Wasn't she wearing a hat?'

'No,' I said.

Danny gestured to the mounds of hats on every available surface, all neatly categorised and labelled. He gave a bitter laugh. 'Why not take one of these! Take two. Take a dozen. Take them all!' And then his face fell again.

I began to edge my way to the door. 'I'd better get to the party.'

Danny nodded miserably. 'I made the most terrible mistake taking Caroline back, Kat. I hope I haven't ruined it with Iris. Have I? Have I ruined it?'

I just smiled and left him to his grief.

At the end of the corridor, flanking the French doors that opened on to the terrace, stood Dawn Jones. She wore a dark-green knee-length apron over a white shirt and dark green leggings. Dawn carried a tray of cocktails that bore identifying flags saying Sunset Safari, Lion's Lair and Zebra Zinger, in an array of vibrant colours that smacked of food-colouring additives. Willow Mutters – who often helped me at Dartmouth Antique Emporium when she was home from university – was identically dressed and manned the other side holding a tray of stemmed glasses of bubbly.

Willow offered me a glass. 'It's not Prosecco. It's the real thing!'

I tasted it and it really was.

'Have you seen the petting zoo yet?' When I laughed and said that I hadn't, she added, 'Out there. On the terrace. You are in for a treat.'

Curious, I left Willow at her post and stepped outside where the soundtrack from *Jungle Book* played in the background. On my left I noticed a row of watering cans bearing the water company's logo – many more than anyone needed in their garden.

But then I saw them.

Dozens of life-sized wild animal sculptures.

'Caroline borrowed the props from the Gipping Bards' production of *Tarzan*,' I heard Delia say to Kizzy Jones, Dawn's mother. 'And of course, she persuaded Malcolm Curley to loan a few of his animals out.'

Of course! The wonderful Malcolm Curley! The sculptures were the work of a retired octogenarian artist who originally made them for fun. Created from polystyrene, bits of wood, and random scrap metal, what had started as a hobby soon became a fixture for tourists. It was no surprise that Caroline had managed to persuade Malcolm to lend her a few, although it looked like he wasn't here in person.

I remembered the first time I had driven through the Bridgetown housing estate in Totnes. I thought I'd entered the twilight zone. Alligators, elephants, and the odd panda peered through hedges or over fences; giant squirrels perched on garage rooftops and monkeys clambered up outside walls. Apparently there are over one hundred sculptures spread along the route that is affectionately known as the Totnes Safari.

Tables laden with platters of finger food – pigs-in-blankets, baked coconut prawns, stuffed mushrooms and a variety of mini-quiches, crudities, and dips – were watched over by Caroline's hand-painted wooden elephants, giraffes, and zebras.

I wished Mum had been here. She would have found it all hilarious.

There was no denying that the first course was a success. All of the partygoers wore Panama hats and a couple of villagers had dressed up, but none were a patch on Yasmine's Jungle Jane.

I looked around for Banu and saw that Crispin had trapped her in the gazebo, her exit barred by a life-sized gorilla. Crispin was casually leaning against the post but had his back to me so I couldn't see his face. But I could see Banu's and she didn't look happy.

Caroline appeared. Her face was flushed. 'Have you seen Danny?'

'Not recently,' I said, which wasn't exactly a lie.

'Do you know what time they're coming?' Caroline asked. 'We're on a tight schedule.'

I didn't need to press for details because suddenly the terrace fell quiet and a lone voice boomed, 'The Earl of Grenville and Lady Lavinia Honeychurch!'

Royalty had arrived.

Chapter Seventeen

The terrace erupted into a round of polite applause and a few sniggers. Although Rupert was dressed in flannel trousers, an open-necked checked shirt and even wore a Panama hat, Lavinia's attire came as a bit of a shock.

I was pleased that she had made a miraculous recovery but startled at what she was wearing. It would appear that Lavinia had been to the same fancy-dress shop as Yasmine. Apart from the fact that Lavinia was painfully thin, flat-chested and carried an adorable little pot belly, she had paired her fake-fur bikini with rubber yard boots that still had wisps of straw attached to the soles.

And then, to everyone's astonishment, Yasmine darted forwards and grabbed Lavinia's hand raising it up in a show of solidarity. 'We sisters. Yes!'

The difference between Yasmine's beauty and self-confidence and poor Lavinia, who was shy at the best of times, was excruciating to see. I couldn't bear it.

I filled the awkward silence by shouting, 'Let's give a round of applause to the Jungle Janes!' and madly started clapping. Everyone joined in. Dawn thrust a Zebra Zinger into Lavinia's hand but Rupert couldn't take his eyes off Yasmine.

I watched her luxuriating in the attention – especially from Rupert. Eric wasn't the only one who noticed either. He put a possessive arm around Yasmine's tiny waist.

I saw the pain on Lavinia's face and my heart went out to her. I couldn't help wondering if Yasmine had done it deliberately.

Lavinia downed her Zebra Zinger. I grabbed two glasses of bubbly from Willow's passing tray and went to join her.

'I'm glad you are feeling better.'

'Much,' Lavinia said as she watched her husband blatantly flirting with Yasmine. 'She's frightfully pretty, isn't she?'

I didn't know what to say.

We watched Banu walk up to the trio and whisper into Yasmine's ear. Yasmine flashed a smile to the two men and followed her mother to the gazebo where Crispin was waiting. A group of partygoers moved into my sightline and Crispin was lost to view.

'Don't you think she's pretty?' Lavinia said again. 'So lovely. So kind. A good friend.'

I wasn't so sure about that.

'Did you and Yasmine choose your matching outfits together?'

'Oh no,' Lavinia said. 'It was a surprise.'

So I was right. Yasmine had done this to humiliate her.

The music stopped abruptly and Caroline's voice boomed across the terrace.

'Now, I want us all to raise our glasses to the future bride and groom!' She gestured for Yasmine and Eric to come to the front.

'You'll be happy to know the nuptials are back on!' Caroline exclaimed. 'Monday at noon at Follaton House registry office followed by a little party at the Hare and Hounds in the Beer Garden with an open bar!'

Eric beamed. Yasmine threw her arms around his neck and squealed with delight. There was more applause and more toasts. Rupert looked on stony-faced.

'And let the safari continue,' Caroline shouted. 'But wait! Before we do, a reminder that the adorable table decorations are for sale. The proceeds go to charity so please – I repeat – please, do not take them off the premises. You'll be able to buy them at the community shop tomorrow for ten pounds. Now . . . onwards! To the Carriage House!'

Delia caught me just as I was getting into my Golf. 'Can we come with you?' Delia jabbed a finger behind her. 'With Iris out of action, Banu has offered to give us a hand. We can't wait for Crispin. He seems to be having a bit of a barney with Eric.'

My heart sank. I'd specifically told Crispin not to exert his 'leverage', and it sounded like this was exactly what he was doing.

Banu frowned. 'What is barney?'

'An argument,' said Delia. 'Your future son-in-law sounded very upset.'

'Men, they get jealous of her,' Banu said with a knowing nod. 'Birdman he look at her much.'

Conversations in the car journey to the Carriage House were filled with Delia's criticism of Caroline's choice of appetisers and that she didn't believe they were homemade. Banu sat silently in the back, cradling her handbag.

I glanced in the rear-view mirror. 'It's good news that Eric and Yasmine are getting married on Monday now. I'm sure you're pleased.'

Her eyes caught mine. She smiled. 'Yes. Very good.'

'And you must be flying to Turkey with them on Tuesday?'

She frowned. 'Excuse?'

'Kat means Eric and Yasmine are away for three weeks,' said Delia. 'When do you fly back to get ready for the family party.'

'Yes. Tuesday,' said Banu.

This was good news for me. My plan to work on Edith and Rupert was back on.

'What a pity that Iris will be missing all the fun,' said Delia.

But she needn't have worried.

As I turned into the tradesmen entrance and headed up the service drive, I could already hear music. A bunch of balloons were tied to the gatepost along with a handwritten sign saying 'Minibus: Park Here For Party'.

I drove straight on and into the carriageway, where we were greeted by my mother, who looked the spitting image of Meryl Streep from the iconic film *Out of Africa*.

'I don't believe it!' Delia said angrily. 'She promised we weren't going to dress up! She promised!'

My mother was notoriously handy with the needle and had a huge chest of dressing-up clothes that she had sewn herself. She did look rather spectacular. She had managed to cover her bruise with make-up and even dug out a long curly wig and styled it like Meryl Streep's character from the film.

'And her wig is terrible!' Delia grumbled. 'Don't you agree, Banu? Don't you think it looks fake?' Delia suffered from alopecia and was a connoisseur on wigs. However, far from pretending the hair was her own, she preferred to flaunt the obvious. This evening her chin-length bob was an intriguing shade of dark plum.

Mum strolled over to greet us, opening Delia's car door and, despite Delia's earlier comment, she was back to business. 'Right, Iris. What do you want us to do?'

The pair scurried away, leaving me to help Banu out of the back of the car. She tripped over her ankle-length kaftan, dropping her handbag and spilling the contents over the stone floor, narrowly missing a pool of yellowing, brownish liquid.

Luckily, Banu wasn't hurt, but as she shovelled random items back into her bag, I saw one of Caroline's giraffes partially hidden in a paper serviette.

Caroline had been specific about not taking the wooden animals home.

Banu's eyes met mine. 'She give it me,' she said as if reading my mind. 'A present.' Banu pushed the giraffe deeper into her bag before zipping it up. She hurried after my mother and Delia.

I caught up with them in the courtyard where trestle tables were laden with food. Wine, beer, and soft drinks were on offer. There were no fancy cocktails this time.

The music changed into a magnificent explosion of harmonies with a deep rhythmic beat. It was perfectly timed as the villagers rolled in from the bus. Everyone, without exception, jogged, swayed, or skipped into the courtyard, obviously assisted by the after-effects of Caroline's cocktails. I heard 'this is more like it!' and 'I hope we can stay here!'

I caught up with my mother at the bar where, to my surprise, Alfred, wearing a Panama hat, was handing out the drinks.

'What music is this? I shouted about the noise.

'"Jersusalema" by Master KG,' she grinned. 'Isn't it amazing? I googled YouTube for happy music with an African theme. Apparently there have been over five hundred and fifty million views and counting.'

I couldn't stop my feet from moving either. 'It's brilliant.'

'Just you see,' Mum said with a knowing look. 'No one will want to move on from here.'

My mobile in my pocket vibrated and when I checked who was calling, it brought me back to reality with a jolt. It was Mallory.

'Kat?' came a faint voice. 'Kat? Are you there? I can't hear you.'

'Hold on,' I shouted. 'I'll go somewhere quiet.'

I went back to the carriageway and slipped through the first red-brick archway into one of the stalls. The immediate silence and peace of the old building seemed to steady my nerves – as did the sight of the bite and hoof marks that peppered the dividers – a reminder that whatever was happening right this minute, would soon pass into history, just like the horses who had lived here all those years ago.

'Can you hear me now?' I asked.

'It sounds like quite a party,' said Mallory. 'Has anyone been eaten by lions yet?'

'Not yet.'

'Good.'

There was an awkward silence until he said, 'I spoke to the vicar and he confirmed the wildlife camera was connected to Ruby's mobile phone, but it's still missing.'

'Oh,' I said.

There was another silence. 'Look, I'm really sorry about this evening.'

'It's okay,' I said. 'Alfred is wearing your hat.'

Yet another silence! It was painful. 'How is the new place?' I said suddenly. 'Larcombe Barn.'

'Oh! How do you know?' said Mallory. 'I was going to tell you earlier but— Who told you?'

'Delia.'

'How would she know?' Mallory sounded genuinely confused. 'I'm renting from a naval officer . . . wait . . . Delia's last name is Evans. Of course. Guy Evans is her son!'

'For a policeman, I'm surprised you didn't make that connection sooner,' I said drily.

'I have made the connection now. Ha!' he chuckled. 'Didn't you have a thing with him?'

'Not exactly a thing,' I shot back. 'But yes, we went out a few times.'

'Is that what you're bothered about? Being back in his house?'

'Why would that bother me?' I was incredulous. Of course it didn't.

'If anyone should be bothered,' said Mallory, 'it's me.'

'It wasn't a serious relationship,' I said. 'And nothing happened between us, as you know.'

I heard a woman's voice in the background. 'Look, I have to go,' said Mallory. 'I'll see you first thing tomorrow morning. Is nine too early?'

'Nine is fine.' And he rang off.

I desperately wanted to ask him who was there but I just didn't want to hear the answer.

I stood for a moment, collecting my thoughts, when I heard angry voices.

Eric and Rupert entered the carriageway and it was clear from both men's postures that they were in the middle of a heated discussion.

I panicked. I didn't want them to see me, so I ducked into one of the stalls.

Chapter Eighteen

I couldn't hear exactly what was being said but when I heard my name, I edged as close to the two men as I dared and stole a look around the corner, withdrawing quickly.

They were standing so close to me that I could have touched them.

They were facing each other. Rupert towered above Eric. He was bristling with barely contained rage, his hands clenched by his sides. Eric, by contrast, seemed amused – almost insolent.

Eric was someone who had always deferred to his master in every possible way, so the power had shifted. He must have some kind of hold over Rupert, and somehow it involved me, which meant that it had to do with moving into my house. Crispin's words that the earl was 'sinking fast' and that he had taken out 'hefty loans' echoed in my mind. Was it remotely possible that his lender was none other than Eric Pugsley? It would go a long way to explaining Eric's sense of entitlement and Rupert's reluctance to entertain any kind of compromise with me. How humiliating for him! Perhaps enlisting Crispin to do some sleuthing hadn't been such a bad idea after all.

'Here they are!' Yasmine strolled in hand in hand with Lavinia – two Jungle Janes together. 'We look for you boys. Come to party! Yes?'

Rupert's face was white with anger. He didn't reply. Instead, he wrenched Lavinia's hand away from Yasmine's and said, 'We're going home.'

Yasmine giggled but grabbed Lavinia's hand to pull her in for a quick hug.

'Get in the car!' Rupert snarled. He stormed out of the carriageway with Lavinia trying hard to keep up with his long strides.

'You argue over me?' Yasmine giggled again. 'Aw. Don't worry *kucak köpeği*.'

I really needed to look up the meaning of that phrase.

Yasmine tucked her hand into the crook of Eric's arm and whispered something in his ear which made him smile. He bent down to kiss her again and when his massive hands started exploring the large naked spaces between the faux-fur leopard-spot bikini, making Yasmine wiggle and squeal, I stepped hastily backwards.

Unfortunately, my foot caught the edge of an unseen wooden ladder that was leaning against the wall, causing it to clatter to the ground.

For a ghastly moment I thought my cover was blown but, as the seconds ticked by and no one called out or even worse, discovered me crouched in the corner, I plucked up the courage to see if they had gone. They had.

I was about to set the ladder back against the wall but stopped when I noticed the two broken rungs a third of the way down from the top. Glancing up, I saw the trapdoor to the hayloft where I was pretty sure my mother had retrieved the boxes of documents. This had to be the ladder. Even though the light was dim, I could see the break was dead in the centre of each, exactly where my mother would have placed her foot. One broken rung was unfortunate, but two? I resolved to take a closer look in the morning.

I headed back to the party just as the music came to an abrupt stop and Caroline was shouting, 'Desserts! To the summer house! Hurry now! We're behind schedule!'

There was a mass exodus across the courtyard and into Honeywell Woods for the ten-minute walk that would take us to the ornamental lake and the summerhouse. I had hoped to walk over with my mother to tell her what I had witnessed in the carriageway but I couldn't see her and was swept along with the throng.

It was just after nine by the time everyone got to the summer house. The sun had set and a full moon hovered in the still night sky.

The summer house had been built at the same time as the Palladian addition to the Hall. Delia had it earmarked as a future tea room but, for tonight, it too was decorated with fairy lights. There was just one table offering wine and beer manned by Willow. Dawn was in charge of an ice-cream cart that not only had a choice of delicious flavours from Salcombe Dairy but a variety of toppings that ranged from hot fudge sauce to nuts and raspberry syrup. The film soundtrack from *The English Patient* played quietly in the background and the mood was mellow.

Given the off-road location there was a distinct lack of chairs, but Delia had thought of this and provided mackintosh squares for those who wanted to sit on the grass, gaze out over the ornamental lake and eat their ice creams.

In fact, Delia had thought of everything. Being so close to the water, a gazillion mosquitoes were out in force. Citronella garden torches lined the banks; bottles of Avon Skin So Soft body spray were being passed around. Delia insisted that it was more effective than Muriel's Miracle Spray, of which there was none to be seen. Nor was there any sign of Alfred, Rupert, or Lavinia.

It seemed that no sooner had we got our ice creams and settled on to our mackintosh squares that it was time to move on again.

'Petits fours! To the Hall!' Caroline yelled. 'Oh – and leave the mackintosh squares. Mrs Evans will be staying behind to fold.'

'Bloody cheek!' Delia exclaimed as she and Mum joined me.

'Caroline deliberately cut me short,' Delia declared. 'I didn't get the full hour.'

'Where's Crispin going?' Mum pointed to Crispin, who was walking in the opposite direction.

'He's going back for a nap,' said Delia. 'It's his last chance to see the nightjar and he's planning on staying up all night to catch it.' She stifled a yawn. 'To be honest, I think this has gone on long enough. Everyone is getting tired.'

It was just before ten when we trailed into the drawing room. Classical music played in the background but was so faint as to be barely audible.

Slowly, the exuberant spirits and laughter evaporated as the partygoers took in the formality of their surroundings.

Some had never stepped inside the Hall, let alone the drawing room with its elaborate cornices and decorative strapwork.

I remembered my first impression of the exquisite room. Red silk wallpaper shared the walls with tapestry hangings. Damask curtains fell graciously from the four casement windows that overlooked the park.

The furniture reflected the Hall's various incarnations from seventeenth-century oak court cupboards to an ugly twentieth-century drinks cabinet. There was the usual plethora of side tables, lamps, and gilt-framed mirrors as well as an overwhelming number of miniatures that took up almost the entire wall to the right of the fireplace. A copper Gibraltar gong stand stood in the corner.

The villagers made small talk, but it felt forced, and the few bursts of laughter unnatural.

Willow and Dawn had reappeared with silver trays carrying an assortment of digestifs in dainty liqueur glasses and some exquisite petits fours that I overheard Caroline say Delia must have bought from Waitrose.

Having skipped appearing at the summer house, Rupert stood in front of the fireplace with his arms folded behind his back looking grumpy. Lavinia was noticeably absent.

Yasmine entered with Eric and Banu. Yasmine seemed awestruck as she took in the splendour of the room. Her eyes drank in the priceless paintings that adorned the walls alongside gilt-framed mirrors. To someone who didn't understand the financial circumstances of most landed gentry in England it would appear that the Earl of Grenville was worth millions of pounds. According to Crispin's discoveries, this couldn't be further from the truth.

Yasmine moved to the credenzas and glass display cabinets. To everyone's shock, she opened the little doors, picking up and inspecting the dowager countess's valuable snuff boxes and curios without any sense of boundaries. Murmurs of disapproval began to circulate the room.

Delia scurried to Eric's side and gestured to where Yasmine was showing Banu a particularly fragile millefiori paperweight. Eric froze, obviously embarrassed. Delia grabbed a paper serviette, marched over to the pair and, with great care, gently took the paperweight away, giving it a quick polish before putting it back and firmly closing the glass door.

Yasmine laughed. She spied the tiger rug and made a beeline for it. There were gasps of shock and then embarrassed laughter as Yasmine dropped beside the rug to stroke the big cat.

'Take picture! Take picture!' cried Yasmine.

Banu grinned, whipped out her mobile and took a few, clearly enjoying her daughter's performance as she writhed on the tiger.

'Good grief!' Mum gasped. 'Who does she think she is? Elinor Glyn?'

'Who?' said Delia.

'She was a racy novelist in the naughty eighteen nineties,' Mum said in a low voice. 'She even stayed here a few times. Let me see if I can remember the rhyme, *Would you like to sin / With Elinor Glyn / On a tiger skin? / Or would you prefer / To err with her / On some other fur*?'

'No one would dare overstep their place were the dowager countess here,' Delia agreed, visibly shaken.

Rupert turned off the music. There was a deafening silence.

Eric's smug arrogance seemed to have vanished as the fellow partygoers and people he had known all his life turned to him with disgust.

He grabbed a moth-eaten throw that had been lying on the back of the sofa and threw it over Yasmine.

'Come along, lass,' he mumbled. 'Let's go home.' Yasmine giggled again and let out a coy meow but no one laughed. 'Get up,' Eric hissed. 'Now!'

Yasmine slowly got to her feet and gave a languid stretch. She tossed the throw aside. As she walked to the door, the revellers parted like the Red Sea. Eric followed with Banu in tow. Everyone began talking at once, some expressing outrage and others stating that Eric was a middle-aged fool.

Rupert stalked to the Gibraltar gong and struck it three times, silencing the room. 'The party is over. Everyone out.'

Within seconds, Delia was snatching glasses out of hands – finished or not – and ordering Dawn and Willow back to the kitchen to help clear up.

We were all outside in under two minutes and those who had come by bus climbed aboard to head back to the village for bed. Caroline stood at the bottom of the steps reminding everyone that they had to return their Panama hats first thing in the morning either at the vicarage or at the community shop.

Mum and I walked back to the Carriage House. As we cleared up the kitchen, we relived the extraordinary scene in the drawing room.

'She went too far with the tiger. I thought his lordship's head would explode,' said Mum. 'Eric will never live that down.'

'Maybe he's coming to his senses,' I agreed.

'Poor little lap dog.'

Seeing my blank look she grinned. 'That's what she calls him – her *kucak köpeği*. Delia looked it up. It means lap dog.'

'Oh, no!' I chuckled. 'I almost feel sorry for him.'

'Delia says she's caught Yasmine several times wandering around on her own in the Hall,' Mum went on.

'*Wandering*?' I exclaimed. 'What do you mean?'

'Oh yes,' Mum nodded. 'And when Delia asked her what she was doing, Yasmine just said she was looking for Lavinia. Not looking for *Lady* Lavinia or addressing her as her ladyship. There's no respect! No respect, at all.'

'I think it's different in Turkey,' I said. 'There's no defined class system there. What I don't like is the way Yasmine is befriending Lavinia. It feels so fake. And she rented that Jungle Jane costume to deliberately make Lavinia look silly.' I felt angry about that and protective of her.

'All the time flirting with Rupert.' Mum said. 'Everyone noticed. If you want my opinion, Yasmine won't be satisfied being Queen of the Scrapyard, she wants to be Queen of Honeychurch Hall!'

'In her dreams,' I said but Mum had a point. I'd seen how Rupert looked at Yasmine.

'I'm just glad that we have Crispin on the case,' said Mum.

'Ah, Crispin,' I said slowly. 'I want to talk to you about him. Perhaps I should let this agreement thing go.'

'Oh darling!' Mum wailed. 'Let's just see what Crispin can do first.'

'No,' I said firmly. 'I've got three weeks to move out. I'll rent a storage unit for my stock. I've got my space at Dartmouth Antique Emporium and, if you don't mind,

I'll come and stay with you for a bit until I find somewhere else.'

Mum's face fell. 'I know you only moved down from London for me,' she said. 'I quite understand if you want to go back. I won't mind. Truly.'

'Of course I don't,' I exclaimed. 'I'll put my flat on the market and find somewhere locally to buy. Maybe nearer Dartmouth.'

As I voiced this decision aloud, I felt much better. I'd miss living on the estate but as Delia had pointed out, Jane's Cottage had never belonged to me. I wanted something permanent.

'And besides, it will be very different when the dowager countess passes on,' I added. 'Rupert could even sell the estate if he wanted to. You're fine. You own the Carriage House.'

'Have you talked to Mallory about any of this?' Mum said suddenly. 'You've not mentioned him once this evening and I didn't want to say anything.'

'Something came up,' I said and pushed the image of the young woman away.

'I'll walk you out,' said Mum. 'Oh wait. You left it behind when you brought the groceries. I don't want her silly potions.' She picked up the copy of *Aunt Muriel's Home Remedies* from the dresser.

I paused before getting into my Golf. 'I think we should get the Mini towed to the garage tomorrow. I'm pretty sure those patches of fluid are brake fluid.'

'It'll be fine,' said Mum. 'You know how much I love to Google . . . well according to Google it's okay to drive. The brakes only felt spongy yesterday. Festive Fun Planners are coming to pick up the tables and whatnot, but we don't need to be here.'

'Okay.'

'Come at ten so we can have a cup of coffee and see what our favourite agony aunt has to say in her column this week,' she said. 'I can guarantee it will be a juicy one.'

We parted with a goodnight hug.

I felt a little clearer now I'd made my decision about moving. Tomorrow I would give Rupert an official move-out date; I'd tell Crispin that I would happily pay for his advice but that I had no more need of it. Thinking of Crispin made me remember the ladder. I'd take a look at that in the bright light of day, too.

I got ready for bed and stepped out on to the terrace, strolling over to the edge of the drive to gaze out at the view. It was a crystal-clear evening with a full moon and a sky filled with a gazillion stars.

I could even make out a satellite slowly sailing through the night sky. Other than the distant sound of a fox and a hoot of an owl I felt an overwhelming sense of peace.

I'd be lying if I said I didn't feel sad about leaving all this but just a few years ago, I hadn't even known of Honeychurch Hall's existence. I was reminded of something my mother always said when a chapter came to an end. 'Why can't the next one be even better?'

And yes, why not?

Times were changing at Honeychurch Hall. Yasmine's outlandish behaviour was a reminder of that.

I went back inside.

When I saw that I'd missed a text from Mallory sending his apologies saying he wouldn't be able to see me in the morning after all, I didn't bother to reply. Perhaps he and I weren't destined to be after all.

This time sleep came quickly and I didn't dream.

Chapter Nineteen

Saturday morning arrived with a high white haze that promised a scorching hot day. If only it would rain! I showered and put on a sleeveless cotton dress.

Mallory had sent two more text messages promising to call me that afternoon but I just didn't know what to say, so all I did was send a thumbs-up emoji.

I wasn't due to meet my mother for another hour so I finally unpacked my suitcase that had been in the boot of the car since yesterday lunchtime.

Ruby's gift was one of the first things I took out. In a strange way, her death was a reminder of how unpredictable life could be and how short it was.

The fifty cigarette cards were slotted into individual plastic pockets for protection. The illustrations were beautifully hand painted. On the reverse, each rose had an anecdote and a little bit of history.

Included in the lot was a battered leather logbook, presumably from the owner of the cigarette cards. It proved to be a garden journal that had belonged to a Jack Morgan. He had chronicled the dates when a specific rose had been bought, planted, pruned, and treated for black spot, aphids, and the usual pests. The logbook had been started in 1935. I flipped through the logbook and came across a recipe for Morgan's Miracle Spray (Nicotine Soap) on the last page.

I grabbed *Aunt Muriel's Home Remedies.* Sure enough, she had created a Miracle Spray. It wouldn't surprise me if Muriel had stolen the recipe. When the former postmistress was alive she had never been exactly honest – as my mother soon found out to her cost.

Resolving to compare the two later, I set them aside and set off to meet my mother.

As I passed Honeychurch Cottages, Delia sprang out from Honeywell Woods and flagged me down.

She was wearing a checked headscarf, leggings and an oversized T-shirt emblazoned with the words: 'Housekeeper: I make dirty look so good'.

I opened the window. 'Good morning!'

'Have you seen him? Have you seen Crispin?'

'No,' I said. 'Why?'

'I thought . . .' She frowned. 'Well. He's not in the shepherd's hut and I've got to do a changeover this morning. He's supposed to be out by ten so I can clean. I've got a young couple from London arriving at three.'

I pointed to Crispin's Audi, which was parked behind Eric's BMW. 'Since his car is there, he can't have gone far.'

'You think?' Delia rolled her eyes. 'I've looked in the walled garden. In fact . . . I haven't seen him since the summer house last night. He didn't come to the Hall for digestifs and petits fours.'

'I thought he went home early to take a nap since he was planning on doing some nocturnal birdwatching.'

'Yes. I thought of that only . . .' Delia reddened. 'I wondered if he might have snuck back to see Iris later.'

'No,' I said. 'I was with Mum until gone midnight.'

'Oh.' Delia seemed relieved. 'So they weren't together.'

'Not when I was there,' I said carefully.

Delia bit her lip. I could tell she had more to say.

'Is something worrying you?' I prompted.

Delia's flush deepened. 'I . . . well . . . when we were driving to the vicarage earlier in the evening he suggested I join him for a nightcap after everyone had gone home. I suppose,' she swallowed hard, 'he must have changed his mind.' Her eyes met mine and I could see how she wished she hadn't told me.

'So you assumed that he'd gone to see my mother instead?' Seriously. What was it with this age group? I remember the first time that I discovered my mother had a healthy appetite for the opposite sex despite her age. I am not sure why I assumed that women got to about sixty and their sex drive vanished.

'But then I couldn't sleep,' Delia went on. 'It was so hot last night that I thought I'd go for a little walk and . . . I went back to the shepherd's hut – it must have been about two, perhaps two-thirty in the morning and he still wasn't there.'

'Why don't we call Mum and ask her if she has seen him today?'

Delia laid a hand on my arm. 'Don't say I'm asking. Please.'

My mother answered on the first ring. 'Where are you? The coffee is made.'

I put Mum on speakerphone so that Delia could hear.

'Is Crispin there?' I asked.

Delia glared at me. I ignored her.

'Crispin? No. Why?' Mum sounded genuinely surprised. 'If he's with anyone it'll be Delia. She was chasing him all last night.'

Delia's eyebrows disappeared under her headscarf.

'Don't be long.' Mum rang off.

'And I wasn't chasing him,' Delia said, hotly. 'He invited me! It was his idea! But what am I to do? He must vacate the shepherd's hut by ten!'

'I don't know what to tell you,' I said. 'Perhaps he left his binoculars in the summer house last night and went back to get them?'

'Oh.' Delia groaned. 'It's such a trek over there. All right. I've really got no choice.'

'Good luck,' I said and drove on.

I found my mother seated at the kitchen table with a cafetière of coffee for us to share, a plate of petits fours that she must have slipped into her handbag from last night, and the *Dipperton Deal*.

She pointed dramatically to the front page and cried. '*Regardez!*'

The lead was in bold black print: 'Festival's Future in Jeopardy: Reward Offered!'

Someone had captured a good photo of the billy goat charging at one of the villagers with the tagline 'Capricious the Killer: One death is one too many in quiet South Hams village.'

'But that's not what happened to Ruby,' I protested. 'Dawn is going to be so upset. Poor Capricious!'

'You know the saying,' said Mum. 'If it bleeds, it leads.'

'And Ruby didn't bleed,' I protested again. 'This is ridiculous!' There were numerous mentions of villagers complaining of lost chances, of sabotage, calling for justice.

'The vicar is offering a huge reward,' she declared.

I pointed to the story in the sidebar with the headline:

HOSEPIPE MOLE IDENTITY STILL UNKNOWN

The number of villagers who have been threatened with fines from the water company has increased to five. One insists she doesn't even own a hosepipe.

'I think it's Caroline,' I said. 'You weren't at the vicarage last night but she had at least half a dozen watering cans sporting the water company logo. She wasn't even trying to hide them.'

'I suppose she could flog them on eBay,' Mum turned the page. 'And here is poor Ruby's obituary. Nice photograph of her.'

Danny had dug out an old black and white photograph of Ruby in her youth, posing on a beach wearing a tight-fitting polka-dot swimming costume. There was an announcement that the funeral service would be the week-end following the festival and that the vicar apologised for any inconvenience this had caused.

'Ready?' Mum turned the page to our favourite column: 'Dear Amanda'.

'Oh!' Mum frowned and flipped through the rest of the newspaper. 'That's odd. Amanda is always on page six. See if you can find her.'

I turned the pages. 'There's no problem page this week.'

The identity of the infamous agony aunt had been a mystery in the village for decades. Although I'd had my suspicions, I would never voice them aloud. It was a turn of phrase, a distinctive comment or a piece of advice that gave her away.

'Well, that's interesting,' Mum said. 'Perhaps it's one of the villagers who's caught that bug. Who do you think it is?'

But before I could answer, Mum's mobile rang.

Checking the caller ID, Mum gave me an eye roll and mouthed the word 'Delia'.

'Good morning—' she began but had to hold the phone away from her ear.

Delia's screams echoed around the kitchen. 'It's Crispin! It's Crispin! He's dead!'

Mum jumped to her feet. 'Where are you?'

'At the summer house!'

Chapter Twenty

By the time Mum and I had hurried through Honeywell Woods on foot, the police were already at the summer house. Delia was wrapped in a thermal blanket and sitting on a mackintosh square, taken from the pile that were still stacked on the table from last night. On the far bank of the ornamental lake was another one covering, presumably, Crispin's body.

Detective Sergeant Clive Banks was hovering nearby already looking hot beneath his heavy black beard. His eyes were fixed on the main drive on the far side of the park, beyond the post-and-rail fence where he had had to leave his car.

Delia scrambled to her feet the moment she saw us and came rushing over. Her headscarf was askew and her wig was missing.

'Oh, Iris,' Delia sobbed. 'It was horrible, horrible!'

'There, there.' Mum pulled her friend into her arms. 'Goodness, you're all wet.'

'He drowned!' she wailed. 'I saw him . . . just floating . . . I jumped in . . . but I was too late!'

'Drowned?' I said sharply. I distinctly remembered the newspaper article that said Crispin couldn't swim and hated the water. Mum's eyes met mine, but instead of remarking on that she mouthed the words, 'Where's her wig?'

'Yes, yes,' Delia gabbled on. 'You were right, Kat. He must have come back for his binoculars.' She pointed to a pair that were lying on the bank. 'Perhaps he got hot and thought he would cool off? Oh! I tried. I tried to save him!'

'It's all right, Delia,' Mum crooned. 'I'm here now. Everything will be all right. Let's sort your hair out shall we?' She readjusted the headscarf.

'The dog stole it,' Delia whispered. 'His lordship has gone to find it.'

'Oh dear.' Mum's eyes met mine. Shock was etched on her face and I could see she was only just holding it together herself. She'd known Crispin for years, so of course she was going to be upset, which was more than I could say for myself. I hadn't liked him from the very beginning and I certainly hadn't liked the way he was so cavalier about finding so-called leverage.

'I tried mouth-to-mouth,' Delia went on. 'I'd wanted to touch those lips all evening but never in a million years did I imagine—'

'Ssh! Of course you didn't,' Mum crooned again and then, 'What did they feel like?'

Delia closed her eyes in memory. 'Like slugs.'

'His lordship is back,' said Clive and straightened his shoulders.

Rupert strolled over with Mr Chips at heel. He was holding Delia's wig aloft. 'No sign of Mallory yet, Sergeant?'

'Not yet, milord,' said Clive.

'I'll take that, milord,' Mum said and Rupert handed her the sodden clump.

'Just managed to stop Mr Chips from burying it,' he muttered. 'Little rascal.'

'Thank you,' Delia said. 'Otherwise I would have had to have borrowed one of Banu's.'

With great care, Mum rearranged Delia's wig and retied the headscarf. 'There, good as new.'

'It feels a bit cold,' Delia mumbled.

'Terrible business,' said Rupert. 'It was just as well that I was out walking and heard Mrs Evans's cries for help.' He pulled out a hip flask. 'Here. Take a snifter.'

Mum handed the flask to Delia and held it up so she could take a sip but Delia grabbed it and took quite a few. When she finally let go, my mother took a sneaky gulp, before giving it back to Rupert.

'Well, Sergeant,' Rupert began. 'What do you think happened here? Was it a bit of fun after I threw everyone out of the drawing room?'

'Er. I don't know, milord,' said Clive.

'I suppose you'll want to question us, like damn Poirot,' he said. 'I can certainly vouch for my whereabouts. I was in bed.'

'Er. I don't know, milord,' said Clive again.

'You'll want everyone to have an alibi, I presume,' said Rupert. 'Not good form for a holidaymaker to drown, however. Won't look good on Tripadvisor – I think that's the website, isn't it, Mrs Evans?'

Delia nodded miserably. 'I'm so sorry, milord.'

'It's not your fault, Delia,' Mum declared. 'Kat said that Crispin couldn't swim. Perhaps he just went for a paddle and didn't realise the water was deep.'

'Good point, Iris,' said Rupert. 'Well. You know where I am if you need me.' And with a sharp whistle, he summoned Mr Chips and they strode away.

I had thought of telling Rupert there and then that I would be moving out, but somehow it didn't seem appropriate in the circumstances. And, try as I might, I couldn't find it in my heart to feel sorry for Crispin.

'He always makes me nervous,' said Clive sheepishly. 'My dad used to get the tremors when the old earl was alive and wanted to talk to him about his roses. I can't help it. I get all tongue-tied. Maybe you're right, Iris. I used to swim in that when I was a nipper and the mud was godawful deep.'

'I didn't feel any mud,' Delia said.

With a cry of relief, Clive pointed across the park to the drive where an ambulance was just pulling up, lights flashing. 'Oh. Thank heavens! Here they come.'

The Cruickshank twins, Little Dipperton's resident paramedics, jumped out and retrieved a stretcher from the rear. They scrambled over the fence as if they were trained marines and trotted over the grass towards us. Another car – Mallory's – pulled up behind it. I felt a rush of nerves but then had to give myself a mental talking to. For whatever reason, Crispin Fellowes had recklessly decided to go for a midnight paddle and it had ended in tragedy. This was not the moment to think about our relationship.

'There's not much we can do here,' said my mother. 'Let's go back to the Carriage House, it's closer than your cottage, Delia. I'll make you a nice cup of hot sweet tea.'

Delia nodded, 'I'd like that but—' She paused. 'What's the time?'

'It's eleven-thirty.'

'Crikey!' She exclaimed. 'I've got new people coming into the shepherd's hut at four! I must clean!'

'You can't do that!' I said, appalled. 'Surely the police need to go inside. What about Crispin's things?'

'I can hardly turn them away,' Delia pointed out. 'They've driven all the way down from London and they've paid! You heard his lordship. We don't want a bad review on Tripadvisor!'

'You're in no fit state to do anything,' Mum said quickly. 'On second thoughts, you should go home and have a hot bath. Kat and I will clean the shepherd's hut for the new folks.'

I regarded my mother with surprise. Since when had she offered to help Delia clean? The same thought must have crossed Delia's mind, too. Her eyes narrowed. 'Why? Were you in there last night after all? Did you lure him to the summer house for a spot of skinny dipping?'

'Oh for goodness sake!' Mum exclaimed. 'You're in shock. You don't know what you're saying. No, Kat and I don't think you should go in there.'

'Leave me out of this!' I raised my hands in mock surrender. But then I guessed the reason for my mother's concern. Who knew what Crispin had in there on my mother's finances!

'Ah, here is Mallory now,' Mum said quickly. 'Let's ask him. I'm sure the shepherd's hut will be out of bounds and no one will be able to go inside anyway.'

As he approached, I could hardly hide my shock. Again, Mallory looked like he hadn't slept. Dark circles bloomed beneath his eyes and he hadn't shaved. I was quite sure he was still wearing the clothes that I had seen him in the day before.

I could see by Mum's expression that she was just as surprised as me.

Mallory said a grim 'good morning' but when his eyes met mine I saw a softness that went a long way to allaying my fears that his feelings for me had changed.

'Delia wants to clear out Crispin's things in the shepherd's hut,' Mum blurted out as if she was telling tales on a schoolfriend.

'Not clear out, Iris,' Delia shot back. 'We've got visitors coming this afternoon. We need his things gone.'

'I'm afraid that won't be possible,' said Mallory. 'We must notify his next of kin.'

'He has a sister called Nancy,' Mum said.

'Do you have a contact number?'

Mum shook her head.

'We should be able to get that information from his mobile,' said Mallory.

Mum blanched. So whatever she had hoped that Delia wouldn't find would almost certainly be discovered by Mallory.

'Have we found his mobile yet, Sergeant?' Mallory asked Clive.

'Not here, sir.' Clive pointed to Crispin's binoculars. 'Just those.'

'Where did you find them?' Mum said sharply.

'On the bank,' said Clive.

'Crispin would never have left them like that,' Mum said. 'They were expensive. At the very least he would have put them on a ledge in the summer house.' She shot me an anxious look. 'I don't like it. Something isn't right.'

'Perhaps the arriving guests can use number two?' Delia said to herself. 'It's empty in preparation for new staff. Yes. I'll pop them in there.'

'Is there a key to the shepherd's hut?' Mallory asked.

'I have a spare,' said Delia. 'But it wasn't locked when I went there this morning around nine.'

'But what about when you went to see him last night – or should I say, at two in the morning?' Mum put in pointedly. 'Was the door unlocked then?'

Delia shot my mother a look of pure venom. 'Thank you for that, Iris. I didn't go inside, if you must know. I just peered in the window. It looked like his bed had been slept in. Oh, and his Panama hat was on the counter. He had definitely gone there first.'

'Crispin told us he was going back for a nap,' Mum reminded her. 'Remember?' She turned to Mallory. 'He was a birdwatcher and specifically hoped to see a nightjar before he went home today. Why would he have come here with his binoculars when the birds he was watching were in the forest behind the walled garden? It makes no sense.'

I could see that Mallory was taking it all in, but all he said was, 'We'll certainly know more about how Crispin met his fate after the autopsy.'

'Two deaths,' Delia said slowly. 'Don't bad things come in threes?'

'It depends if you are superstitious,' Mum said. 'Isn't that right, Officer?'

'And I'm not,' Mallory declared. 'For now, I suggest you all go home. I'll be in touch and you, Mrs Evans, need to take it easy today. You've had the most terrible shock.'

'Thank you.' Delia thought for a moment and then said, 'I trust you are settling into Larcombe Barn.'

Mallory gave a polite smile. 'Very much, thank you.'

'If there is anything you need, anything at all,' Delia went on. 'I have the spare set of keys that Guy gave me.'

'Thank you. Excuse me.' And Mallory walked away.

'Larcombe Barn?' Mum said sharply and zeroed in on me. 'You never told me.'

'Didn't she?' Delia feigned surprise but was clearly glad that there was something else my mother didn't know first.

'I only found out myself yesterday,' I said.

Delia readjusted her wig and headscarf.

'What did you mean by borrowing one of Banu's wigs?' Mum said suddenly.

'Oh we wig wearers are very astute,' Delia declared. 'Although personally, I don't think iron grey is her colour. It makes her look so much older than she is.'

The three of us left the police by the ornamental lake. Delia insisted she was okay to walk back to her house and besides, she said, 'Now I have to sort out number two for my guests.'

It was only when we got to the carriageway that my mother gave way to her grief. She made a strange gulping sound. 'Oh, Kat. Crispin hated swimming! Why would he go for a swim?'

The same thought had been swirling in my mind too. 'I wish I knew. Come on, I'll make us a fresh pot of coffee.'

We settled back at the kitchen table with a plate of chocolate digestives and our drinks. Mum didn't eat and nor did I.

'We know he went to the shepherd's hut because his hat was there and his bed had been slept in,' said Mum. 'So what made him go back to the summer house when he told me how much he wanted to spend his last night looking for a nightjar in the walled garden?'

'To get his binoculars?' I said.

Mum shook her head. 'No. When he left the summer house, they were round his neck. He would never have just put them down on the grass. I'm so upset!' She reached for a Kleenex and dabbed at one eye. 'Crispin was always so good to me. He always looked after me. What am I going to do now? There will never be anyone I will trust like Crispin.' She started to cry quietly into her tissue.

I scooted my chair closer to hers and put my arm around her shoulders. 'Oh Mum. I'm so sorry.'

She blew her nose. 'I think this is my fault.'

A familiar sense of dread seeped into my stomach. 'What do you mean? How can it be your fault?'

'I should never have involved Alfred—'

'Alfred? What do you mean?'

But before she could explain we heard the familiar roar of a motorbike. Moments later, the vicar burst into the kitchen brandishing Ruby's distinctive mobile phone and swinging his helmet.

His face was white and he was deeply distressed. 'Caroline did it! Caroline killed my mother!'

Chapter Twenty-One

Danny allowed himself to be led into the kitchen and helped into a chair. He was in a terrible state.

'My mother was right,' he whimpered. 'I should never have taken Caroline back. I should be with you, Iris.'

'Don't be silly,' Mum said firmly. 'Get him a brandy, Katherine. He doesn't know what he's saying.'

'Where did you find Ruby's mobile?' I asked.

'In the vestry,' said Danny.

'The vestry?' I was confused. 'In the church? How on earth did it get in there?'

'I was praying to the Lord for the phone to appear and when I went into the vestry, it was on my desk. My prayers were answered.'

'Well, that's good news.' Mum's tone was brisk. 'But I'm quite sure there is a logical explanation as to how it came to be there.'

'Danny! Danny!' came a hysterical female voice. And this time it was Caroline who burst into the kitchen.

Her face was ashen. 'I can explain! I can explain everything!'

Mum pulled out a chair for Caroline to tumble into. Caroline then dissolved into uncontrollable sobs.

'You'd better get another glass,' Mum said to me.

'I'll make it four,' I muttered. 'I think we could all do with one.'

Moments later I was back with a tray of crystal tumblers and my mother had the Courvoisier out. She poured a generous slug into each.

'Well?' Danny regarded his wife with disgust. 'We're listening!' But he didn't give Caroline a chance to explain. He let fly a torrent of abuse that was most un-Christian like. We heard how Caroline had never liked his mother; how Caroline had made her life miserable; how Caroline had been jealous of Ruby's roses. Next, Caroline turned on my mother and accused her of influencing Danny and ruining her marriage. It was unbelievable.

'Silence!' Mum shouted. 'Stop this! Enough.'

Danny and Caroline stopped.

'Let Caroline explain herself, Danny,' Mum said firmly.

'It was an accident.' Caroline pulled a clump of Kleenex out of her pocket and dabbed at her nose. 'Will I have to go to prison?'

'That's for the police to decide,' Danny said coldly.

'Don't worry,' Mum said. 'I doubt if it'll be a murder charge. Probably manslaughter.'

Caroline started crying again. She really was an ugly crier. 'What's everyone in the village going to think? I'll never live it down!'

I thought of Danny's reward for any information leading to the goat incident and if my hunch was right about Caroline being the water company mole, I doubted if their marriage would survive so much scandal.

'How was I to know the old bag had a weak heart?' Caroline whined.

'There was nothing wrong with my mother's heart!' Danny exclaimed. 'She was as strong as an ox.'

'I just let one goat in,' wailed Caroline. 'Just one. But they all came at once. A stampede! I swear. I nearly got trampled to death! I cracked two ribs! That billy goat was so aggressive. Look.'

She whipped up her blouse, giving us an eyeful of a full-coverage bra in a shade of lime green. Sure enough, her rib cage was black and blue. It looked very painful and certainly explained the discomfort I'd witnessed on Thursday afternoon when Caroline attempted a three-point turn up at Jane's Cottage.

'And then I left,' Caroline went on. 'I was frightened. I didn't see Ruby! I swear. She wasn't there! She wasn't even there! Please, Danny. Please don't tell the police!'

'He doesn't have a choice,' Mum said with exaggerated dismay. 'Unfortunately, that train has left the station, Caroline. And naturally, the evidence must be on Ruby's phone, and you knew that, which was why it mysteriously vanished from the kitchen.'

'So you did steal the phone!' Danny said. 'Having sworn that you hadn't seen it.'

'I . . . yes . . . I did.' Caroline's face crumpled again. 'But I felt compelled to return it. It was like a voice telling me to put it in the vestry. So I did.'

'I'm sorry, Caroline.' His voice was icy. 'But this is the last straw.'

'I see. I see how it is. You all hate me,' Caroline ran on. 'You all judge me just because I left Danny for a short while. A very short while. I made a mistake!' She looked around in desperation. 'Don't we all make mistakes?'

She drained her brandy, replacing the glass on the table with a loud thump.

'As you are confessing all,' Mum began, 'perhaps you'd like to admit to being the mole in the village.'

'Mole?' Danny sat bolt upright. 'Is this to do with the hosepipe ban?'

Something switched in Caroline's demeanour. 'Oh so what!' she said bitterly. 'Yes. It was me. Doesn't anyone care about saving the planet? What a selfish lot you all are! I was just doing my bit. That's all. And besides, those roses . . . those should have been my roses. Not Ruby's! That bit of the garden should belong to the vicarage but oh no!' Caroline's face was twisted with hate. 'Danny had to move the boundary to please his wretched mother.'

'Anyone want a top up?' said Mum. 'Because I do.'

'I think you should go back to the house.' Danny's voice was quiet, which felt more chilling somehow. 'We will talk later and I will decide what to do.'

'No need, sweetie,' said Caroline. 'I did my best for this village. No one had ever had such a successful party – everyone loved the petting zoo – but what thanks do I get? None!' She got to her feet. 'Good luck with everything, Daniel. You'll be hearing from my solicitors.'

'You'll be hearing from mine!' Danny retorted. 'And no doubt the police will want to talk to you!'

'Oh goodie.' Caroline's voice was laced with sarcasm. 'I can hardly wait.'

And with that, she stormed out of the kitchen, leaving Mum and I utterly gobsmacked.

Danny put his head in his hands, muttering to himself. I caught random words – 'mole, goats, roses . . .'

'Presumably the evidence is on Ruby's mobile,' Mum said gingerly. 'Kat and I would quite like to see it.'

Silently, Danny handed it to my mother. I scurried to her side, not wanting to miss a moment of this revelation.

'Presumably you know the password?' Mum said.

'Nightjar,' Danny muttered.

'You do it.' Mum handed me the mobile. I entered the password and found the wildlife camera app that was already open.

'Danny, do you want to show us what we're supposed to be looking at?' Mum suggested. 'Otherwise, we're going to be watching hours of nothing.'

Danny seemed to pull himself together. In fact, he almost cheered up. He brought out a notepad. 'I jotted down the timecodes.'

The app was easy to navigate. There had been three wildlife cameras installed in Ruby's garden, all with different views, concentrated on the various bird tables, the nesting boxes in the trees and, fortunately, the entrance to the rose garden where I had found Ruby's body. We huddled over the tiny screen and soon were transfixed.

One goat came into the frame. Slowly at first, followed by a shadowy figure. And then, a torrent of goats shot by, including Capricious, who was hard to miss with his long horns. The shadowy figure was swiftly knocked aside but not before Caroline's shocked face looked straight at the camera before disappearing under a deluge of hooves.

'Caroline was certainly right about the stampede,' I said.

And then things seemed to settle down. The goats drifted in and out of frame, chomping happily on whatever prize-winning flowers and vegetables they could snatch.

There was no sign of Ruby, and when I pointed that out, Mum said, 'But perhaps she just wasn't captured on camera.'

'Did Caroline know about Ruby's wildlife cameras?' I asked Danny.

'She knew she had them but I don't think she realised they were synced to Ruby's mobile phone.'

'So Caroline must have gone back to End Cottage the first chance she could,' I said. 'Because the police had been looking for it.'

Iris regarded Danny. 'I hate to say this, but the footage doesn't really prove anything.'

'Of course it does!' Danny protested.

'All you've shown us is Caroline and the goats,' Mum said. 'There's no evidence of her opening the gate and letting them into Ruby's garden. I thought you had proof that Caroline had killed Ruby. Those were your words when you came in.'

'It's obvious,' Danny began. 'Mother was out of frame. There had to have been a scuffle between them off-camera.'

'That won't secure a conviction,' Mum declared. 'I know these things. I watch a lot of crime shows.' She returned the mobile and topped up her glass yet again.

'Can we watch the footage for a bit longer, Danny,' I asked.

So we did. The seconds turned into minutes but nothing came up on the screen.

'This is a waste of time,' Mum moaned.

'Wait, it's Ruby!' I exclaimed. 'Look!'

Ruby entered the frame. She was in her nightdress and slippers and seemed very distressed. She began hurling whatever objects came to hand – plastic flower pots, her stick, bamboo canes, suet balls – to shoo the goats away from her flower beds.

We watched as Ruby went into the greenhouse and emerged with a large plastic spray bottle with a nozzle gun. She disappeared, and moments later reappeared on camera at the arched entrance to her rose garden. Ruby pointed the nozzle at the goats and hit the trigger. Brown liquid spewed out in bursts. Capricious charged, knocking the bottle, which fell apart, drenching her nightdress in brown sludge.

Ruby stood there. The goats wandered off and the screen was blank once more.

And that was it.

'Something must have happened after this,' I said. 'Can we fast forward a bit more?'

Danny did so and after a few back-and-forths, we finally saw Ruby lying in the foetal position I had found her in. We reviewed the footage several times and as far as we could tell, Caroline had not come back.

'Ruby's heart must have given out,' Mum insisted.

'No,' Danny said, exasperated. 'As I already told you, Mother did not have heart problems.' He seemed defeated as he slipped the mobile back into his pocket. 'I need to think. I'd appreciate you keeping this quiet. At the moment, only you are aware of Caroline's involvement.'

'How horribly awkward for you, Danny,' Mum said. 'What are you going to do about the reward? Everyone will want to know who the culprit is. And don't get me started on the hosepipe ban.'

Danny ran his fingers through his hair. 'I . . . I just don't know what to do. I need to pray.'

'You'd better hope for a quick answer,' Mum said. 'Ruby's death isn't the only thing that Mallory is involved in at the moment.'

Danny frowned. 'Excuse me?'

'Haven't you heard?' When there was still no reaction, Mum added, 'One of the,' she struggled to find the right word, 'guests at the Safari Supper drowned last night in the ornamental lake. Of course I'm not saying that Caroline had anything to do with *that*, but apparently there was a bit of a car accident in the lanes a few days ago. Kat overheard—'

'Yes I know about that,' Danny said sharply. 'What? Are you implying that my wife is a serial killer? She murdered my mother and then she decided to kill off a random guest at a party?'

His anger took us both aback and was a reminder of how he usually was in the pulpit – preaching fire and brimstone – not this wreck of a man who had just lost his mother.

'Of course not.' I glared at Mum. 'And besides, Caroline went back with everyone on the minibus.'

Danny stood up. 'Thank you for the brandy. I apologise for my outburst but I'm very upset. I may need some time to get through this, Iris, and it's not a reflection on my feelings for you, but I can assure you that I will soon be a free man.'

And with that, he grabbed his motorcycle helmet and dashed from the kitchen.

'Be careful what you wish for,' I muttered, 'You'd better tell him sooner or later that you're not interested anymore.'

'I don't need to hear that from you, thank you very much,' Mum said. 'You can make yourself useful. Follow me to the garage.'

I got into my Golf and did as I was told, shouting, 'I still think we should get a tow truck.'

But my mother didn't listen, nor did she get very far.

As she reversed her Mini out of the carriageway, it didn't stop. It kept on going, and going, and going . . . eventually hitting one of the stone pillars that flanked the entrance. There was a sickening crash of metal, a rumble as the pillar collapsed into a pile of rubble, followed by a loud bang as the airbag went off. The balloon shot out of its compartment and hit my mother in the face.

And, with perfect timing, Mallory's car appeared.

Chapter Twenty-Two

'And don't say I told you so in front of your boyfriend,' said Mum as she held a packet of frozen peas over her other eye. She was coated in fine white powder and there was a lingering smell of burned rubber. 'He'll think I'm irresponsible.'

We were back in the kitchen again, alone for a few moments, while Mallory was looking at her Mini.

'Not irresponsible. Accident-prone perhaps,' I said. 'You need something other than frozen peas over that eye. You look like you've been in a fight.'

There was a polite knock and Mallory stepped into the room, making Mum and me jump.

Again, I thought how exhausted Mallory looked and, again, when our eyes met, I was relieved to see the softness was still there. But just as quickly it was gone as he turned to my mother.

'That was quite a knock,' he said. 'How is that eye?'

'It matches the other one,' Mum retorted.

'Did your foot slip off the pedal?' Mallory asked.

'No,' Mum said. 'I was braking hard but nothing happened.'

'Yes. I thought as much,' he said. 'I'm afraid the pillars have collapsed across the entrance. We won't be able to tow your car until the rubble has been cleared away.'

'Oh dear,' Mum said. 'Festive Fun Planners won't be able to get into the courtyard.'

'Don't worry, Eric is on his way,' said Mallory.

'We'd rather not involve Eric,' I said hastily. 'Coffee?'

Gesturing to the brandy bottle and the four empty tumblers he raised an eyebrow. 'Not offering me brandy?'

'It's been a very stressful day,' I said.

'The coffee will be cold by now,' Mum said. 'Make him a fresh one.'

'Cold coffee on a hot day sounds good enough to me.'

I jumped up to fetch him a cup but put it in a glass and added plenty of ice.

Mallory gestured for me to sit down at the kitchen table. 'When was the last time you drove your car, Iris?'

'The car was perfectly driveable on Thursday,' said Mum.

'You said the brakes were a little spongy,' I reminded her, but decided against mentioning the near miss we'd had at Cropper's Corner. There was no point.

Mallory looked worried. 'The brake fluid reservoir was completely empty. I also looked at the carriageway floor and saw traces of brake fluid, which means that you've had the leak for quite some time.'

'The Mini passed its MOT ten days ago.' Mum said defensively. 'You can check with the garage if you don't believe me.'

'Mum, it's okay.' I rested a hand gently on her arm. 'Mallory isn't accusing you of anything.' His eyes met mine. 'Crispin's death has been a big shock.'

'For all of us,' Mum said hastily. 'And Ruby's death, too. Two deaths! Did Kat tell you that Caroline confessed to letting the goats into Ruby's garden? It's all on camera.'

'Yes. Caroline called me herself,' said Mallory. 'She sounded very upset.'

'Oh.' Mum's face fell, then brightened. 'So she'll be facing a charge of manslaughter, no doubt.'

'I'm not here to talk about Caroline,' said Mallory. 'I'm here to talk about something else.' He paused before adding, 'How well did you know Crispin Fellowes, Iris?'

'Me?' Mum exclaimed. 'Me? Why? He was just holidaying here. A birdwatcher, apparently. I mean, we spoke a little bit. He had a glass of Pimm's one evening, but no. Not really.'

I glared at her in frustration. What was the point in hiding something that was bound to come out!

Mallory flipped through his notes. 'That's strange, because according to Delia, you spent yesterday morning with Crispin at Hope Cove birdwatching.'

She turned on me, her voice heavy with accusation. 'You told Delia?'

'No, Mum,' I said wearily. 'I didn't. Delia went to the

Safari Supper with Crispin and I suspect he mentioned it. You may as well tell Mallory the whole truth.'

'If you wouldn't mind,' said Mallory. 'It would make things go much more quickly.'

There was a long, lengthy pause as Mum hesitated and then, 'Fine,' she declared. 'Crispin is my financial adviser. End of.'

'*And*?' I mouthed the word, *Poole*. 'Isn't there something else you want to tell Mallory?'

'And nothing, Katherine.' Mum folded her arms and sat back in her chair. I felt the familiar surge of exasperation with my mother's inability to be honest.

'Just so we're clear,' said Mallory. 'Are you saying that Crispin Fellowes was your financial adviser for your Krystalle Storm endeavours?'

'Yes,' Mum said. 'He handles – handled – everything.'

'This must be a very difficult conversation for you to have, because,' he took a deep breath, 'at this point, we're not sure whether Crispin's death was an accident or something a little more sinister.'

Mallory pulled out a plastic bag marked 'Evidence'. Inside was a scrap of paper with something handwritten in spidery writing which I wasn't close enough to read. 'It would seem that Crispin Fellowes had an enemy.' He showed the bag to my mother. 'Do you recognise this handwriting?'

I saw a flicker of recognition cross my mother's face. 'No.' She shook her head slowly. 'No. I don't recognise it at all. No. Definitely not.' She paused. 'Where did you find it?'

'Can I have a look?' I asked.

Mallory handed me the bag. I shook my head, too. 'I don't recognise it either.'

'No problem.' Mallory slipped it back into his pocket.

'Where did you say you found it?'

'I didn't say,' said Mallory mildly. 'But, since you are asking, it was in a tea caddy in the shepherd's hut.'

'A tea caddy! ' Mum exclaimed. 'How extraordinary!'

'I thought it extraordinary too, Iris,' said Mallory.

'So it could have been left in there for anyone to find,' said Mum. 'Perhaps the visitors who were staying there before didn't drink tea so they wouldn't have found it.'

'Can you tell us what it says?' I asked.

'I'll read it, shall I?' Mallory didn't take it out again, instead he read from his notebook. '"If you even think about exposing me, it will be the last mistake you ever make. This is your one and only warning."' Mallory cocked his head. 'What did Crispin find? What could be so incriminating to force whoever this concerned to write such a note?'

Before Danny had burst into the kitchen, my mother had started to tell me that she should never have dismissed Alfred's reservations. Like me, Alfred had been suspicious of Crispin. I'd seen it in his face.

I thought of last night's event. Although Alfred had been at the Carriage House manning the bar for the main course, he'd not been at the summer house for ice cream or at the Hall for digestifs and petits fours.

'Was the note signed?' Mum asked, gingerly.

'Should it have been?' Mallory asked.

Mum let out a huge rush of air, clearly having been holding her breath. 'Then I can't see how we can help you, Officer.'

'That's not a problem,' said Mallory. 'We're hoping to lift some fingerprints from the note which we will run through our database.'

'Database?' Mum squeaked. 'Whatever for? But surely that implies that there could be someone with a . . . criminal record . . . in the village!'

'It could,' Mallory agreed. 'But at the same time, if there is someone with a criminal record in the village who had nothing to do with the note, he or she will be ruled out.'

'Did you find anything else of interest in the shepherd's hut?' Mum's question seemed innocent enough, but I knew her well.

'We've now got Crispin's laptop as well as his mobile,' said Mallory. 'So we'll see what that brings forth.'

'Wouldn't they be password protected?' Mum asked.

'That won't be a problem.' Mallory stared at my mother steadily until she looked away. 'We already have a forensics expert working on that right now.'

'You do?' Mum whispered. 'Good. Good.'

Mum caught my eye. 'Kat and I have thought that it was suspicious, too. He didn't like the water. He couldn't swim. I just don't understand what can have happened.'

'How long had Crispin been your financial adviser?' Mallory asked with his pencil poised. He clearly wasn't going to let this go.

'Twenty-five years, give or take a month or two,' Mum said. 'He was working at Goldfinch Publishing when I got my first contract.' Her eyes filled with tears. 'He . . . he was a dear friend.'

I reached for her hand. 'I'm sorry, Mum.'

'And I'm sorry for your loss, too.' Mallory sounded sincere. He flipped through his notes. 'Delia mentioned that his stay at the shepherd's hut was last minute, and that he was going on to the Isles of Scilly afterwards.'

'That's right,' Mum said. 'He was part of the nightjar network – you know, the same group of bird enthusiasts that Ruby belonged to. That's why he stopped off in Little Dipperton. It was a coincidence really.'

'Really?' Mallory said. 'I would say it was a bit of a detour. When was the last time you met with Crispin?'

Mum blinked. 'I don't understand.'

'Has he been here before?'

'No,' said Mum. 'We rarely met. So it was a lovely surprise.'

Mallory continued to scribble in his notepad. 'So you didn't conduct any business here at all?'

Mum didn't answer.

Mallory sighed. 'No worries. We'll know when we've accessed his briefcase and logged on to his laptop.'

'Oh! You mean *that* kind of business!' Mum exclaimed. 'He was helping Kat with her problem, but it wasn't exactly business-business.'

'What problem?' Mallory turned to me. He looked concerned.

'It's nothing, honestly,' I said.

'Kat received a letter from his lordship ordering her to leave Jane's Cottage and the gatehouses in three weeks,' Mum blurted out.

Mallory seemed shocked. 'But . . . why didn't you tell me?'

'I haven't had a chance,' I protested. 'And besides, it doesn't matter now because I've decided I'm leaving anyway.'

'That seems extreme,' Mallory remarked. 'I wish you had said something. Why? What's happened?'

'Let me tell you,' Mum began. 'I'm assuming you know all about my neighbour Eric Pugsley's upcoming nuptials to his young bride. Eric runs the scrapyard and banger racing meetings. He and Yasmine met in Turkey. His lordship decided to kick Kat out of her home – a home that was promised to her by the dowager countess – so that Eric and Yasmine can move in.'

'And I told you, Mum,' I said firmly. 'I'm fine with that decision.'

'I see,' said Mallory. 'And what did Crispin advise?'

'I didn't have any rights,' I said. 'I only have a licence to occupy the properties. It's not a contract.'

'*And*?' Mum glared at me. 'Kat won't tell you but I will. Eric has been fiddling the books.'

'How do you know this?' Mallory asked.

'Eric asked Kat to value a couple of rings and he wanted a blank invoice so he could fill in the description himself,' Mum said. 'Isn't that right, Kat? Tell him.'

I nodded.

This bit of news didn't produce any reaction at all. Mallory just said, 'Anything else?'

'Yes, there is,' she said. 'I had an unpredictable upbringing – life on the road, really. My adopted family ran a travelling fair and boxing emporium. That's how I met Frank – Kat's father. He was a tax inspector investigating ticket sales fraud.' Her face grew wistful. 'Frank and I eloped but I've never regretted it. Not once. We were very happy.'

'Go on,' said Mallory.

'Crispin is well-connected in financial circles. He thought if there was some way to persuade Eric to change his mind about moving into Jane's Cottage—'

'You mean, to blackmail him?' Mallory said bluntly.

Mum winced. 'Leverage was the word he used.'

Mallory stiffened. 'And Eric knew that Crispin had discovered this?'

'What do you think?'

Even though my mother and Eric had never seen eye to eye, I didn't like what she was doing and I was pretty sure I knew why she was doing it. To take the heat off Alfred.

'Tell Mallory what you heard in the carriageway, Kat,' Mum went on. 'Eric and his lordship were arguing and it was about Kat!'

'Mum!' I protested. 'I only heard my name—'

'That's all I'm prepared to say.' Mum raised her hands in mock surrender. 'But if you want my opinion, if anyone had a grudge against Crispin, it's Eric.'

'But surely it's up to the earl if he wants Kat to leave.' Mallory turned to me. Our eyes locked. 'Isn't it?'

'Ah, but here's the thing,' Mum's eyes flashed. 'Kat thinks that Eric must have some kind of hold over his lordship! And Crispin might have—'

'Ay-up,' came a familiar voice. There was a curt knock on the kitchen door and Eric popped his head in.

A tide of red raced up my mother's neck. I didn't know where to look. Had Eric been listening to our conversation? It was mortifying. She really needed to lock her back door.

Chapter Twenty-Three

'You could have knocked!' Mum jumped to her feet. 'What do you want?'

Eric reddened. 'Eh?'

'I asked Eric for his help, Iris,' said Mallory smoothly.

'Got the tractor outside,' said Eric.

'We don't need you,' Mum said rudely. 'Jimmy is going to send out a tow truck.'

'Did you call him?' said Eric.

'Not yet,' Mum retorted.

Eric gave a small smile. 'Jimmy's on holiday. What happened? Accelerator got jammed, eh?'

'No,' said Mum. 'As a matter of fact, my brakes failed.'

'I can take a look at 'er if you like,' Eric said gruffly.

'What? And charge me for it and then ask for a blank receipt?' Mum shot a triumphant look at Mallory.

Eric's flush deepened. He seemed different today. There was none of the swagger that we'd got used to seeing. Not only that, he was back in his old clothes – jeans and a brown T-shirt with 'Pugsley's Bangers' emblazoned on the front with a caricature of a beaten-up car shaped like a sausage.

'You here!' Yasmine entered the kitchen. She was wearing skin-tight jodhpurs and a tight shirt. She'd tied her long hair back in a ponytail and was immaculate as usual.

'I look everywhere!' She walked up to Eric and gave him a kiss on his cheek but this time, Eric didn't return it.

I couldn't help wondering if Yasmine's antics in the drawing room the night before had made Eric have second thoughts about his nuptials.

Mallory stepped forward. 'We haven't met,' he said. 'I'm Detective Inspector Mallory and you must be—?'

'Yasmine, Eric's fiancée,' Mum put in when Eric didn't answer.

Yasmine zeroed in on Mallory. 'Oh. Poor bird man dead,' she said. 'I hear. Very sad. What happen?'

'Crispin drowned,' Mum declared.

'Bad to swim at night,' Yasmine said. 'Maybe he crump?'

Mum frowned. 'Oh, you mean he got cramp. No. Crispin didn't like the water. He couldn't swim so he would never have gone in there just for a late-night dip.'

Yasmine's mouth dropped. 'You think bad thing happen?'

'At this stage, we're not ruling anything out,' said Mallory.

Yasmine reached for Eric's hand. 'We sleep. But Mama saw man outside late.'

Mallory turned to a fresh page in his ever-ready notebook. 'Would you know what time?'

Yasmine shrugged. 'Mama smoke cigarette outside. Delia forbid inside. Man walk past her. Maybe twelve? One?'

'But why would he do that?' Mum said. 'There aren't nightjars in the lane. Crispin was watching for them in the walled garden. Why would he go looking for them in the lane?'

'Unless . . .' I had a sudden thought. 'Didn't Delia say she and Crispin had planned to have a nightcap? Maybe he was going to her cottage? Or perhaps that's when he was going back to get his binoculars.'

'And your mother is—?'

'Banu,' said Yasmine.

'Surname?' Mallory asked.

'A-Y-D-I-N, Aydin,' said Eric.

'Not bird man,' said Yasmine suddenly. 'No. Horse man.'

Mum gave a cry and quickly turned away. My stomach dropped.

'Horse man?' Mallory said.

'He looks after the horses,' said Eric. 'Alfred Bushman.'

'No,' Mum said firmly. 'No, no, no. That can't be right.'

'Why not right?' Yasmine said with wide-eyed wonder. 'Horse man only at second party. Not third. And no bird man at fourth.'

Mum's face had turned white. 'Well . . . where was Eric in the early hours?'

'With me.' Yasmine squeezed Eric's hand tightly and leaned into him. Again, he didn't reciprocate.

'Oh really?' My mother's voice was heavy with sarcasm. 'How do you know he didn't slip out? You don't share a bedroom. Everyone knows . . . well . . . never mind.'

'Everyone knows what, Iris?' Mallory prompted.

'Put it this way,' said Mum. 'The marriage won't be consummated until after the wedding on Monday and Banu is making sure of that. She's her chaperone.'

Mallory's eyes widened but he kept a straight face.

'How old-fashioned you are,' Yasmine laughed in that tinkly laugh she had. 'There are other things couples can—'

'Okay, I think we get the picture,' I jumped in.

A tiny smile crinkled at the corner of Mallory's mouth.

'Well, regardless, Eric could have still nipped out when you were sleeping,' Mum mumbled.

Mallory raised a quizzical brow. 'Eric? Did you?'

'I was asleep all night,' he said, and snatched his hand away. 'I didn't hear anything.'

'There!' Yasmine was triumphant. 'He sleep!'

'How convenient,' Mum said. 'Of course you would give him an alibi, wouldn't you? Did he tell you about the argument he was having with Crispin?'

Confusion flickered across Yasmine's face.

I looked over at Mallory, who was saying nothing but seeing everything. I expected him to intervene but he didn't.

'You don't remember?' Mum said.

'Oh *that*!' Yasmine laughed again. 'It was about me. I flirt with Crispin. Eric did not like. It was joke.'

She tried to take Eric's hand but he kept it out of reach. 'Let's get this car moved.'

He abruptly left the kitchen with Yasmine trotting after him.

Mum and I locked eyes. I caught her expression and knew she was thinking the same thing as I was.

There was trouble in paradise.

'Shall we?' said Mallory and gestured for Mum and me to go first.

We filed out of the kitchen and into the carriageway where Eric was peering at the splodges and trails of yellowish-brown liquid. 'That looks like brake fluid.'

'We know that,' said Mum icily.

Between Mallory and Eric, they moved the rubble to one side. Yasmine fluttered about praising Eric's efforts. He ignored her.

Finally, the entrance was clear, allowing Eric to manoeuvre his tractor and tow-hitch into the courtyard. He had the Mini winched up in minutes.

Even though Mum's car had not been moving very fast, the impact had damaged all of the rear and side panels.

'I'll tow 'er to the garage,' Eric said. 'Leave 'er until Monday.'

'Thank you,' Mum said grudgingly.

He faffed about tightening straps to check the car was secure, then stopped to inspect the underside of the chassis.

Eric took out his mobile and touched the flashlight, peering very closely at what I assumed were the brake lines.

'You don't need to do that,' Mum said.

Eric raised a hand and continued his inspection as we looked on. When he stepped back, his expression was grave. 'Nipple clamps,' he declared. 'They've been deliberately loosened.'

'Excuse me?' Mum said.

Mallory strode to join him. 'Are you sure.'

'Yeah,' Eric pointed to something I couldn't see. 'You loosen 'em with a spanner. The fluid seeps out real slow.' He turned to Iris. 'Did the brakes feel spongy for a bit?'

Mum hesitated. 'Well. Yes.'

'And then suddenly nothing?' Eric asked.

'Yes,' Mum said. 'My foot was flat on the floor.'

'You can drive quite a bit with loose nipples,' Eric went on keenly. 'But then once the fluid has gone, you've got no brakes. See?' He tapped the chassis, as if patting an old horse. 'If you want my opinion, loosening those nipples was deliberate.'

'But . . . but . . .' Mum sounded flustered. 'That's ridiculous! Why would someone do that to my car?'

Eric shrugged. 'You only need a spanner, like.' He turned to Mallory. 'Ready?'

'I'll follow you to the garage,' said Mallory. 'Then we can have a little chat.'

'I come,' said Yasmine.

'Aren't you helping Lady Lavinia at the stables?' said Eric in an accusing voice. 'You're dressed for it.'

'Oh!' Yasmine looked hurt. She pointed to the BMW. 'I take?'

Eric's car was just visible out on the service road, along with a large flatbed truck with 'Festive Fun Planners' painted on the side which had just rocked up.

'You drove in it here, so why bother to ask?' Eric turned away leaving Yasmine looking as if she was about to burst into tears. I almost felt sorry for her. She trailed after him again.

Mum leaned in and whispered. 'I reckon the wedding is off and I reckon it's because Eric is coming to his senses after that shameful performance Yasmine put on in the drawing room last night.'

The Festive Fun Planners truck rumbled into the courtyard. Two burly men got out to load up the trestle tables and take down the bunting and fairy lights.

'We need to talk, Mum,' I said and pointed to the Carriage House.

'But—'

'They don't need our help. Into the kitchen please,' I said firmly.

'So,' I began when we were both seated at the table again. 'When are you going to tell me what's really going on? I'm not stupid. I know you were deliberately distracting Mallory by throwing Eric under the bus.'

'But you were the one who said Eric is fiddling the books and heaven knows what else!'

'I know Alfred wrote that note,' I persisted. 'Well? *Did* he have anything to do with Crispin's death?'

Mum's face crumpled. 'I don't know. Oh, I can see him making a few threats, perhaps throwing a punch here and there, but why? It doesn't make sense. I'm not the one Crispin is investigating!'

And then it was glaringly obvious. 'If Crispin was looking into everyone's business, perhaps he found out about Alfred's past and that's what Alfred discovered in the shepherd's hut. His warning to Crispin was very clear.'

'I know,' she whispered.

'Maybe Crispin threatened to tell her ladyship. Maybe he wanted money for his silence?' I thought for a moment. 'Was that why you changed your mind about going to Hope Cove yesterday? Alfred wanted Crispin out of the way so he could have a snoop around.'

'All right,' Mum admitted. 'It's true. I did. But if Alfred had left that note, it was still in the tea caddy, so we don't even know if Crispin saw it.'

I gave a heavy sigh. 'I don't know what's going on with Alfred and you or, for that matter, what Crispin was up to either. It all sounds very dodgy to me.'

'Poor Crispin,' said Mum. 'What am I going to do without him?'

'Well, if Alfred is involved in some way, you might find yourself in prison after all.'

'Don't be ridiculous!' Mum exclaimed.

'An accessory after the fact? Obstructing the course of justice? Just be careful. That's all I'm saying.'

'I'm going to have a lie down,' Mum said suddenly. 'You've given me a headache.'

I needed some alone time too. The events of the day had really begun to take their toll.

Just a moment later, Mallory sent me a text to say that he would come by later because he had something to tell me.

So this was it.

Chapter Twenty-Four

The minutes ticked by slowly as I waited for Mallory to come.

Restless and distracted, I picked up Jack Morgan's logbook and turned to the page where he'd listed the ingredients for Morgan's Miracle Spray (Nicotine Soap). I brought out *Aunt Muriel's Home Remedies* book and turned to the recipe for hers. Whereas Jack's focused on garden plants and making your roses 'shine', Muriel's was 'all purpose' and promised the following benefits: soothes arthritis and most skin conditions, repels mosquitos, erases crayon marks off walls, cleans candlewax from carpets and kills off aphids, black spot, and spider mites.

As I compared the two, a shocking picture began to develop. The ingredients in both were the same, but the quantities were critically different. Morgan's Miracle Spray quoted his in milligrams but Muriel's were in grams. Even more telling was that Morgan's stipulated only using six cigarettes and Muriel recommended sixty!

I ramped up my laptop and did some research, only to discover that nicotine is one of the deadliest poisons known to man. Just sixty milligrams of the stuff is all it takes to kill a healthy adult, meaning if you were to eat eight cigarettes, there's a good chance you'd end up dead. I re-read that line three times.

Fatal poisonings usually resulted from swallowing tobacco, administering tobacco enemas – heaven forbid – or absorption through the skin.

One of the main reasons why nicotine poisonings don't occur more often is because the early warning signs are so unpleasant – acute nausea, drooling, dizziness, vomiting and breathing difficulties. Recovery was fast as long as the source was removed quickly.

Nicotine soap, that is, miracle spray, was easy to make. Cigarettes were soaked in alcohol or some other solvent for a few hours or ideally, overnight, and then it was good to go. Again, I thought of Ruby's bathroom and the brown sludge. There was no doubt now that she had been making her own.

I read on, mesmerised by nicotine case studies from the late nineteenth century to the early twentieth century that seemed specifically to affect gardeners and florists who used the go-to formula of homemade nicotine soap.

One medical journal chronicled the extraordinary fate of a gardener who sat on a work bench on which something called Nica-Fume Liquid – a forty per cent solution of free nicotine – had been spilled. I read, 'A palm-sized solution soaked through his clothes. Fifteen minutes later he began vomiting and sweating profusely before falling into unconsciousness. He was taken to hospital in a semi-comatose state, writhing and moaning and gasping for breath, but the following day his symptoms had all but disappeared. Discharged from the hospital, he went home wearing the same clothes he had arrived in. These had been kept in a paper bag and, according to the patient, were still damp from the nicotine solution. Within an hour of leaving the hospital the gardener was again seized with nausea, vomiting, and sweating and was readmitted.'

I thought of Capricious knocking the plastic bottle out of Ruby's hands and the brownish stain on her nightdress. I just knew this was what had happened to Ruby! The nicotine must have soaked through her clothes but it had taken a while for the poison to be absorbed through her skin. She collapsed and lay there, presumably terrified as to what was happening but powerless to do anything to save herself.

What a truly horrible way to die.

Something was niggling away in the back of my mind. Muriel had boasted that her nicotine spray was all-purpose. I'd seen bottles of the stuff everywhere. Crispin had taken it to Hope Cove that morning and when my mother had returned she had complained of feeling nauseous. Perhaps it hadn't been sunstroke, after all. And then there was Lavinia, who had to cut her ride short with Yasmine because she wasn't feeling well. I had seen Lavinia put the spray on her arms to ward off mosquitoes.

Could it be that this mysterious bug that was sweeping through the village was none other than the effects of Muriel's toxic Miracle Spray?

The dowager countess! I distinctly remembered Banu saying she had been massaging Edith's limbs for her arthritis. Edith was slowly being poisoned and no one had guessed. Perhaps this was what had happened to Crispin. He'd slathered himself in the stuff, gone back to the lake to get his binoculars and collapsed and fallen in.

My mind was racing. I was desperate to share my theory with Mallory. But Muriel's Miracle Spray would have to be analysed first, just in case I was wrong. Muriel had been a bit of a legend in the village and, as the years passed, her reputation had become almost saintly.

When I heard the sound of an approaching car and saw headlights, I was ecstatic. It was Mallory.

But then my initial euphoria about my nicotine theory evaporated. Just for a few moments I'd forgotten about the young woman at the service station or Mallory's ominous text saying he needed to talk to me.

I hung back, but I needn't have worried. Mallory leapt out of his car and in just a few strides, he had caught me up in his arms, holding me so tight I could hardly breathe.

It was not what I expected and all the doubts I'd had about our relationship melted away. Neither of us spoke. We just held each other.

Slowly he lessened his grip and then stepped back, his eyes searching mine.

'Are you okay?' he said. 'Are we okay?'

I cracked a small smile. 'Define okay?'

'Let's sit down.' He gestured to the wicker loveseat on the terrace. 'Look. I need to tell you something.'

'And I have something to tell you about Ruby,' I said quickly, desperate not to hear what he had to say.

'All right. I'm listening.' He took my hand and led me to the loveseat.

'Would you like something to drink?' I said.

'In a minute. Just tell me what you have to tell me.' He sounded impatient but as I shared my theory about not just Ruby's death, possibly Crispin's too as well as the mysterious illness affecting some of the villagers, he soon paid attention.

'It's easy to confirm,' he said. 'I'll send a sample to the lab. We'll test for nicotine poisoning for Ruby and for Crispin. I'm impressed.' He brushed a lock of hair out of my eyes. I saw the hunger in his and felt myself blush. We were going to be okay.

'That will take ages though.' I couldn't dismiss a sense of dread that time was running out for the dowager countess. I wanted answers now! If nicotine was not the cause of her deteriorating health, then that was fair enough. But if it was? Then it really *would* be a miracle!

'It won't.' He gave a small smile. 'You seem to forget—'

'I haven't forgotten,' I cut in. I didn't want to hear about his ex-girlfriend and superior officer who managed to fast-track anything Mallory asked for.

'I'll make the call now.' He stood up and stepped a few feet away for privacy. He had his back to me but I heard him laugh, and when he returned he was smiling. 'Sometimes it's handy to have friends in high places.' He sat down next to me. 'There is just one problem with your theory about Crispin.'

'Which is?'

'There was a small puncture wound behind his ear,' said Mallory. 'I'm asking you to keep this strictly between us until we get the toxicology report back.'

'Oh.' I felt disappointed. 'A mosquito bite perhaps?'

'I'm not ruling anything out,' he said. 'Crispin had been in the water overnight. The inflammation from any kind of bite had gone. Let's get all the tests back before we scare everyone about this legendary potion.'

'I'll show you Jack Morgan's logbook,' I said. 'You'll see what I mean.'

'Later, not now.' He took my hand again. 'Look, I want to talk to you about Alfred.'

So this was what Mallory wanted to talk about. Not 'us' at all.

'Until we can access Crispin's computer and mobile phone, the jury is still out on who – if anyone – is responsible for his death. I spoke to Eric at great length,' Mallory went on. 'He admitted his ticket sales were not always declared and he also admitted to doing a bit of creative accounting.'

'Wow,' I said. 'What with Caroline confessing all, and now Eric. You must have a gift!'

'Maybe.' Mallory said. 'Eric also told me that he had loaned a considerable sum of money to the earl.'

I had had my suspicions and told Mallory so.

'Not only that,' Mallory went on. 'The earl offered Jane's Cottage and the two gatehouses as collateral for that loan.'

My jaw dropped. 'So that must have been what Rupert and Eric were arguing about in the carriageway. I didn't think Rupert wanted me to leave.'

'Maybe,' said Mallory slowly. 'I don't know Eric personally, but he told me the wedding was off and so was his decision to live here or use the gatehouses for whatever he had been planning on using them for.'

I was shocked and didn't know what to say.

'So, don't you see?' Mallory went on. 'Whatever leverage Crispin claimed to have over Eric, didn't work. He freely admitted all this to me. Apart from the fact that he had a solid alibi, Eric had no motive to get rid of Crispin at all.' He gave a heavy sigh. 'Which leaves Alfred.'

'Have you spoken to Alfred?' I asked. 'What did Alfred say?'

'He told me that he was attending to a sick horse,' said Mallory. 'Unfortunately, no one can verify that this was the case. And we do have Banu witnessing Alfred walking down the lane in the early hours.'

'Oh.' My heart sank. I knew nothing about any sick horse. All I remembered was Alfred leaving the Carriage House after the main course and not seeing him again.

'I can't say more at this stage,' said Mallory, 'But I just wanted to warn you that we are getting a warrant to search his flat tomorrow.'

I felt sick.

'Kat,' Mallory said gently. 'We can't choose our family. Believe me, if anyone knows about that it's me.'

He took a deep breath. 'The reason why I couldn't come to the Safari Supper concerns my niece,' he said. 'Her name is Polly and she is my eldest sister's only daughter.'

I was surprised. 'I didn't know you had a sister.'

'I have two, and an older brother as well,' said Mallory. 'All of whom you will meet one day, but this concerns Polly.'

'Okay,' I said.

'I had promised Stevie – that's my sister – to keep this to myself but I could see from your reaction and the wall that you put up the moment I had to cancel on Friday, that it could ruin what we have.'

I was clenching my fists and made a conscious effort to relax. 'Okay,' I said again.

'What we have is special, Kat,' Mallory went on. 'I don't want to jeopardise that. You must trust me.'

'Is that who I saw you with at the service station on Friday?' I said.

Mallory looked baffled. 'I don't follow.'

'I thought you saw me,' I said. 'I was with my mother.'

'Why on earth didn't you say something?' Mallory seemed incredulous. 'You thought . . .? Kat, she's twenty-two!'

I felt my face redden. 'I wasn't that close to see how old she was,' I mumbled. 'So why is she here?'

Mallory's expression hardened. 'Unfortunately Polly broke her parole.'

I was stunned. 'Parole?'

'As I told you, we can't choose our families,' he said. 'My brother-in-law died about five years ago and Polly went off the rails. This last incident got her prison time – three years in fact.'

'What on earth did she do?' I exclaimed. 'Rob a bank?'

'Not exactly,' he said. 'She got in with the wrong crowd. Diamond-switching scams—'

'Diamonds!' I squeaked.

'Shoplifting. You name it,' Mallory said, hardly able to believe it himself judging by his bewilderment. 'All because of this man who is much older than her: she was so infatuated with him that she happily took the fall. That is, until he dumped her.'

'I just don't know what to say other than I'm sorry.'

'The court wanted to frighten her so gave her time,' he said. 'Polly only served a year of her three-year sentence and got an early release.'

'But that's good news, isn't it?'

'It would have been had she not breached her condition of bail. There are exclusion zones, places she cannot go as a condition of her early release which she deliberately ignored.' He gave another heavy sigh. 'The new satellite tracking tags are so accurate that they can record the second someone steps into their garden, and Polly did more than that.'

I waited for him to continue.

'This *boyfriend* of hers broke up with her,' he said. 'She didn't think twice and went to confront him. Stevie called me in a panic so I dropped everything, including you.'

'I understand, truly,' I said and I did. 'Where is Polly now?'

'Staying at Larcombe Barn with strict instructions that she cannot leave the premises or go outside. I'll be driving her back to East Sutton Park – it's an open prison near Maidstone – on Monday. She should have been taken straight back but I pulled in a favour which I would never normally do.'

I knew it had to have been very serious for Mallory to go against his principles and loved him all the more for considering family first. 'I am so grateful that you have told me all this.' Grateful didn't even cut it. Yet again I'd been quick to judge a situation without being aware of all the facts and nearly ruined everything.

He stood up. 'I'd better get home. Polly is a town mouse and finds Larcombe Barn spooky.'

I walked with him to his car. We embraced and he kissed my forehead gently.

'Wait,' I said. 'Is there anything I can do to help? With Polly that is. Can I go and keep her company – at least until you take her back on Monday. You're consumed by this case and must feel pulled in all directions.'

He gave a sigh. 'Thank you but no. Yes, I told her about you but she doesn't know what you know about her. Not yet, anyway.'

I watched his taillights disappear and stood outside for a moment, taking in the beauty of my surroundings. Knowing I didn't have to move after all was such a huge relief and knowing that Mallory and I were a real couple made me so happy. But then I thought of Alfred and my joy turned to dread.

Mallory may have bent the rules for Polly but there was no question of him doing the same for a man with a track record like Alfred's.

When sleep finally came, it was accompanied by the dawn chorus.

Chapter Twenty-Five

It was nearly eleven when the phone woke me up with a jolt. I'd overslept! But when I heard Mallory's voice, telling me to get to the Carriage House as quickly as possible, I leapt out of bed.

Mallory was waiting for me in the carriageway. He was alone.

I scrambled out of my car. 'What's happened? Where is Mum?'

He gently caught my arm and turned me around to face him. I looked into his compassionate eyes. 'She'll be all right, but she's had a terrible shock. I just wanted to prepare you.'

I found my mother seated at the kitchen table staring into an untouched balloon of brandy. I dashed to her side and threw my arms around her.

'I'm so sorry,' I said. 'Everything is going to be okay. Just you see.'

'I feel so betrayed,' Mum whispered. 'All those years. I can't believe it.

'I'm sure Alfred was doing it to protect you, Mum,' I said. 'I'm sure that will be taken into consideration.'

'Alfred?' Mum said sharply. 'What's this got to do with Alfred?'

'Oh.' I was puzzled. 'But . . . I don't understand.'

'It's got nothing to do with Alfred,' Mum's tone was harsh. 'No. It's that little creep Crispin, and he deserved all he got!'

'Crispin?' I looked from Mallory to my mother in confusion. 'What's going on?'

Mallory pulled out a chair and gestured for me to sit.

'Crispin Fellowes works for HMRC,' Mallory said bluntly.

'Excuse me? HMRC. As in—'

'Yes Katherine,' Mum put in. 'His Majesty's Revenue and Customs. The tax man. Just like your father did.'

'But that's not possible. He's . . .' I shook my head. 'I don't understand. Isn't he your financial adviser?'

Mallory opened his notebook but he didn't need to consult it. 'Crispin Fellowes has been employed by HMRC for the past twenty-two years. Yes, he runs his own financial consultancy business on the side but his full-time job is for the government. You do understand what this means, don't you?'

'I'm sorry,' I said. 'But I don't.'

'Crispin has been handling Iris's taxes but only declaring a minute proportion of what she has really been earning.'

'You mean, he's . . . he's been *embezzling*?'

'I trusted him with my life!' Mum said. 'I never saw a reason not to.'

'How could you not have known?' I rounded on my mother in horror. 'What about your bank statements? Your royalty statements? Didn't you check them?'

Mum shrugged. 'Your father always handled our money so I was more than happy for Crispin to do all that, too. Crispin paid all my bills and I paid him a monthly retainer. Why shouldn't I have trusted him? I always had plenty of money. It never occurred to me to think otherwise.'

'The statements?' I said slowly. 'That must be why Crispin wanted you to shred them.' Seeing Mum's blank look I shared my new theory – a theory that just popped into my head five seconds ago. 'Because if you had looked at them properly and checked the deposits against your bank statements, you would have noticed that they wouldn't have tallied. You should have had a lot more money in your bank account than you actually do.'

'I don't understand royalty statements,' Mum said. 'They make no sense to me.'

I turned to Mallory. 'The royalty statements were always sent by Goldfinch Press – that's Mum's publisher – care of my post box in the village,' I said. 'They came in a brown envelope. I would then hand them over to my mother. Remember, Mum, you always insisted on having hard copies.'

'Because I'm old-fashioned,' Mum said. 'Although Crispin had wanted me to go paperless. I said it would be like going without underwear and no thank you.'

A flicker of a smile crossed Mallory's features.

'Technology is so advanced these days there are many ways to get the information,' Mallory mused. 'What people don't realise is that HMRC know everything about everyone. They are automatically informed about income, royalties and yes, cash transactions. Any sum over £2,000 gets an instant flag or a SAR – that is, a suspicious activity report.'

My jaw dropped. 'Seriously?'

'People think they can get away with being paid under the table or cash in hand but everything is tracked,' Mallory went on. 'When Fergal Grimes went over the limit and smuggled in the extra cash, it was flagged and reported by Border Control. Iris told me about Alfred's channel dashes to withdraw her money—'

'Yes,' Mum said. '*My* money which is legal! Ten thousand pounds is legal!'

'And that she called Crispin for advice . . .'

'Crispin told me not to panic,' Mum took up the story. 'He said the timing was good because he was on his way to the Isles of Scilly to do some bird watching. He said he would "pop in" to sort it out. *Pop in!*'

'Forensic accounting will be able to prove everything,' said Mallory. 'I don't think it was only your mother who he was embezzling. Obviously, I haven't had time to do a deep dive but I have seen enough on his laptop to know what he was up to.'

'You found the password?' I said.

Mallory gave a small smile. 'I think I went through the name of every bird in the British Isles, but in the end it turned out to be—'

'Nightjar,' Mum muttered. 'The lying thieving . . .'

'It was the same password for his mobile,' Mallory went on. 'He and Ruby exchanged many texts about bird sightings. In one thing he was truthful. Crispin was passionate about his hobby.' He paused for a moment. 'Crispin's call logs have proved very enlightening. The moment you rang him about Fergal Grimes's arrest, he rang his contact in Border Control.'

'So that's why Fergal Grimes was allowed to go free,' I said.

'Crispin's contact lists will prove very useful in exposing other corrupt officials,' said Mallory. 'A corrupt HMRC employee can falsify everything should he choose. No wonder he was able to get confidential information on whomever he pleased and use that as so-called leverage.'

'I feel such an idiot,' Mum said miserably.

'You didn't know,' I said but then I remembered something odd. 'Crispin seemed very interested in how Banu entered the country.'

'Yasmine's mother?' Mallory flicked back through his notebook. 'Banu Aydin?"

'Crispin told me that she wasn't travelling with Yasmine and, for some reason, he thought it was significant but then he was distracted by Yasmine's arrival dressed as Jungle Jane.'

Mallory raised an eyebrow. 'So he didn't say why?'

'He wanted their IDs,' I said. 'He was going to ask the vicar because they would have had to have given him the information for the parish records.'

Mallory wrote it down.

'And you know why?' Mum exploded. But she didn't wait for anyone to ask. 'Because he was looking for *leverage* on those two women, too. Well, he won't be *leveraging* anyone ever again.' She slumped forward and put her head in her hands.

'I know this is hard for you,' Mallory began. 'But we'll get to the bottom of it all, Iris. Just to confirm: you say you got hard copies of all your statements – royalty and bank?'

'Yes,' she nodded.

'You mentioned earlier that you didn't use email,' Mallory said. 'I know the publisher posted your royalty statements to Kat. What about the bank statements?'

'They were posted from Crispin,' said Mum.

'Not from the bank?' Mallory's eyes narrowed. 'You're sure?'

'Positive.'

'Good,' said Mallory. 'Those are the bank statements I want to see.'

'Oh no!' Mum exclaimed. 'Everything has been shredded!'

'Shredded,' I said. 'But not thrown away. Alfred kept them, remember?'

Mallory blanched. 'They can certainly be reassembled but it'll take a very long time. I have a feeling that the bank statements sent to you by Crispin were almost certainly forgeries created just for you, and that's what we need. Evidence.'

'We'll sort it, Mum,' I said and looked to Mallory for reassurance.

Mum went very quiet. In fact, unnaturally so. She bit her lip in anguish and clenched her hands tightly together.

'It'll be okay, just you see,' I said.

When she looked up and her eyes met mine, I was alarmed at what I saw. It was fear.

'Mum—?'

'I think . . .' She swallowed hard, almost struggling to speak. 'The more I think about it . . . yes. I think he wanted me gone.'

'Gone?' I echoed. 'What do you mean?'

'Crispin must have known he would be found out. All those questions you were asking. The talk of the audit. Not doing what he asked about burning the documents,' she raced on. 'Oh Kat. That walk to Bolt Tail. I know I wasn't feeling well but he deliberately took me up there.'

'What do you mean?' Mallory said sharply.

'He was going to push me off the cliff,' she whispered. 'And what about the ladder?'

'The broken rungs,' I nodded. 'I saw them. There was something odd about the way the wood had snapped. I'll show them to Mallory. Oh gosh. And the brakes? Mum! Do you think he had something to do with your brakes?'

'I don't know,' she said, adding in a small voice. 'I trusted him.'

Mallory went very still. 'Did you tell Alfred any of this?'

'Not exactly,' Mum said.

'I just mentioned that we shouldn't get rid of the documents, that's all,' I jumped in.

Mallory regarded my mother with suspicion. I did too.

'But perhaps Crispin found something out about Alfred,' Mallory said which was exactly what I had begun to believe, too. 'And Alfred wrote that note.'

Mum hesitated. 'Even if he did write it – which I'm not saying he did – how would Alfred get Crispin to the lake? Have you seen how small Alfred is? He might be strong but it's quite a trek from the walled garden to the park. And what are you implying? That Alfred did what? Beat him up? Did Crispin have any bruises? No! Was there any blood? No!'

I could see that Mum was getting upset but she was making an excellent point. My nicotine theory seemed far more likely but, when I spouted Occam's razor about the simplest answer usually being the right one, was a little hurt when Mallory shut me down with a sharp look and shake of the head.

He stood up. 'For now, I would concentrate on getting those shredded bank statements, Iris,' he said. 'And let the police do our job. Kat? A word?'

I followed him out of the kitchen again. He always seemed to be wanting to have a 'word', and usually it wasn't a good one.

Out in the carriageway, his expression grew grave. 'Whether Crispin's death was an accident or deliberate, and if Alfred was responsible or not, won't change the very real possibility that your mother could face jail time for tax fraud.'

I thought I had misheard. 'But that's not her fault! It's Crispin's! He's been embezzling her money! You know he has. You just told us!'

'Ssh. Hear me out,' he said gently. 'Iris would have to prove that she had no knowledge of Crispin doing this. Would she be able to prove ignorance?'

My heart sank. 'I don't know.'

'We really need to see those bank statements that Crispin sent her. And try not to worry.'

'Worry!' I exclaimed. 'I'm worried sick!'

An alert sounded from his pocket. He pulled out his mobile and glanced at the caller ID. 'I'm sorry, Kat,' he said. 'The search warrant has come through. We're going to Alfred's flat. I just want you to be prepared for the worst.'

The moment he left, my mother emerged from the shadows. I'd never seen her look so worried. 'Alfred wouldn't do it. I know he wouldn't. And what were you about to say about Occam's something or other and nicotine?'

'Let's focus on you,' I said briskly changing the subject. 'Did Alfred tell you where he left those dustbin liners?'

Mum nodded. 'In one of the potting sheds in the walled garden.'

'Good,' I said. 'Let's go.'

Chapter Twenty-Six

Crispin's Audi was still parked outside the walled garden but, as I drew up behind it, Delia emerged from her cottage at number one. She spotted us and came over, her eyes alight with mischief. We hadn't even got out of the car.

'Oh no,' Mum murmured. 'She's the last person I want to see today.'

I opened the window.

'I was just on my way to see you! I have news!' Delia leaned in and frowned. 'You look a bit ropey, Iris. I don't think I've ever seen you without your lipstick. Is everything all right?'

'Mum's still upset about Crispin,' I said which was partially true.

'Upset?' Delia declared. 'If anyone's upset it should be me! I was the one who found him. Every time I see his car I get triggered. I think I've got PTSD. Anyway, you won't believe it.'

'I'm sure I will,' Mum said rudely.

'Remember the guests who were supposed to stay in the shepherd's hut?' Delia put her hand on the roof of the car, ready for a long chat. 'They went to the pub in the end. I called in a favour. They were only in number two for all of five minutes.' She indicated Eric's cottage. 'They wanted privacy, not folks fighting.'

Mum perked up, suddenly interested. 'Who? Eric and Yasmine? Eric and Banu? Yasmine and Banu?'

'Yes. All of them,' Delia nodded. 'You should have heard them going at it hammer and tongs. For someone who doesn't speak very good English Yasmine certainly knows a few swear words, let me tell you. Eric stormed out. Then Yasmine and Banu got into it – in Turkish of course but I got the gist. And then sometime in the middle of the night, I heard a car drive away and when I got up this morning, the Skoda was gone.'

'Oh yes, we knew that the wedding was off,' Mum said airily and shot me a look of triumph because we had heard that piece of news first from Mallory.

'You'd like to think so, but no,' Delia said her triumph, trumping ours. 'I asked Yasmine and she said her mother had gone back to Turkey to prepare for the big family party. Yasmine looked as if she had been crying all night, poor mite. But you're right. Eric nearly ended it. Yasmine told me it was touch and go.'

'Touch and go, how?' Mum prompted.

Delia looked over her shoulder as if to check no one was around. 'I don't think Yasmine's home but you never know.' She lowered her voice. 'Eric wanted to pull out but,' her voice grew even lower, 'I think they did it.'

'Did what?' Mum said loudly.

Delia's eyes widened and she turned pink. 'Well, Banu left didn't she so Yasmine didn't have her chaperone anymore.' She nodded furiously. 'Yes. I'm sure of it. And then she guilted Eric into going ahead with it and said he'd have to marry her now. Plus they've got a guest list of about a hundred strong and it's too expensive to cancel.'

'How do you know all this?' Mum demanded. 'I suppose you've been listening at your bedroom wall again.'

Delia stiffened. 'I thought you'd be interested.'

'We saw Eric this morning and he didn't look like a man who had finally had his way,' said Mum. 'He looked as if he was being led to the gallows. I bet he still calls it off.'

I frowned. 'Wasn't Banu supposed to be one of the witnesses at the registry office tomorrow?'

'They've asked me now,' Delia beamed. 'I get on very well with Yasmine. *Very* well. She's like a daughter to me.'

'Who is the other witness?' Mum declared. 'I'm not doing it.'

'There's no chance of that,' Delia shot back. 'Yasmine asked Lady Lavinia. They're like sisters.'

'Daughters, sisters,' Mum sneered. 'I'm surprised you're not flying out to Turkey for the party.'

The sarcasm was lost on Delia. 'I'm too busy for parties. It would be easy if it was a quick hop from Exeter Airport but the trek to Heathrow . . . that takes far too long.'

'Is that where Banu is flying from?' I said. 'Going to Heathrow in that old car?'

'She told me Eric said it was roadworthy,' said Delia. 'Parking for three weeks is going to cost a pretty penny, let me tell you that. And then they're all back at the end of the month.'

I waited for Delia to ask about my moving plans but she didn't.

'Is that it?' said Mum. 'Is that your news?'

'Oh no, there's more!' Delia grinned. 'Remember those wooden table pieces that Caroline had at the vicarage?'

'What about them?' Mum said.

'When I spoke to Doreen she told me that Caroline was freaking out.' Delia paused in the annoying, dramatic way that was a habit of hers. 'Guess why?'

'Oh, you mean because Caroline's the village mole and she was the one who let the goats out.' Mum rolled her eyes. 'That's old news.'

'No, not that.' Delia waited again, barely able to contain her glee.

'Spit it out,' Mum said.

'There was a recall on all the carvings,' she said. 'Apparently those red beads with the little black spots that she stuck on for eyes are rosary peas and if they fall out they could be dangerous.'

'Rosary peas.' The name seemed familiar but I wasn't sure why.

'Dangerous, how?' Mum said.

Delia blinked. 'She didn't say but I'm guessing they could get stuck up a kiddie's nose. She'll have to reimburse everyone and I bet she's already spent the money.'

Delia's mobile rang.

Raising a finger presumably a sign for us to wait, Delia dragged it out of her pocket and glanced at the screen. 'It's Lady Lavinia.' She hit the button. 'Good afternoon milady. I was just . . . what? Oh!' All the colour drained from Delia's face. 'Yes. Yes. Of course. I can be there in ten minutes if I pedal fast.'

She ended the call with an expression on her face that gave me the chills.

'It's the dowager countess,' Delia seemed unable to get the words out. 'I . . . I . . .'

Mum clutched at her throat. 'She's dead!'

Delia shook her head vehemently. 'No. Lady Edith has been taken away in an ambulance. She was having trouble breathing. Couldn't keep any food down. Not even water. Oh. This is the end. This is it. I've got to go. She'll need a change of clothes and . . .' But we didn't hear anything else. Delia mounted her bicycle and pedalled frantically away.

'Oh, Kat. I can't bear it if something happens to her ladyship,' Mum whispered. 'Delia said that death comes in threes—'

'She's not dead yet,' I said sharply. 'You mustn't think that way. I've got a hunch – I might be wrong but I pray I'm right.'

When I told Mum about Muriel's toxic miracle spray, she was stunned.

'I know that Banu was using it to ease Edith's arthritis,' I went on. 'If Edith is suffering from nicotine poisoning, then she should make a full recovery—'

'The spray!' Mum exclaimed. 'Crispin gave it to me at Hope Cove.'

'Did he use any himself?'

'No.' Mum shook her head. 'He said that Delia told him to use Avon Skin So Soft. She didn't like the spray. Come to think of it, it did have a funny smell.'

'That was why you felt so ill. I don't think it was sunstroke. I know Edith will pull through,' I said more to reassure myself than anything else. 'She has to.'

I reversed through the tall gates and into the walled garden, parking as close as I could to the glasshouses so that we didn't have too far to haul the dustbin liners.

Under Delia's supervision the garden had been transformed. The perimeter paths that divided the grounds into four equal sections were now fashioned a little on the famous colour-themed gardens at Sissinghurst Castle in Sussex. Only the far corner retained the original wild look ('nothing but weeds,' my mother had said) but it had been planted deliberately to attract the bees and birds. Beyond the ivy-clad boundary wall was dense woodland and some young conifers, which was where the elusive nightjar was supposed to nest. The shepherd's hut was behind a twelve-foot-high screen of woven hazel panels which now had police do-not-cross tape – as if we needed reminding.

Gesturing to the glasshouses that hugged the boundary wall, I said, 'Come on, let's get this over and done with.'

'How about using that?' Mum pointed to a red metal wheelbarrow that was resting against the wall.

I went to get it but as I wheeled it over the front tray brace collapsed.

'Well honestly!' my mother exclaimed. 'I suppose this was made in China.'

'I don't think you can say things like that these days, Mum.'

We entered the first glasshouse that opened into a series of connecting glasshouses. Doors lined the back wall that led to the various storerooms and potting sheds.

'Did Alfred tell you which one he left them in?' I asked.

'It's the third one,' said Mum. 'Or maybe the fourth.'

In the golden age of the country house, a Victorian glasshouse was a symbol of wealth and prestige, and these were no exception. Now, although empty and swept clean, it was easy to imagine what they would have been like filled with an abundance of hothouse plants and exotic fruits. Ferns, palms, and orchids would have been grown in some; others would be bursting with oranges and nectarines, peaches and figs. I'd heard talk of resurrecting these beauties – another of Delia's ideas to attract visitors – but it would take a lot of work and expense.

I followed Mum through to the third glasshouse. She pointed to a rear door that was set in the wall. 'In there.'

When she pushed it open the smell hit me straight away. 'Ugh. Cigarette smoke!'

Mum wrinkled her nose. 'Crispin said he saw Banu sneaking in here all the time for a quick puff.'

'I thought she was doing the nicotine patch,' I said.

'I think she just said that to placate Delia.'

We stepped inside. The storeroom was an empty shell with a few iron hooks on the walls that would have been used to hang garden implements. A small high window covered in cobwebs ran along the top of the wall near the ceiling, giving some light to the gloomy area.

'Nothing in here,' I said. 'What about trying in there?'

A latch-door led to an adjoining room. It was windowless and dark. I felt for a light switch, not expecting to find one, and surprised when I did. I flipped the switch.

The small room was lined with shelves and a narrow workbench where a white plastic bag with 'Duty-Free Schiphol Airport' printed on it in red, lay next to a large stone and a random piece of slate the size of a saucer.

It looked out of place. Curious, I picked up the bag and peered inside. 'What on earth! Look, Mum.'

She peered inside too. 'Well I never! That's one of Delia's pudding basins. It's got the Grenville crest on it.' She seemed outraged. 'What's Banu doing with that? That's stealing! What else is in there?'

'I don't think we should look,' I said. 'What if she comes back?'

'How can she come back?' Mum said. 'She's on her way to Turkey.' She paused. 'If you won't, I will.' Mum quickly tipped the items out of the bag and on to the workbench.

She set out a wooden giraffe that I was sure was the same one that Banu had taken from the party – although this one didn't have eyes – an empty bottle of nail polish remover, and a navy hard-shell eyewear case.

We looked at each other in confusion.

'I suppose I was hoping for a snuff box or something,' Mum muttered and put the items back into the bag, taking care not to damage the basin. 'We'll take it. The giraffe's not hers either, and since I've never seen either of them wear glasses, maybe Banu pinched those too.'

I was getting twitchy. 'Look, there's another door over there. Let's try that.'

But when we did, the door was locked and there was no key.

'Blast! I bet the bags are in there,' Mum said. 'Alfred must have kept the key. We'll go and get it.'

Something must have given me away.

'What's the matter,' Mum said sharply. 'You've got that funny look on your face.'

I knew I had to tell her. 'Mallory has a warrant to search Alfred's flat. He's doing it right now.'

'And you didn't think to tell me!' Mum shrieked. 'And that's where we're going *right now*. Quickly!'

Yasmine was waiting by my car. Her eyes darted to the Duty-Free bag. 'Ah. You find?'

'Yes, we find and this belongs to Delia.' Mum took out the pudding basin and waved it at her.

Yasmine shrugged. 'Mama. She like to smoke there. Use as ashtray. I take?'

'I take this,' Mum held on to the pudding basin and thrust the bag at her. 'You take that.'

Yasmine looked inside the bag. 'Ah, Mama has the diabetes. She need. She sick.'

But before I could comment my mother was already sitting in my car and gesturing for me to hurry.

We set off for Alfred's flat. 'That was weird. I didn't see any cigarettes in that shed and the basin hasn't been used as an ashtray.'

'I don't care,' said Mum. 'I only care about Alfred.'

I parked next to the archway and Mum hurried on ahead. I grabbed my mobile and followed.

The stable yard was empty. Mallory must have been and gone. The horses were in their stables, resting in the afternoon heat. In the summer months, their routines were reversed. They were turned out at night and kept inside during the day and it was far too hot to ride until late afternoon.

As I waited for my mother to return, I checked my mobile. There was a voicemail from Mallory. It was long and detailed and made my heart sink.

Things did not look good for Alfred.

Mum emerged at the top of the steps that led to Alfred's flat above. 'He's not here! I couldn't find the key.' She joined me. 'Oh – what's wrong? You've gone that funny colour again.'

I knew that the only way was to tell it to my mother straight. 'Alfred has been taken to the police station.'

Mum reached behind and sank on to a step. 'Oh no!'

'Alfred claims he has an alibi which they are going to check out, but Mallory didn't say what it was.' I tried to sound confident but, deep down, I was filled with a dreadful foreboding. 'Alfred has not been charged with anything at this stage, Mum. He's only helping police with their enquiries.'

'Helping police with their enquiries?' Her voice was heavy with scorn. 'We all know what *that* means. They already think he's guilty. It's that stupid note.'

'So you *did* know about the note!'

'Not exactly,' Mum said. 'But I thought the handwriting looked familiar.'

I took a deep breath. 'Mallory found a spanner and a small hacksaw in Alfred's flat along with a map of Hope Cove and Bolt Tail. Alfred admitted that he'd taken them from Crispin's suitcase which he found stored under the two-seater in the shepherd's hut.'

Mum looked blank. 'A spanner? A hacksaw? A map? How can that possibly incriminate Alfred?'

'Eric said you only needed a spanner to loosen the nipple clamps on your brakes to create a slow leak,' I said. 'I'm guessing that the hacksaw could have been used to partially saw through those ladder rungs. I haven't a clue about the map.'

'But surely, that's good news!' Mum enthused. 'It's proof that Crispin was out to get rid of me. And that map! I bet that was where he planned on pushing me off – oh Kat. If that lovely couple hadn't appeared with their dog when they did, I wouldn't be here.'

'I know,' I said. 'But you are.' I took another deep breath. 'The problem is that nothing can actually be *proved* on Crispin's end—'

'Well Alfred is hardly going to try to bump off his own sister!' Mum said with scorn.

'Of course not,' I said. 'But there was a witness. Banu.'

'Who isn't here now,' Mum pointed out.

'But it provides Alfred with a motive to take matters into his own hands. Don't you see?'

'When you put it like that . . . Oh dear.' Mum's face fell. 'But I still don't know why Crispin would have gone with Alfred to the summer house. The note made no mention of meeting him there, did it?'

I didn't know what to say, so I said nothing.

'Kat! Oh golly. So glad to see you.' Lavinia strode into the stable yard in her usual dishevelled state. My thoughts went immediately to Edith.

'Have you any news?' I said.

'No.' Lavinia bit her lip. 'Frightfully worried. Rupert's there. Must go too, but . . . where is Alfred?'

'Alfred is helping the police with their enquiries,' Mum said firmly.

Lavinia brightened. 'Will he be long?'

'We're not sure how long he will be,' I said. 'Can I help with the horses at all?'

'Would you?' Lavinia said eagerly. 'Must go to Edith.'

'I can take care of the evening feed and turn then out if you tell me what you need me to do. I'm more than happy to ride, too.'

'Oh golly. That would be *ab-so-lutely* super,' said Lavinia. 'You're the only person Edith would trust with Tinkerbell.'

'Tinkerbell,' I said faintly. I had never ridden Edith's beloved mare before.

'She's desperate to get out,' Lavinia said. 'Side-saddle, yah?'

'Good grief, no, sorry!' I exclaimed. Although I had ridden side-saddle there was no way I would feel confident enough on Tinkerbell. She was notoriously skittish.

Lavinia's face fell. 'Oh. I'm sure she won't mind astride just this once.'

I wasn't sure if Lavinia meant Edith or the mare.

'What about Jupiter and Duchess?' I said. 'Could Yasmine ride out with me?'

'Oh golly, no,' Lavinia turned pink. 'Edith was livid when Alfred told her I'd let her ride. *Livid*. So no.'

'I don't mind taking them out afterwards,' I said. 'I can ride one and lead the other.'

'No need,' said Lavinia. 'Jupiter can skip a ride and Duchess had colic on Friday night so Alfred wants her to rest up.'

'On Friday night?' Mum said sharply. 'The night of the Safari Supper? What time would that have been?'

Lavinia frowned. 'About nine. They were in the small paddock but Alfred noticed Duchess had been kicking her belly. He was frightfully worried.'

Mum grabbed my arm, hardly able to contain her excitement. 'Alfred was with Duchess! How long for, milady?'

'All night,' said Lavinia. 'Can't leave a horse with colic. Twisted gut, you know. Vet came out.'

'The vet came out!' Mum trilled happily. 'Thank heavens! The vet came out!'

It sounded like Alfred had his alibi. But it didn't explain why Banu said she had seen Alfred walking in the service drive in the early hours of the morning. He would never have left a sick horse.

Promising Lavinia I would take great care of Tinkerbell Lavinia gave me instructions on what to do before scurrying away.

'I'm going straight to the police station to get Alfred out,' said Mum. 'Oh, blast! I don't have my car!'

'You can take mine,' I said. 'Just drop me home so I can change and I can walk from there.'

But when we reached my house, Mum groaned. 'What's *he* doing here.'

It was Eric. He was on foot and he was alone.

Chapter Twenty-Seven

Eric took a few steps forwards as if to open Mum's car door, but then changed his mind and waited. He seemed awkward and self-conscious.

Mum and I got out. I handed her my car keys.

'No Yasmine?' I asked Eric.

'She's gone shopping in Exeter,' he said.

'I'll be off,' said Mum. 'Can't stop.'

'I left a note for Jimmy, like,' Eric said quickly. 'He'll know what to do first thing Monday. I rang my mate in Torquay who will see you right with the bodywork.'

'Oh.' Mum seemed taken aback. 'Well, thank you. But I must go.'

'Good luck, Mum,' I said. 'Let me know what happens.'

She gave a grim nod and slid into the driver seat. Mum adjusted the rear-view mirror and pulled on her seatbelt. Eric continued to hover as if he wanted to say more. With a sinking heart I suspected that since the wedding was back on, so was my eviction.

Mum executed a perfect three-point turn and sped away.

'I'm in a bit of a hurry too,' I said.

'Sorry, but . . .' Eric seemed all tongue-tied. 'With her ladyship poorly and Lady Lavinia wanting to stay at the hospital, I thought . . . Yasmine thought . . . would you be our second witness, like.'

This was something I absolutely did not want to do.

'You're still going ahead, even with the dowager countess close to death?' I had hoped this wasn't true, but part of me did think having a wedding in such circumstances was just not right. 'What if Lady Edith dies?'

Eric swallowed, showing me that Adam's apple again, but he just looked miserable and certainly not a man about to marry the woman of his dreams.

'Yasmine won't wait another minute,' he said. 'Not now. And with her Ma already gone ahead. It's going to be a big party. I don't suppose you and Iris would like to—?'

'Come?' I cut in. 'No. Sorry.'

I looked at him standing there. A shadow of the man of just a few days ago who was glowing with love. I suppose it was daunting celebrating a wedding among strangers – especially since most of them probably wouldn't speak any English.

I felt an unexpected surge of compassion.

'If you have any doubts at all,' I said. 'It's not too late to cancel. Do you think Yasmine will be happy here? She seemed a little . . . well . . .' I struggled to be tactful, 'A little out of her depth at the Hall on Friday evening.'

Eric reddened. 'She didn't understand. She's Turkish, see. They're not like that over there. No earls or lords and all that. She was upset. Crying like. Got into a big fight with her ma about it too.'

'Over the tiger?'

Eric nodded.

I didn't believe that for a minute. I'd seen how Banu hadn't hesitated to snap a few photographs on her mobile. It was obvious that mother and daughter found the whole thing a huge joke.

'She was scared I'd call off the wedding,' Eric went on.

'Did you?' I said.

'Well, yeah, but then, Banu blamed herself,' said Eric. 'Thought we needed alone time. And now she's gone, it's good. Yeah. We're good.' He nodded again but I felt he was convincing himself.

'Delia mentioned that Banu had driven herself to Heathrow airport,' I said. 'I hope that car gets her there.'

'Yeah, me too,' said Eric. 'It was a bit sudden like. I didn't hear her leave.'

'Was she able to change her airline ticket at such short notice?' I asked.

Eric shrugged. 'I guess. Yasmine said there are lots of connecting flights through Amsterdam.'

'Ah, Schiphol airport.' I thought of the Duty-Free bag that we'd found in the potting shed with its peculiar contents. 'Look, I'm sorry Mum and I won't be able to come to your wedding party. I appreciate the invitation.'

'You're welcome.' And still Eric wouldn't leave!

'You were right,' he finally blurted out. 'Yasmine doesn't want to live in your place. She thinks it's too small and now she wants us to live in her villa, part-time like.'

'Really?' I was very relieved to hear it. 'I'm sure it's lovely.'

'Yeah but . . .' He swallowed yet again. 'It's not England, is it? I've lived here all my life. I just . . .' He shook his head. 'I wonder what Vera would have said.'

Vera. Was Eric still hung up on his dead wife? I was definitely not getting into that conversation. 'I'm sure she'd be happy for you.'

'I never changed my will,' Eric said. 'Just couldn't do it.'

This was a surprise. 'You haven't?'

Eric shook his head. 'Vera was till death us do part.'

I was exasperated. 'Eric. Vera is dead. You do realise what this means. If something were to happen to you, figuring out your will would be a total mess.'

'No not that Vera, my Vera,' he said. 'Vera's niece. We call her LV. Little Vera. Lives out in Australia with Vera's sister-in-law's brother's nephew or second cousin. Or something.'

I was stunned. 'But what about Yasmine?'

Eric looked blank. 'What about Yasmine? She told me she loved me just the way I am.'

I just didn't know what to make of it all. 'But what about the scrapyard and all the bits of land you own all over the place? You need to get those sorted.'

'Oh that,' he said dismissively. 'Yeah. Everything goes back to his lordship. So you see, Yasmine really is marrying me for love.'

I was stumped for what to say. 'Well. Good. Look, I'm sorry but I've got to go. I'm riding Tinkerbell and I need to do it because it's supposed to rain later.' I wasn't sure if that was true but the air certainly felt heavy enough for a good old storm.

'Right then,' he said. 'So see you Monday at noon.'

I forced a smile. 'Delia and I will be there.'

And with that, he turned away and wandered down the hill, striking the look of a lost and somewhat forlorn man about to embark on a rather uncertain future.

I changed into jodhpurs, tied back my hair, and grabbed my riding helmet. As always whenever I rode alone, I took a mobile phone with me and slipped it into a crossbody leather pouch.

As I walked to the stables, Mum called me on my mobile.

'Mallory won't let Alfred go.' She sounded distressed. 'Not until he's spoken to the vet, who is somewhere on the River Dart in his canoe.'

'Canoe?'

'Apparently Ian Masters is an avid canoeist,' said Mum. 'He can't be reached until this evening. Mallory can hold Alfred without charge for twenty-four hours.'

'Don't worry,' I said. 'We know Alfred has an alibi.'

'It's not that,' Mum said. 'Mallory knows everything about him. His rap sheet, what he's been in prison for and for how long. I don't think I realised just how much of a criminal Alfred really was. But he's been going straight for years! I'm desperately worried. I lied to her ladyship.' The phone went quiet for a moment. I was certain I heard a sob. 'What if Mallory tells her ladyship and Alfred gets the sack?'

'If he's innocent, there's no reason for Mallory to tell the family,' I said.

'Could you talk to Mallory? Please, Kat.'

In light of Mallory's own family problems with his niece, I grudgingly agreed.

Luckily, my call went to voicemail. I didn't want to leave a message about Alfred on Mallory's mobile but I told him that the dowager countess had been taken to hospital and that I was going riding on Edith's much-loved mare and to wish me luck.

Back in the stables, I was having second thoughts about riding Tinkerbell alone. Tacking her up was a challenge. She wouldn't stand still, and when I tried to tighten her girth, she blew her belly out. I was feeling anxious and knew I had to get a grip, otherwise Tinkerbell would pick up on it.

I was just about to lead her out of her loosebox when my mobile rang. It was Lavinia.

'How is Edith?' I asked.

'A little better,' said Lavinia. 'I told her you were riding Tinkerbell. She said to let her have her head along Hopton's Crest to get rid of fizz then go through Larcombe Woods. It's a frightfully easy trail.' She continued with a detailed list of instructions of where I could canter, where I should walk and what to avoid; that Tinkerbell was spooked by odd-shaped boulders and plastic bags. I was to take a riding crop so she would know who was boss, but never use it.

I felt as if I was looking after the crown jewels, which I suppose, as far as Edith was concerned. I was.

Finally, we set off.

Chapter Twenty-Eight

It was just gone five and the air was hot and still, shimmering with heat waves that distorted the horizon.

Hopton's Crest was one of my favourite bridleways. The ridge, once lush and green, was now hardened mud marked by brittle clumps of withering vegetation. I urged Tinkerbell into a gentle canter, her hooves kicked up small clouds of dust. She tossed her head, anxious to go faster. I could feel the strength of her powerful haunches under the saddle and marvelled at how someone as small as Edith could ride her – and ride her side-saddle, too.

I let Tinkerbell have her head. I felt a surge of adrenalin. My body seemed to melt into hers as we thundered along the ridge with the wind stinging my eyes. The landscape stretched out in a seemingly endless expanse of parched grass and scrubland.

Tinkerbell's pounding hooves made it easy to imagine Royalist troops galloping along this track, following

Sir Ralph Hopton, their commander and leader, who secured the south-west of England for Charles I.

As the bridleway began to narrow, I sat down in the saddle and gently pulled on her reins, bringing her into a trot and then finally, a walk. She wasn't even sweating. I was exhilarated and my head felt wonderfully clear. All my worries and concerns had been blown away by the wind. I felt a rush of affection for Edith's mare and patted her shoulder, whispering affectionate nonsense in her ear. She was such a beautiful horse.

I stopped to take in the scenery, and that's when I felt the first twinge of alarm. Storm clouds were gathering over distant Dartmoor. Even though they seemed far enough away, Tinkerbell must have sensed my concern, because she started side-stepping and spooking at imaginary ghosts.

I hesitated. The quickest way home was to skirt the quarry. Following the path that Edith had wanted would take at least an hour. I didn't want to risk it.

Gently, I turned her into a narrow opening in the trees. We followed the animal track, winding our way down hill and eventually coming to a three-way junction of green lanes – now called unmetalled roads. This was Larcombe Cross and it was marked by an ancient standing stone embedded in a triangle of dead grass coated in dust.

One lane led up to Larcombe Barn, Mallory's new home; the second eventually came out in the village behind the church, but the one we were going to take descended to the quarry through thick woodland, finally arriving at the rear of what Harry, the ten-year-old heir to the Grenville title, who was away with the Sea Scouts, referred to as the Black Forest.

Ignoring the warning sign that this was a no-through road for vehicles, we picked our way along the rutted track. Although wide enough for a car to begin with, it grew narrower and narrower until it became no more than a very overgrown footpath. The steep banks of slate, stones and blackened moss rising on both sides made the track claustrophobic – and, should a car venture this way, it could never turn around.

As we made our descent I was struck by how quickly the temperature dropped the closer we got to the abandoned quarry.

I hadn't ridden this way for a long time and felt the familiar shiver of apprehension that I always experienced in these woods. Was it the ruined mining village, the underground shafts and abandoned pieces of machinery or was it the knowledge that just a few yards away, lay a gaping quarry only hidden by crumbling dry stone walls, claimed by the virulent thick banks of laurel?

It felt desolate, cold, and unfriendly. Even the usual chirping of birds and rustling of small creatures seemed eerily absent.

Tinkerbell wasn't happy. Each step she took felt hesitant. She was jittery. Her shoes slipped on the slate surface. Twice she stumbled, causing me to snatch at her reins, which she hated, tossing her head and stamping her feet. My stomach was in knots. Coming this way had been a terrible mistake. The perimeter path was only fifty feet away, but it felt like it could have been a hundred.

In a rush of cascading pebbles and stones Tinkerbell half-slid down to the pathway. From here the ground levelled out. The old stone wall, once a sturdy boundary, was now a crumbling relic, interspersed with spindly shrubs, coated in dust.

Beyond it, the ground sloped sharply downward. The steep incline was dotted with hardy weeds and tufts of dead grass that clung to the rocky surface. The air was thick with the scent of damp earth and vegetation along with the stench of dank water.

We were close enough now to see the sheer cliff face disappear into the blackness where the quarry's waters gleamed dark and menacing. Larcombe Quarry was rumoured to be over two hundred feet deep and used to be a well-known catchment for numerous abandoned cars and old bits of farm machinery.

I kept us away from the edge, hugging the far bank which was over-run with more laurel, a mass of intertwining branches that climbed up the hillside. What vegetation there was had withered away to reveal the old iron rails for the quarry carts that used to haul slate up to the top where the winch and engine house had long fallen into disrepair.

I glanced down at the quarry, shocked to see how far the water level had dropped. Several yards below was a shelf-like ledge in colours of gold, browns and ochres that would usually have been hidden beneath the water.

It followed the natural contours of the rock face and ran around the open pit.

I began to feel uneasy and Tinkerbell soon picked up my mood, prancing about, weaving from side to side, and freezing and snorting at imaginary goblins. I kept my weight down and low in the saddle, my hands light on the reins and just focused on the track ahead. Once we had rounded this upcoming bend, we would be leaving the quarry behind us.

And that's when I saw it.

It was a blue Skoda. The chassis had got beached on a small rocky outcrop two-thirds of the way down the slope.

At first I thought I was imagining things, but when I saw the passenger door painted in a distinctive shade of pink, I knew I wasn't. Banu was supposed to be on her way back to Turkey. Yasmine was thirty miles away in Exeter, and I'd only seen Eric an hour ago.

What was that old car doing here?

I reined Tinkerbell in to take a closer look. Fresh tyre tracks had carved a path through the vegetation. The car must have gone over through the gap in the broken-down wall.

A prickling sensation made me feel that I was being watched but I couldn't see anyone. The air felt thicker here, menacing. It was as if a malevolent force was lurking somewhere in the eerie silence.

I had to get away, and Tinkerbell, who had started snorting and dancing again, was more than ready to go.

A distant roll of thunder boomed in the leaden sky.

Tinkerbell leapt backwards, rearing up and whinnying in fear. I clung tightly to her withers – not daring to pull on the reins in case I hauled her over. My hands slipped. As she dropped down, I pitched over her shoulder and landed heavily on my back.

Instinctively, I dropped my riding crop, but I kept hold of the reins, telling myself I mustn't let go; I mustn't let Tinkerbell gallop free.

The sky lit up with a blinding flash and crackle of distant lightning, sending Tinkerbell almost mad with fear.

Terrified, she sped backwards as I clung on for dear life, hoping my weight would slow her down. I didn't even feel my bare arms being torn and scraped along the stony, rough ground. Tinkerbell continued to back up, dragging me with her, but another boom of thunder sent her rearing up again, filled with terror.

All I could see were her hooves, pawing at the air, flailing above my face. As they hurtled down towards me, I had to let go, only rolling aside before they hit the ground.

And then Tinkerbell was off, head flung back, nostrils flaring, reins dangling between her legs, in the direction of Larcombe Cross.

I was distraught and in terrible pain from my fall. There was a deep gash on my arm that was bleeding heavily, but my only thought was for Tinkerbell's safety.

The Skoda was forgotten as a dozen scenarios raced through my head; terrible things that could befall the frightened mare and, if something should happen to her, how could I ever face Edith again?

I dragged myself to my feet. I had to find her. I started up the track but then stopped. It was futile. My only hope was that she would find her way home.

But there would be no one there to greet her. Only Eric.

It wasn't even thundering anymore. It sounded as if the storm had missed us. I was angry with myself for thinking I could navigate a short cut. This was all my fault.

I had to contact Eric. My fingers were shaking as I pulled my mobile out of my pouch. The screen was cracked but the phone still worked. I set off again for higher ground to get a signal.

But then I heard a car approaching. Unbelievably, it was heading in my direction. I started moving again but froze as the engine's sound shifted. The violent revs were filled with urgency, the driver alternating rapidly between the accelerator and brakes. The driver was trying to turn around!

Then, with a high-pitched whine, Eric's BMW came into view, reversing swiftly.

The roof was down and two poles, secured with rope, jutted out over the boot.

It was Yasmine.

I went numb. My mind wouldn't work; I couldn't understand what was happening. Why she was here? Was this a rescue mission? Where was Banu?

Instinctively, I turned tail and fled. I had to find somewhere to hide. In two quick strides I was on the other side of the low wall, crawling desperately to a clump of bushes. Forcing my way through the gnarled roots, I pulled myself into a tight ball and waited.

Yasmine turned off the engine and climbed over the back seat – the track was too narrow to open a car door. She slipped across the boot of the car, turning to pull out the two poles, one by one. Her movements were fast and determined.

I heard the poles being dragged across the stony path. Yasmine passed so close to my hiding place that I could smell her. Not the sweet, floral scent that I'd come to associate with her before, but something more primal. She was panting with exertion.

My heart was pounding so loudly that I was certain she must know I was there. She was just yards below, giving me an uninterrupted view. I drew back deeper into the branches, praying that she wouldn't look up.

Yasmine skittered down over the stones, dragging a pole in each hand before dropping them next to the Skoda. She took something out of her back pocket. When she flicked her wrist, I saw what it was. A switchblade.

She paused.

Yasmine moved to the boot of the car, knife at the ready, but she couldn't open it. Digging the tip of the blade into the lock her movements became more frantic. In exasperation she slammed both fists on the boot and uttered a cry of anger.

And then I guessed. Banu must be in there. Trapped? Or dead? Yasmine's actions were not those of someone on a rescue mission.

I was gripped by a feeling of such terror that I could hardly watch.

Yasmine closed the switchblade and slipped it back into her pocket. She manoeuvred a pole under each rear wheel and began pushing down hard on one, before moving to the other in an attempt to jimmy the car free.

Nothing was happening. The Skoda wouldn't budge.

Yasmine moved to the front of the car, clearing away rocks and digging into the ground. Her movements were more frantic now. Desperate. She returned to the poles and suddenly the car broke free and rushed the final yards down the slope into the quarry, sending a plume of water skyward.

Yasmine stood there watching the Skoda float. I could hear the muffled sound of water filling the car; the hiss of bubbles as they raced up to the surface echoing around the quarry walls. The Skoda's nose tilted and then, in a violent rush, the dark water swallowed the little car.

It was gone.

Yasmine stood motionless, staring out over the dark water.

My mind raced through different scenarios – Yasmine took Banu to the railway station to catch a train, but there were no trains that ran during the night; Yasmine drove her to an airport, found a taxi, hitched a lift home. I refused to believe the simplest explanation – that Banu was dead.

Sweat trickled down my spine. I felt sick as reality began to sink in.

Banu and Yasmine were not mother and daughter.

I thought of the bizarre scene with the tiger and how Banu was taking photographs of Yasmine. There had been something malicious about it all. A shared joy. Like two teenagers enjoying a prank.

All my suspicions as to the reason behind Eric's whirlwind courtship and hasty marriage began to make sense.

It had been Banu who had introduced Yasmine to Eric in the beginning. She'd believed that he owned Honeychurch Hall and I was pretty sure he wouldn't have disillusioned her.

They thought he was loaded.

Yasmine had played her part well. Banu had been the chaperone to ensure the key to Eric's bed depended on a wedding ring, and when it looked like Eric had changed his mind, Yasmine had given him what he wanted and guilted him into the marriage. They had to marry in England to make sure that Yasmine inherited all his money.

It was a honeytrap. The two women must have worked as a pair but then something happened and they fell out.

I thought of Eric's honeymoon destination. The Kale Konak Cave Hotel was remote and surrounded by rocky outcrops – plenty of places for an accident to happen. Hadn't Crispin planned something like that for my mother on Bolt Tail?

Crispin.

I distinctly remembered the scene between Crispin and Banu at the Safari Supper. I'd been so focused on finding chinks in Eric's armour that I hadn't given his so-called 'mother-in-law' a second thought – that was, until Crispin made that strange remark about how Banu had entered the country.

When Crispin started delving into Eric's past, he had poked a dangerous bear. I was certain that the women were involved in Crispin's death, I just didn't know how. Banu had attempted to frame Alfred. Yasmine had given Eric an alibi for that night, but I still didn't understand how he didn't hear anything. Was he really that heavy a sleeper?

Yasmine turned to make her way up the hillside, leaving the poles where they were.

I caught a glimpse of her face. It was a hard, unreadable mask.

I stayed deathly still.

Every bone in my body ached and the cut on my arm was bleeding heavily.

I waited for the sound of the car to start.

It didn't.

Every second seemed to stretch into an eternity. The quarry was eerily silent.

And then.

'I can see you, Kat.'

My heart almost stopped.

The tip of my riding crop appeared from above, jabbing me hard on the shoulder. I turned and looked up through the branches. Yasmine's eyes, cold and cruel, met mine.

'You know, I saw Tinkerbell at Larcombe Cross,' she mused in perfect English without the trace of an accent.

'Almost hit her with my car. I expected to find Lavinia somewhere, but not you.'

I was desperate to ask if Tinkerbell was okay but the words just wouldn't come.

She laughed. 'Are you going to come out?' Yasmine poked my shoulder again. Harder this time. 'Or shall I come and get you? I think you already know that I have a knife and I'm very good at using it.'

'Is that what you did to Banu?' I said. 'Your *friend*. I know she's not your mother.'

'She was never my friend,' Yasmine said coldly. 'She was the one who caused all this.'

'This?' I tried to keep my voice steady. 'What do you mean by this?'

'Come out and I'll tell you,' Yasmine said. 'Or I can come in. Nice and cosy but you won't like it.'

I crawled out of my hiding place. Yasmine held my riding crop in one hand. In the other she grabbed my injured arm.

I cried out.

'Oooh, that looks painful.' Her fingers dug into my flesh. It hurt. 'You're bleeding.'

'If you leave now, you stand a chance of getting away,' I gasped.

'Oh. Thanks for your permission,' she said.

'The police will be here at any minute,' I bluffed, praying that Yasmine hadn't heard about Edith being whisked to hospital and everyone with her. 'Tinkerbell will be back at the stables by now. Lavinia knew I was riding this way.'

'You think I'm stupid?' She shook her head. 'I just don't know what to do with you.' She frowned then brightened. 'Yes. I know.' She pointed the riding crop in the direction of where I had originally been heading with Tinkerbell. 'Go and wait there. Close your eyes and count to a hundred. Off you go.'

I didn't trust her. 'Why?'

'How *ab-so-lutely* beastly for her.' Yasmine mimicked Lavinia's voice. 'A *frightful* fall. She hit her head you know. Such a tragic accident. But then riding is dangerous.'

'Eric never changed his will, Yasmine,' I said quickly. 'He told me. What money he has, still goes to his first wife's estate. The scrapyard and bits of land he has don't even belong to him. They all belong to the earl.' I wasn't sure if this was true but I plunged on. 'It's just the way things are done here in England.'

Yasmine stared at me, her hand gripping the riding crop, but I could see a tiny hesitation. Her expression hardened. 'You lie. He loaned money to Rupert,' she said. 'Your house as collateral—'

'Oh *that*,' I said dismissively. 'I think you'll find it was a gentleman's agreement. It won't stand up in a court of law. It's over, Yasmine.'

'For you, maybe,' she said. 'But not for me.'

'You'll be arrested the moment you get to the airport.'

There was flicker of confusion.

'Didn't you know?' I pressed on. 'Crispin worked for the government, for Border Control in fact.' This wasn't strictly true. 'He found out who you really are and Interpol have been tracking your movements ever since you got here.' This was a blatant lie but I could see that I had struck a nerve. 'Crispin had your IDs and passports. He knew how you came into the country. He knew that Banu travelled through Amsterdam and that she wasn't your mother.' This last was a wild guess but it worked.

'Banu was an idiot!' Yasmine exploded. 'I told her not to come this one time. I told her just to meet us at the caves but she just turned up.'

'The caves?' I said sharply. 'Where you're going on your honeymoon?' I knew then that my hunch had been right. Eric would have gone to his death. 'You both killed Crispin didn't you?'

Yasmine stopped. It was as if she knew she had said too much. 'He drowned,' she said simply. 'We were *all* sleeping. Very, very deeply.'

She glanced at the Etruscan ring on her finger. But I caught the significance.

'You drugged him,' I whispered. 'Of course you did. And you drugged Banu. That's how you got her into the boot of the car.'

Yasmine rolled her eyes. 'Clever you. You can't prove a thing. Crispin just took a midnight dip.'

'How *did* you get Crispin to the lake?' I said. 'I'm interested.'

'The wheelbarrow,' Yasmine said with a smirk.

'Pity you put the binoculars on the bank,' I said. 'Crispin would never have done that.'

'That was Banu!' Yasmine snarled.

'You also didn't know that Crispin was afraid of water,' I said. 'He'd never have gone for a swim and, because of that, the police are running toxicology tests to see what really killed him.'

Yasmine went very still. 'That was Banu. Not me.'

'But you would say that, wouldn't you?' I said. 'With Banu dead, everything will fall on you. Why did you kill her?'

Yasmine gave a bitter laugh. 'I just didn't need her anymore.'

I caught a flash of movement and the shock on Yasmine's face as she pitched forward and crashed heavily on to the track.

I was face to face with Banu. But this Banu had long, dark hair. Dirty, dishevelled, and angry, she was clutching a heavy stick. Swinging it, she stepped towards me.

Yasmine staggered to her feet and launched herself at Banu, using the riding crop in one hand and the switch-blade in the other.

I saw my chance and scrambled up the bank, falling, scrabbling, to reach the BMW. Sobbing, I clambered over the boot to get into the driver's seat, and then realised the keys weren't there.

The two women were screaming and fighting. I'd have to go the other way – somewhere neither could follow me in a car.

I retraced my steps just as there was a blood-curdling scream and a cry of 'No!'

I turned and saw Banu roll all the way down the slope, reach the edge, and drop into the quarry. There was a splash as she hit the water.

Yasmine spun around. Our eyes met, but she turned and ran back to the car, leaving me paralysed with horror.

I wanted to run for help but I couldn't leave Banu. The water would have broken her fall and she might still be alive.

With a roar and the sound of tyres spinning on the rough stones, Yasmine drove away but then she slammed on the brakes. She was coming back for Banu, she had to be.

I saw her toss a lighted match out of the window.

Chapter Twenty-Nine

The speed at which the fire took hold was horrifying.

Flames raced towards me from the dry brush.

Flames raced up the hill, engulfing trees and turning them into blackened pillars with mind-blowing speed.

I'd never outrun the fire. My only chance to survive was getting to the water, but the flames had already jumped the track and were hungrily devouring the dried moss and lichen.

My knees were shaking so badly I could hardly stand. Coughing and spluttering I stood at the top of the steep slope above the quarry.

I pulled up my shirt and put it over my nostrils so I could breathe without coughing. Ash rained down, smoke filled the sky, obscuring the sun with an eerie brown haze. The heat was intense. I descended the steep slope, struggling to keep my balance as my feet skidded over the loose stones, throwing me on to my bottom as I made a desperate descent. Every tree I reached for came away in my hand.

I got to the edge of the quarry and stopped. The exposed shelf was further down than I thought. Ten feet, maybe more. It was a wall of sheer granite. I would never get back up, but I would die if I didn't move.

I dropped to my knees, turned around and tried to lower myself as far down as I could but the edge held no handholds and I dropped, landing badly on my ankle.

I lay there, in excruciating pain as I was overcome with nausea and the familiar fizzing and tingling sensation that accompanied a broken bone. I could hear sobbing and I realised it was coming from me.

Yasmine had got away. Banu must have drowned. When Tinkerbell was found without me, I would be a tragic casualty of a summer wildfire.

The orange sky grew darker as thick, heavy clouds rolled in. Thunder roared overhead, each crack splitting the dark sky with blinding flashes of lightning. Rain came down in sheets.

The storm had finally come.

Shivering violently, I dragged myself into a sitting position, and that's when I saw her.

Further along the shelf, Banu was trying to attract my attention. She was alive and distressed. I could never get to her from here even if I could walk.

Her gestures became more frenzied as she pointed to the rock face around to my left.

Torrents of water were pouring through a crevice.

The level of the quarry was already rising. I caught the stench of dirt and mud and the metallic tang of the submerged cars rising with it.

Within minutes, the water was lapping at my feet. The coldness took my breath away. They say the cold water is one of the main causes of death for swimmers in a quarry. Banu lay slumped against the rock face, unable to stand.

I felt this extraordinary sense of peace. I've heard people say that grace is bestowed by celestial beings on those who are facing their death.

I felt sad that I'd never really know Mallory or have his children. I was in love with him. I knew that now. Who would look after my mother? The bigger issues gave way to trivia – what would happen to Ruby's cigarette card collection, who would water my flowers – something else I'd heard people do when their end is inevitable.

The water had reached my waist. I had stopped shaking. I didn't even notice the pain in my ankle anymore. I felt nothing.

I closed my eyes and waited.

Suddenly, the downpour ceased, leaving an eerie silence. I heard the distant thrum of helicopter blades echoing around the quarry, growing louder with each passing moment.

Banu was screaming and waving for help. Not that she would have been heard.

I opened my eyes and looked up. Framed by a watery blue sky, a red and white Search and Rescue helicopter hovered overhead. The side door slid open, and a man in a harness, wearing a helmet and visor appeared. He was secured by a sturdy cable. He signalled to the pilot before beginning his descent.

The rope swung out carrying him towards me. It felt like a dream and I was just a spectator, but then the man extended a hand to me and said, 'I've got you.'

It was Mallory.

My Mallory.

Chapter Thirty

It was lunchtime the following day when Mallory arrived at the Carriage House with an enormous bunch of flowers.

I'd spent the night in hospital getting my ankle set and the nasty cut on my arm sewn up. Although it was only a small break, I'd be on crutches for a few weeks.

I was back in my old room and being waited on hand and foot by my mother. I still felt shaken by my near-death experience and truly grateful to be alive.

Mum left us together. The moment she closed my bedroom door, Mallory pulled me into his arms and we just held each other.

There was no need for words.

'Tell me everything,' I said finally. So Mallory did.

'It was Polly who raised the alarm,' he said. 'Tinkerbell galloped up to Larcombe Barn. Polly knew that something had happened to the rider but she also knew she couldn't go and find out. Polly managed to get her into one of the old barns and stayed with her in there until help came.'

I was impressed. 'That was brave of her.'

'Polly grew up with horses,' he said. 'Her satellite tag triggered the alert and I immediately got the call. When I spoke to her, she was in a panic. She was worried that the fire would reach Larcombe Barn but she refused to leave Tinkerbell. I knew you had gone riding because you'd left me a message. Polly described the horse as a chestnut mare. I still had Alfred in custody. He called Lavinia and she told us it must be Tinkerbell.'

'Is Tinkerbell going to be okay?' I asked.

'The horse is fine,' he said.

'I'm very grateful to Polly,' I said. 'And I know that Edith will be, too.'

'I thought you'd also like to know that if the dowager countess continues to improve, she'll be discharged tomorrow.'

'What will happen to Polly? Will she be in even more trouble? I owe her everything.' I thought of those last terrifying moments when I didn't think I would make it. 'If it hadn't been for Polly—'

'But here you are,' he said gently. 'Here *we* are.'

I nodded, trying not to cry. I was still an emotional and physical wreck.

I thought of Banu and asked if he had spoken to her.

Mallory shook his head. 'The doctors won't let me talk to her yet. She has a shattered pelvis and broke her leg in two places.'

'What about Yasmine?'

Mallory's expression grew hard. 'She's still at large. We've a national security alert and "be on the lookout" alerts on all airports, railway stations and ports. We found Eric's BMW. She'd abandoned it at a service station off the M5 at Junction 13. Yasmine stole another car which was spotted on CCTV. Oh, we'll catch her. She won't get away.'

He went on to tell me that as well as the local police force, there were half a dozen police and law enforcement bodies that were already involved in the manhunt. 'The National Crime Agency, Interpol, the UK Border Force, Europol, to name just a few.'

'Good,' I whispered. 'She's a cold-blooded murderer. They both are.'

'What we do know however, is that Banu is only forty and Yasmine is thirty-five.'

My jaw dropped. 'Banu looked so much older! And Yasmine so much younger.'

'A wig, makeup and, in Yasmine's case,' said Mallory, 'plenty of Botox.'

I forced a smile. 'I did think that Banu's dazzling white teeth were a little at odds with her dowdy appearance.'

Mallory squeezed my hand. 'Eric had a lucky escape. You saved his life.'

'I think we should credit the goats with that,' I said wryly. 'Oh, and Muriel's Miracle Spray.'

'The lab report confirmed that Ruby died from the nicotine solution that she had spilled over her nightdress,' said Mallory. 'It was absorbed into her skin. By the time the symptoms appeared, she had collapsed and no one was there to save her.'

'Poor Ruby,' I whispered. 'But, how did you manage to get the results so quickly?'

'Susan fast-tracked—'

'I know who Susan is,' I said, surprised that I no longer felt threatened by Mallory's ex-girlfriend.

'But here's the strange thing,' said Mallory. 'Crispin had no trace of nicotine in his bloodstream but there were traces of another toxic substance. We're still waiting on that.'

I was struck by a horrible thought. 'If Ruby hadn't died, the vicar would never have cancelled the wedding. But that means . . .' I felt sick.

'What?' he said.

'Crispin would still be alive,' I said. 'If I hadn't cut my trip short, I wouldn't have got the eviction letter until Crispin had gone home and he wouldn't have started digging around—'

'And Crispin would have got away with his crimes, too, Kat.' Mallory's expression grew serious. '*All* of them.'

My stomach dropped as I thought of what could have happened to my mother if he had. It didn't bear thinking about.

'Doreen Mutters confirmed that Crispin purchased the spanner, the hacksaw and the map in the community shop,' he went on. 'The saw marks on the ladder rungs match the teeth in the hacksaw. Of course we'll never be able to prove he did that, or that he tampered with Iris's brakes or that he planned a fatal accident on Bolt Tail. But investigations will be made into uncovering the corrupt officials he had been working with over the years.'

'But with Crispin dead, what happens to my mother now?'

'It'll take a very long time to go through all the documents that were shredded and put the pieces together,' he said. 'My guess is that Crispin created his own template to generate fake bank statements which will go a long way to help prove Iris's innocence.'

'But she is innocent!' I said sharply.

'It's not as easy as all that,' he protested. 'Crispin is dead. Alfred crossing the Channel to draw out cash will obviously seem suspicious. I'm sorry. But this problem isn't just going to go away.' He squeezed my hand again. 'Remember what I said about family? We're not responsible for what other people do.'

'I know that,' I said miserably.

'But we can support and love them regardless.'

'What about Alfred?' I said suddenly. 'Are you going to say something to the family about his past?'

Mallory smiled. 'I don't know what you're talking about.' He kissed my forehead and stood up. 'I've got to go. I've got to drive Polly back to Maidstone tonight.'

'Please thank her for me again,' I said. 'I hope to meet her one day.'

Chapter Thirty-One

The day of the Little Dipperton Flower and Produce Festival dawned overcast with scattered showers.

The heavy rain of the past week had turned the park into a quagmire, keeping Eric busy pulling cars out of the mud with his tractor. I'd expected him to be devastated about Yasmine's deception, but he seemed relieved and was certainly enjoying his new-found fame.

Aunt Muriel's Home Remedies was pulled off the shelves and flyers were distributed warning everyone to dispose of their homemade miracle sprays wearing rubber gloves. Bottles were to be taken to the recycling centre and put in the designated Hazardous Waste container.

Villagers exchanged war stories and shared their afflictions. Poor Bethany, Muriel's niece was mortified. It turned out that it was she who had transposed the ingredients from Muriel's handwritten notes, misreading the quantities after a coffee spill.

Thankfully, the dowager countess made a full recovery and was able to present the trophies. She created a Ruby Rose Trophy in Ruby's memory. Mum picked up the cup for the best heirloom tomatoes but spent most of the afternoon avoiding Danny, who was trailing after her like a lovesick puppy dog. There was no sign of Caroline.

It was just as Mallory and I were leaving the park that I heard a familiar voice call out my name.

My stomach did a flip-flop. I hadn't seen my ex-boyfriend for many months. Shawn seemed different, more confident somehow, although I saw his passion for steam trains was still very much in evidence given that his sweatshirt bore the slogan, 'Rolling Stock Rocks'.

He gestured for Ned and Jasper, his twin boys, to join us. It was good to see them again. I marvelled at how much they'd grown and how their interest in soccer and dinosaurs had not waned.

And then a pretty woman in her late thirties waved and came over with a little girl in plaits in tow.

I felt arms slide around my waist and Mallory say, 'Ah, glad you could make it, Shawn. Good to see you again, Gilly.'

Introductions were made all round and it turned out that Gilly was a senior investigating officer for the National Crime Agency. She and Shawn worked together. The little girl with plaits was Rachel, Gilly's daughter.

'I'm between husbands.' Gilly said mischievously. She looked at Shawn, who rolled his eyes and laughed.

'I love teasing him,' she said. 'No more husbands for me.'

Shawn turned pink.

'I think you're going to like what they have to say,' said Mallory.

'You go first, Shawn,' said Gilly.

'Yasmine was picked up at St Pancras station trying to board the Eurostar to Paris,' said Shawn. 'She swears she was frightened for her life and that Banu was the ringleader—'

'Which, of course, isn't true,' said Gilly.

'And Banu claims it was all Yasmine's idea—'

'Banu Aydin's real name is Donita Lis,' Gilly continued. 'She isn't Turkish, she's Albanian, operating under many fake identities.'

'The passport!' I exclaimed. 'Crispin discovered Banu wasn't who she said she was. That's what triggered the whole thing!'

I listened with astonishment as Gilly revealed that Yasmine had already disposed of three husbands in the last seven years.

'They began with small-time theft and scams,' said Shawn.

'Earmarking lonely business men or bachelors out on a stag night—'

'In hotel bars—'

'In cities and holiday resorts.' Gilly smiled at Shawn and he smiled back, clearly enjoying their to-and-fro banter.

'One would distract the mark,' said Shawn, 'While the other laced his drink with a cocktail of sleeping pills—'

'The Etruscan ring.' I exclaimed. 'I knew it!'

Shawn nodded. 'There were traces of powder in the hidden compartment that we can confirm was a mixture of Ambien, Restoril and Halcion.'

'When the victim came round and discovered what had happened,' Gilly continued, 'Obviously, he could never report it.'

'But they were getting older,' said Shawn. 'They couldn't keep it up forever. Yasmine was pragmatic, planning for the future. She was stashing her wealth away. The villa she showed Eric was her own—'

'Banu was a gambler,' Gilly cut in. 'She was tired of doing the dirty work. The last husband's death caused too many questions and Yasmine wanted to cut all ties with Banu and told her their partnership was over—'

'But Banu wouldn't have it,' said Shawn. 'She turned up all the same.'

'I think Banu was secretly in love with her,' said Gilly. 'Yasmine's betrayal was devastating. She knew she'd been drugged that night. But fortunately, the car got stuck, it triggered the lock and Banu was able to escape.'

'And the rest, as they say,' smiled Mallory. 'Is history.'

'We'll keep you posted.' Shawn locked eyes with Gilly, leaving me in no doubt that they were far more than colleagues. The twins grabbed Rachel's hand and the trio ran off, followed by Shawn and Gilly.

I was genuinely pleased for them. I knew I could have never made Shawn happy, nor he me.

'Are you okay,' said Mallory gently.

I smiled. 'Very much so.'

'Then allow me to carry you back to my car.' He scooped me up in his arms and I flung mine around his neck.

'I cannot wait to be able to walk properly again,' I moaned.

'There is just one piece of the puzzle that I am hoping you can answer,' he said as he carried me with seemingly effortless ease.

I clung on. 'I'll try.'

'The results came back from Crispin's autopsy,' he said. 'That mysterious substance was abrin.'

'I don't know what that is,' I said.

'It's also known as a rosary pea,' said Mallory. 'The bright red berries have black spots and look like ladybirds. They're often use to decorate souvenirs, but not many people realise they are seventy times more toxic than ricin.'

I gasped. 'The giraffe! Caroline used rosary peas to decorate the wooden sculptures. Banu had smuggled one out in her handbag. Mum and I found it in the potting shed minus the eyes!'

'You're sure?' Mallory sounded excited. 'What else did you find?'

'Odd things,' I said. 'An empty bottle of nail polish remover—'

'Acetone,' he nodded. 'The abrin would need to be mixed with a solvent. The berries would have to be crushed—'

'Yes!' I exclaimed. 'There was a piece of slate; a stone . . .' I couldn't keep the excitement out of my voice. 'Banu must have used the stone to do that and then mixed the granules with the acetone in Delia's pudding basin but . . .' I frowned. 'If Crispin was drugged, how could she have made him swallow it?'

'Was there anything else?'

'Only a hard-shell case for glasses,' I shrugged. 'Although, this sounds weird, Yasmine made a very strange comment. She said that Banu had diabetes. Believe me, she was definitely packing away the ice cream at the summer house that night.'

'Hah!' Mallory clapped his hands. 'A diabetes kit would contain a syringe. We need to find that bag.'

'No chance of that,' I said. 'Yasmine took it.'

'It doesn't matter,' said Mallory. 'It sounds like Banu and Yasmine will be happily throwing each other under the bus.'

It was much later when we were sitting out on the terrace that Mallory suddenly stood up.

'You're going already?' I was disappointed. 'It's not even ten.'

'I want to show you something.' He helped me to my feet and scooped me up in his arms again.

'I could get used to this,' I laughed.

We set off across the grass, away from Jane's Cottage towards the edge of the forest. The terrain gently sloped downward, giving way to the open, rugged beauty of Dartmoor.

Moonlight filtered through the clouds, dappling the ground with patches of light and shadow.

Mallory stopped in a clearing. He set me down and drew me into the shadows.

'What are we doing here?' I said.

'Ssh.' He held his fingers to his lips. 'Just wait.'

It was deathly quiet.

And then I heard it. A low, throaty churr that gradually grew louder and more persistent. It was like a vibrating trill that was both haunting and captivating. I'd never heard anything like it before.

Mallory nudged me and pointed to what looked like brownish mulch on the forest floor, a few feet from where we were hiding.

At first I couldn't see anything, but as the moon emerged from the clouds again, a ray of light shone down on a patch of dead leaves. As my eyes adjusted to the gloom, the leaves moved. I could make out a large head, a short neck, long wings, and a tail.

It was a bird.

Unable to contain my excitement, I whispered, 'Oh, look!'

There was a rustling and an indignant raspy squawk as the nightjar took flight. We watched her gain altitude, the rhythmic beating of her wings the only sound in the still night.

We stood there, silent, neither wanting to break the spell until he whispered, 'You never did tell me why you came home early.'

'What do you think?' I asked softly.

Our eyes locked and for a moment, he didn't answer.

And then he smiled. 'Because we belong together.'

Acknowledgements

It is a well-known fact that most writers find it harder to write the acknowledgments than the actual novel. I'm no exception. Honestly, composing a tweet is challenging enough – this is a whole other level.

Recently, I was asked if I worried about running out of ideas. The answer is, never. In fact, I don't think I'll ever have enough time in my life to write all the books I want to write. Ideas are everywhere.

The spark for this mystery began with a village flyer announcing the annual safari supper fundraiser. Instead of moving across the veld to spot exotic animals, guests would enjoy a travelling dinner party, to enjoy a different course at a different home. What an excellent setting for . . . murder.

Speaking of safaris, I've been itching to include our very own Totnes Safari. If you haven't done the drive through Bridgetown, you're missing out. Created by octogenarian artist Malcolm Curley, there are over 200 extraordinary sculptures made from recycled materials, which range from leopards to unicorns, peering over hedges or lurking on garage roofs. If you don't believe me, you can find him on Facebook.

For the record, the characters in my Honeychurch novels are purely fictional and bear no resemblance to anyone, living or dead (truly) – with two exceptions: the aforementioned Malcolm Curley and a Billy goat called Capricious. His owner, Nicola de Pulford, is the legendary photographer for the annual British Farmers Calendar.

I'd like to give a special thanks to Kevin Butterworth for filling me in on loose nipple clamps and small hacksaws (yes, really). And to Detective Inspector Steve Davies and Detective Inspector Mark Smeaton for making sure I got the crime details right. You have been warned – HMRC knows everything.

My heartfelt thanks to:

Andra St. Ivanyi and Dr. Linda Sterry for schooling me on sedatives. In the spirit of transparency, I also asked ChatGPT but it politely suggested I see a doctor about my insomnia instead.

Clare Smith, auction-house aficionado, neighbour and friend, for suggesting the Etruscan ring. Who knew? I know what I want for Christmas.

My long-suffering boss of twenty-five years, Mark Davis, Chairman and CEO of Davis Elen Advertising in Los Angeles. Thank you for your never-ending support and enthusiasm.

My wonderful agents, Dominick Abel and David Grossman. Thank you for taking such good care of me on both sides of the Atlantic.

My incredible publishing team at Constable, with a special thank you to publishing director Krystyna Green (my fellow canine enthusiast and dream editor), editorial manager Rebecca Sheppard and sharp-eyed copyeditor Colin Murray. Also, to Liane Payne, thank you for the beautiful map of Honeychurch Hall.

My multi-talented VA, Krissy Lilljedhal, who keeps me on track. Did anyone seriously believe it was me doing all those amazing graphics on social media?

To my family and non-writer friends who wisely steer clear in the final weeks of a book deadline: your patience and willingness to celebrate with me (briefly, before I dive into the next project) mean everything.

Special love to my beautiful daughter Sarah (and grandson, Leo!), my 95-year-old Mum (who reads everything I write with her giant magnifying glass), and, of course, to the canine gods for my elderly Vizsla, Draco. Athena, we miss you every day.

And finally, to the readers, libraries and booksellers who give life to our books – without you, these stories would never see the light of day. Thank you!